Rescue

Book 3 in
After the Fall Series

A Novel

By David Nees

Copyright © 2019 David E. Nees

All rights reserved.

To keep up with my new releases, please visit my website at www.davidnees.com. Scroll down to the bottom of the landing page to the section titled, "Follow the Adventure" to join my reader list.

You can also click "Follow" under my picture on the Amazon book page and Amazon will let you know when I release a new work.

ISBN 9781094898339

Manufactured in the United States

For Carla

It's an exciting journey with much more to come.

Grateful thanks for to my beta readers, Eric, Chris, and Ed. Your insightful and detailed comments are key to turning my rough agate into a polished (gem) stone. I appreciate your generosity of time.

And thank you, Catherine, for your careful proofreading. Proofreading is hard. There are so many words, so many opportunities for mistakes. You and Carla help remove those pesky problems, greatly improving the text.

Cover art by Onur Aksoy. You can find his work at https://www.onegraphica.com/

Rescue
Book 3 in *After the Fall* series

"Not to punish evil is equivalent to authorizing it." –
Leonardo Da Vinci

*"He who loses wealth loses much; he who loses a friend
loses more; but he that loses his courage loses all."* –
Miguel de Cervantes

*"The superior man does not, even for the space of a
single meal, act contrary to virtue. In moments of haste,
he cleaves to it. In seasons of danger, he cleaves to it."* –
Confucius

Chapter 1

Jason studied the man in front of him. He was in his late thirties, unkempt, grizzled. He had a hard look about him, now tempered by concern. He was probably worried about what can happen to a messenger of bad news. He had reason to be.

"So, you traveled all these miles by foot to bring me this demand?" The man nodded, concern starting to show. "And your name is Bud?"

"I already told you. What the hell are you doing keeping me locked up? I didn't have anything to do with this and you got no reason to hold me. I was just following orders."

"You must have known your message wouldn't be well received."

The man glared back at Jason. "Go to hell."

"How did Knoxville hear about us? Why would they think we had anything of value?"

He shook his head. "I ain't telling you anything more than what I already said. You need to load up a hundred pounds of gold and jewels and take them out to Gatlinburg. Then you'll get your two men back, Gibbs and Turner."

"That's all?" The man nodded again. "And your boss, this 'Chairman' guy, figured I would just agree to this?" The man nodded. "I need to know more."

"Tough. I don't know more."

"Are my two men in good shape? Are they being well treated?

Bud just glared at him. "How the hell would I know?"

"You have no idea?"

"I heard the black guy was beat up some. Heard he was acting belligerent and some of the boys didn't like that. Serves him right."

Jason stood up. "Wait here," he said.

"You let me loose," Bud shouted after him. "You can't keep me locked up in this piss-ant jail. Who do you think you all are in this town? The Chairman finds you treatin' me this way, he'll make you pay. You don't know him. He'll destroy this town, you mess with me."

Jason didn't answer and quickly walked out of the room, locking it behind him. He met Kevin Cameron in the hall.

"What do you think?" Kevin asked.

"I'm stunned," Jason replied. "First that Rodney and Billy got caught, second that someone would try to shake us down."

"Rodney wouldn't talk to anyone about all the loot Stansky had assembled, so how would they know about it?"

"Billy wouldn't tell. Hell, he didn't even know about it," Jason replied.

"Word must have drifted west from some of the militia who escaped—"

"Or men from Roper's squad. They might know." Jason shook his head, making a decision. "It doesn't matter. I need you to put this man in restraints, leg irons, cuffs and waist belt."

"Why?"

"He's been an SOB since he got here and gave us his message. He's complaining about us keeping him locked up, not treating him with respect. Says the Chairman's going to make us pay for mistreating him. And he refuses to give me any information about the situation in Knoxville. I need to know more about what's going on there and I don't have a lot of time. I'm going to have a private conversation with him."

Kevin gave Jason a long, questioning look. "I don't know what you're planning, but don't do anything rash. We have rule of law now, not gangster law. Remember that."

Jason knew his face betrayed his hard intent. "Nothing rash. But I am going to stretch the boundaries a bit." He could tell those words didn't give Kevin much comfort.

A half hour later, Jason led the man out of the mayor's office and down to the street. They drove out of the city, departing from the northern gate. They angled west through the abandoned suburbs with the foothills of the Appalachian Mountains showing ahead.

As they drove, the man tried more than once to start a conversation, but Jason didn't speak. Nor did he look at him. They entered the forest, now two hours outside of Hillsboro. Jason stopped the car and motioned for the man to get out.

"Where are you taking me? Why are we out here? You act like a tough guy with me in chains. You take them off and we'll see who's tough. Dumb hick. Just pay the ransom and let me go, you got no right to treat me like this." His comments came with increasing anxiety in his voice.

Jason did not answer. He picked up his backpack and motioned for the man to walk ahead. Jason's mind raced with conflicting thoughts. Before this messenger showed up, he was a happy, content man, even if harassed by administrative details as temporary mayor of Hillsboro. He had a wonderful wife, a son and two step daughters, one married to Kevin Cameron, now head of the police department for the town. He thought he had put his days as a warrior behind him in the post-EMP world.

Since the EMP attack on the U.S., Hillsboro had come under the control of a gangster named Joe Stansky. When Stansky threatened Jason and his family and friends in their rural valley, they initiated an uprising that overthrew the gangster and freed Hillsboro from his clutches. Since then the town had worked on getting electricity and some level of communications going. The increased trappings of the pre-EMP world had given Jason and everyone else a false sense that their world was returning to normal.

Then this kidnapping and extortion demand. It brought home the fact that the country was still unsettled with no central authority. There was still danger outside of the city; danger that could intrude on their lives. The times still required hard people. He now had to put aside his gentle nature as he did once before and become the warrior, the killer, a dangerous man for a dangerous time.

He had to get information from his captive, even if he had to be brutal to get it. His stomach churned at what he was about to do.

Ten minutes later Jason halted next to a large red oak tree. Without a word he dropped his backpack and took out two short boards. He taped Bud's hands flat to the boards. He took a hammer and a nail from the pack. Next, he released one of Bud's wrists from the cuffs and before the man could react, he forced his arm out to the tree and nailed the board into the trunk.

"What're you doing?" Bud's gravelly voice now was filled with fear.

Without a word, Jason repeated his steps with Bud's other hand. The man was now standing, facing the tree, with his arms wrapped around it, his hands effectively nailed to the trunk.

"What're you gonna to do?" Bud asked again. "You got no reason to hurt me. I just delivered the message. I don't have anything else to say to you.

Jason said nothing. He left Bud nailed to the tree and left to gather up some dead branches and kindling. Bringing them back, he lit a small fire behind the man. Then he walked back into the trees. He was looking for an Ironwood tree. It was very dense and hard to burn. It would work perfectly for what he had in mind. He returned a few minutes later with a fresh limb he had cut. He built up the fire and laid the end of the stick in the growing bed of coals.

"You gonna burn me? Damn you. You're a coward. Turn me loose." Bud was now squirming and beginning to hyperventilate in fear.

Got to be hard. Can't let him think I can be reasoned with. It will save both of us a lot of pain.

"Bud, I need some information and you're going to give it to me. I don't have a lot of time and I don't have much patience."

"I ain't telling you anything! You don't know the Chairman. He's one you don't cross. He's gonna take over the whole south one day. Say's he saw it in a vision, and I believe him. You hurt me, he'll come after you and your city. Just do what you're told. I don't know anything else."

"If you keep to that story it is going to be very painful for you."

"Go to hell!"

Jason turned the stick in the coals. "I'm going to ask you some questions. I want to know everything you know. You're going to tell me everything and I'm going to write it down. Later you'll draw me a map. When we're done, I'll be able to see the place with your eyes, as if I had been there myself."

Bud cranked his head over, looking at Jason with a mixture of fear and anger. He shook his head. "I ain't helping you. I don't know anything but what I said."

Suddenly Jason took out his hunting knife and thrust it in front of Buddy's face. "I've got two good men out there, one of them may be hurt and I need to go get them."

"You'll get yourself killed." Bud almost sneered at him. "The Chairman got too many men."

"It's not me that is going to get killed. I'm going to do the killing." He took his knife and put it to Buddy's left hand. He placed the blade half way down the little finger. "I'm going to start cutting your fingers until you tell me what I want to know."

"He'll kill me if I tell you everything."

"I'll kill you if you don't. Or I'll send you back with two bloody stumps for hands and you'll die slowly of starvation. You think anyone will take care of a cripple with no fingers?"

Jason began to press down on the blade, cutting into one of Bud's fingers.

Bud screamed in pain and started cursing at Jason. "Damn you! I told you I don't know nothing. You got no right."

"First question. Where's his headquarters?"

I don't know anything, I'm telling you. They just picked me to deliver the message."

"You say 'I don't know' a lot."

Jason pushed down on the blade. The man screamed, his body jerked against the tree. Blood spurted from the severed digit. Jason grabbed the Ironwood stick from the fire and stuck it to the end of Buddy's finger.

Bud screamed again, even louder.

"Scream all you want. There's no one to hear you. Now I'm going to ask you again. Tell me everything about this Chairman and his setup. You ready to do that, or do I have to take the next finger off?"

Bud shook his head. "No, no more."

"Now you're being smart."

"I'm a dead man."

"Bud, I got no time for this. I'm going to cut another finger. You're going to talk or you're going to die."

"Okay, okay." He threw his head back. "Oh God it hurts."

"The hurt increases with each finger." Jason put his face up close to Bud. "You want to feel real pain? I can deliver more pain than you can imagine. You're standing between me and rescuing my friends. You don't want to be in that position."

He stepped back. "Now again, where's the Chairman's headquarters?"

"In the Knoxville County Building. It's next to the courthouse."

"How many men does the Chairman have?"

"I don't know. Please."

Jason put his knife to the man's next finger.

"Hundreds. It's a lot. Stop. I really don't know how many."

Jason released his pressure on the knife,

"He's got the whole city under his control, so it's a lot of men. He's got the police and a city militia. Knoxville's gonna rule the south with him in charge."

"How well are they armed?"

The man made no pretense of holding back now. He was obviously in great pain.

"M16s, M14s. He cleaned out the armories."

"Heavy weapons?"

"I don't—"

Jason increased the pressure on his knife. It started into the flesh.

"Mortars, RPGs, machine guns! I've seen them."

"Anything else?"

"I seen some big guns, cannons. But I don't know if they work.

"How well trained are the men?"

"All of 'em are trained, but some not so well. We do some practicing but don't use live ammo. The officers say it needs to be saved."

"You're in the militia. Tell me more about the troops, where they are kept, how they're organized, is there an elite group?"

For the next hour the man gave Jason more detail including where he thought the prisoners were being kept and how the county building and courthouse were defended. Jason withdrew his knife from the man's finger and began to write down the information, asking clarifying questions when needed.

I'm a dead man," Bud said again when they were done.

"Maybe, maybe not. At least you have most of your fingers. I could be sending you back with stumps." Now we're going back to town. You're going to remain in our custody while I go for my friends. If I find you've lied to me about these details, when I get back I'll take you back out into these woods, strip you, and stake you out on the ground for the insects and animals to feed on. You'd better hope a mountain lion comes across you before any dogs or wolves. You'll die quicker. The dogs and wolves will eat you alive and you'll be screaming for death before you get it."

Bud shuddered. "I'm telling the truth, but you're going to get yourself killed."

"A lot of people have said that to me, and they're all dead."

Chapter 2

When Jason arrived back at the police station, Kevin was waiting for him.

"What the hell happened?" he exclaimed when he saw Bud.

"He needs some attention, but he'll be all right. That stump should be disinfected and bandaged properly."

Kevin sent a militia soldier off to the hospital to bring a nurse back to attend to the prisoner. Jason headed into Kevin's office while Kevin instructed a police officer to put Bud back in his cell and give him some food, water, and an extra pillow on which to rest his injured hand. After everyone got into action, he closed the door to the office.

"Jason, you've got some explaining to do. I'm the acting police chief and this looks too much like what we had before. I hope to hell you got a good reason for this or you're going to have some big problems with the town council."

Jason sat down heavily in a chair next to the desk. He sighed. "We've got a big problem. One that's going to change everything."

"What do you mean? I know Rodney and Billy have been taken hostage, but we can work that out and free them."

"You think so?" Jason looked at Kevin who was taking a seat behind the desk. "You think that will be the end of it?"

"We pay them, we get the guys back. What else is there? What did you learn?"

"This guy, the Chairman they call him, he's taken over Knoxville. They know about us. They've heard stories about how much wealth, resources we've collected as a town—Joe Stansky's loot. They think we're rolling in resources, gold, fuel, guns, ammunition. I'm afraid we're going to be a target."

"It's all rumors, you know how they get exaggerated."

"But that's what they'll believe, the exaggerations. You think they'll stop with a hundred pounds? They're just testing us. They'll come back, with lots of men. According to Bud, this Chairman's got plans to rule the south and that probably includes us. He's got a militia like Joe had and probably a couple of hundred elite men."

"But why come all the way here?"

"Resources. Apparently, he's in a battle of dominance with Nashville. That's what's standing in his way to expanding his rule."

Kevin just gave him a questioning look. "So, Knoxville will take the time to come all the way here if it will help them get stronger. It's cities against cities?"

"Cities becoming city-states, becoming regional powers. You had that in Italy nearly to the twentieth century."

Kevin put his elbows on the desk and held his head in his hands. "So why the mutilation? Why cut the man's finger off? That's pretty brutal and, frankly that doesn't seem like you at all."

"Yeah. It's not like me...or like what I am now. But there was a time, before you came upon us in the valley—"

"I know. You led the massacre of Big Jacks' gang. We saw the results of that battle."

"And there was more, before Big Jacks. I was a violent person then. I had to be. I saw people I loved killed, brutally and I wasn't going to let that happen to my new family."

"But why torture this guy? What good did that do?"

"We don't have much time. I needed to get the full story with no chance of deception. Believe me, I didn't like it, but I got the full picture. Now he's going to draw me a map of the town—show me where everything is."

Kevin looked at the older man, nearing forty; his father-in-law. It seemed odd, since they were only about ten years apart in age. It seemed out of place to be criticizing him since he was also the acting mayor.

"Jason, I have to report this to the town council. Too many people have seen this guy and know that you took him into the woods. This won't go over well."

"That's okay. I expected you would have to do that. Don't worry about it."

"You'll probably lose your job."

Jason smiled at him. "That's not a problem. I've got another imperative now. It's time to turn this mayor work over to someone else."

Jason had been chosen to be the temporary mayor of Hillsboro after the defeat of Joe Stansky and his gang. Everyone thought the heroes of the battle, Jason, Catherine and Kevin, should play a large, public role as the city restructured itself around new leadership. Jason became the Mayor, Kevin was made Chief of Security and Catherine was made the diplomatic representative to the nearby towns that had been brutalized by Stansky's gang.

"So, your quitting?"

"I'm quitting. I'm going to go get our two men back."

Kevin stared at Jason, weighing what he just said. "You mean, not pay the ransom. That means going to fight and try to free them. Am I right?"

Jason nodded.

"That doesn't sound like such a good idea. You'll need a lot of help and that could get them killed. It's like declaring war on Knoxville."

Jason shook his head, his face was dark, unreadable to Kevin. "Not war; I'm going alone."

"That's *really* not a good idea. I should at least put a squad together and go with you."

"No, you can't. You have to stay here and prepare Hillsboro."

"But going alone?"

"I'm a trained sniper, the best shot in the city. I'm experienced in the woods and fought in Iraq. I know combat, sniping, both in an urban environment and in the forest. If necessary, I'll take out the key people and while they're in disarray, free Rodney and Billy. We'll fight our way out if we need to, but we'll get out. I'm going to bring them back."

"Jason, none of this makes sense. It's like you've lost your perspective. Billy and Rodney set out on their own journey. Are we really responsible for them? If anything, I'm more responsible since Rodney was my sergeant."

"They're part of our tribe. It's all tribal now." Jason stood up. "I'm going now. I have to break this to Anne. Get that map out of Bud. Make sure he understands that if he doesn't, or it isn't accurate, he gets another session with me in the woods. We need to get a good drawing. My life may depend on it." He started for the door, then turned back to Kevin. "And get the town council together tomorrow at noon. I'm going to address them. It's important."

"They're going to want to have a say in this," Kevin said as Jason left his office.

Chapter 3

That night Jason played with his two-year-old son, Adam, for a long time after dinner. They wrestled, played hide and seek and Adam had a number of romps around their living room on his dad's back squealing with delight. Playtime culminated in a quick ride up the stairs hanging on for dear life while Anne shouted for Jason to be careful.

After putting the boy to sleep, Jason and Anne went downstairs and sat on the couch. They lived in an older neighborhood, near Charlie Cook, the prior police chief, and Mary, his wife. The houses were built in the forties and fifties, bungalow style with sloped roofs covering the front porches. Sarah, Anne's younger daughter, was now seventeen and was spending the night at a friend's house nearby. Catherine, her older daughter, was married to Kevin and lived a block away, much to Anne's delight. She looked forward to becoming a grandmother someday.

After telling Anne what he planned to do, Jason was met with fierce opposition.

"You cannot do this," Anne said. Her face was set hard with anger. "You have a duty to your family, especially Adam. You risked your life to free Hillsboro and after that we agreed, I agreed, to go along with you being mayor to help the town get back on its feet. But this," she slammed her fist onto her thigh, "is too much."

Jason sat quietly. She could see he was waiting for her to get all her objections out. She felt desperate to find the words that would change his mind. She knew how hard he could be once he made a decision. "We all love Billy and Rodney. I know you feel a sense of responsibility for Billy especially, but he's a grown man and he made his decision to go off with Rodney and try to get to Missouri. You don't owe them your life. Your duty is here to your family, not to them."

"Anne, I don't expect you to understand, but let me explain."

"How can I understand? You have a life here, with me, with us. You said we'd spend some time, a couple of years in town, and then we'd go back to the valley. You told me you wanted to be a boring farmer and make babies." She stood up and stepped back from him. Then she turned and leaned over, grabbing his head in her hands, "How can we do that if you go off to Tennessee?" She began to cry. Angry tears ran down her face.

Jason reached up to her. "No, no, no," she said backing away. "Don't do this to me...to us, your family."

"Anne, I first left Hillsboro because I didn't want to be involved in the violence, the corruption I saw coming. But I had to kill two men just to get out of town. Later, as you know, Sam and Judy befriended me and they were brutally murdered, and worse, by a gang. I sought vengeance on them. From that time on I was alone. I lived for myself. Then I found you and the girls. You let me into your life and gave me something to live for."

"I know. You needed someone to take care of." Her voice was filled with grief.

"My first wife called me a sheep dog. Always trying to save or help people. She said I hired too many needy people in the gym I ran. It's just how I'm wired."

Anne sat down next to him. "Well save us. Take care of us. Don't run off and leave us."

Jason exhaled. "We're fine here. All our family. The whole town actually, even though I'm worried what might happen. But Rodney and Billy are part of us. I went from being alone, to taking care of our family, then to taking care of our valley and then to rescuing the town. Our circle has grown. We're a tribe now and that includes the family, the valley, Hillsboro and the Jessup and Early clans outside the city walls."

Anne kept staring at Jason, this man she loved, who had saved her and the girls and brought them joy and security out of the chaos of the post-EMP world they now lived in. "It's too much. It's too hard. You don't have to do this. It's not your fight."

Jason shook his head and slowly stood. "It is my fight. It's all our fight. The clan has to stick together or it fails. The town is in danger, not just Billy and Rodney. Knoxville will come for more if we bow to their demands."

"No!" she shouted and got up, running out of the room.

Later Jason went outside and sat on the porch steps, listening to the soft sounds of the evening, smelling the slight breeze that drifted in gentle swirls around the house, sniffing out the odors of cooking, fresh tilled dirt, the faint perfume of some unknown blossom hidden by the night. It was spring and the air had never seemed cleaner. The heaviness of what he was about to undertake slowly crept over him. The hardness inside began to soften as the husband and father reasserted itself. Quiet sobs came flowing out from deep inside of him. Sobs for the injury he caused today, sobs for the hurt he was causing this night and sobs for what he was going to have to become to rescue Rodney and Billy. Within all that though, there was no waiver of purpose, only sadness.

A half hour later, Anne quietly came out and sat down beside him. She put her arm through his and pulled herself close to his side. No words were spoken. She just held her man as he sobbed in the night. Finally she spoke.

"I know how you are. I don't understand this drive to rescue, to be the knight in shining armor, but I know that's a part of who you are. And I know that is part of why you came to us and how you prevailed over those gangs. It scares me though. I don't want you to go. With all my heart I don't want you to go—for myself and for our family."

She shifted around to look at him in the dim evening light. "I know you have to do this. What drives you to it is what makes you who you are. I love you. I'll pray for you while you're gone. But you must promise me you'll come back." Her voice was now soft but fierce. "You promise. You come back, Jason Richards. You have a son to raise and more children to bring into this crazy world."

Jason put his arms around her and they embraced. "I promise. I will come back."

Chapter 4

The next day the town council assembled in the city's town hall. They had moved back to the pre-EMP government building. The bank where Joe Stansky had his offices was a distasteful reminder of the corrupt past that everyone wanted to put behind them. By now most everyone had heard the story of Jason's abusive interrogation of the prisoner. The room buzzed with conversation.

Jason watched the growing assembly, now inflated by curious onlookers to the day's meeting. *Smelling blood in the water?* Jason could not hold back a grim smile. There was Steve Warner, an electrician and head of the underground resistance that helped overthrow Stansky's gang; Bob Jackson, who headed the water mill project, Dr. Janet Morgan who ran the hospital. Kevin was there. He had a position on the council as head of security along with Catherine as the town's diplomat. Among the members of the council was Raymond Culver, a past school administrator. Jason frowned. He knew he would be at this meeting, but it didn't make Jason feel any better. Raymond, Dr. Culver as he liked to be called, was a pain in the ass. He was a constant critic to all the real-world security mechanisms Jason had worked to instill. It seemed to Jason that Raymond Culver wanted to go back to a state of pretend bliss and forget that they lived in a shattered world with danger everywhere.

Oh well, I'll deal with him. I've been doing it for a year now.

Catherine came up to him while people were taking their seats. Her face was full of questions as she looked at him. "Can you explain what you did?"

"I'll explain it to the whole group. You may not accept it, but it will be the truth."

She touched his arm and turned to go to her seat. Jason caught Anne's eye as she entered and sat in the visitor's section. They smiled at each other.

When the room had filled up, Jason smacked the gavel on the sound block. It took three strikes to bring the room to order.

"First of all," he announced, "since we have many visitors, I need to remind you to remain quiet. This is a town council meeting, not an open forum. We are happy to have you listen in, but there will be no time to open the session up to visitor questions."

"Why can't we make this an open forum?" Raymond Culver asked.

Jason paused. *Can't let him get under my skin. Keep to my agenda.* "Because I have a lot of ground to cover and we don't have all day. In fact we only have half a day." There were a few snickers from the council. Many members had similar feelings about Dr. Culver.

"I just think that because of what has taken place the public may want to weigh in."

Jason smiled at the man. "We'll see if that is possible. Your request is duly noted." He made it sound like he was putting the request in the round file.

Turning his attention to the rest of the council, Jason started his speech.

"I'm sure you have all heard of my interrogation of a prisoner we have in our jail." Heads nodded.

"I did this because I needed to get correct information without any obfuscation or deception. And I needed to get it in a hurry. You're aware that a person called the

Chairman has taken over Knoxville, Tennessee...think of Joe Stansky and you will get the picture. He's turned the city into a criminal enterprise and you know he's captured Rodney Gibbs and Billy Turner. You also know about the ransom demand.

"What you don't know is that this Chairman is expanding. He's threatening Johnson City to our north and, according to our prisoner he's going to start a campaign against Chattanooga to the southwest of us. That hasn't happened yet, but if you think about it, he's working to encircle Hillsboro.

"The word out there is that we are rich in resources, not just gold and jewels, but fuel, weapons and ammunition. There's truth in that. You know how much Joe acquired and how much we acquired in emptying that abandoned FEMA warehouse in Lenoir."

"That was theft," Raymond Culver called out. "I opposed that action."

"You are out of order. Please refrain from shouting out while I have the floor or I'll have to remove you from the meeting. But you are right, you opposed that action. We are all aware of your position.

"Now my point is we are a target, fat and rich with resources. The Chairman won't be satisfied with the hundred pounds of gold and jewels he's asking for. There's not that much use for them at this point in a barter economy. He's testing us. Seeing if we'll bow to his demands.

"I've given a lot of thought about what to do, what is the best course of action, for Rodney and Billy, and for Hillsboro. These, by the way, are not mutually exclusive issues. I've got a list of proposals to present to the council for a vote along with an announcement."

Jason took a piece of paper that he had labored over all morning. He took a deep breath.

"Please hold your comments until I'm finished. First, I'm resigning as mayor of Hillsboro effective the end of this meeting." There was a muttering among the council members and the visitors.

"Quiet please." Jason said, before continuing. "First I recommend that the council approve Steve Warner as temporary mayor until elections can be arranged. As you all know Steve lead the resistance group here in town. This effort meant not only giving up many privileges accorded other technicians but also endangering him and his family. He will make a fine leader and I hope he'll be elected to a full term.

"Next I want the council to separate the police from the militia. It's time for a civil police force. I'm proposing Les Hammond as the new Chief of Police. He can be advised by Charlie Cook who handled himself with honor in defeating Stansky.

"I propose the council continue to develop the citizen's addition to the militia. Kevin Cameron should be put in charge of this group. As I have spoken before on this subject, we should look to Switzerland as our model. Every healthy male between the ages of eighteen and thirty-four is required to serve in the militia. All are issued a rifle which they keep at home. I would expand that to every able-bodied adult in our town. They should know how to fire a rifle and should be assigned one. They should be ready to defend the town when called upon."

He took a breath and then continued before anyone could interrupt. "You could also look to Israel as a model. We live in perilous times. What you see going on in Knoxville is happening in Nashville. In fact those two cities might come to blows. So far, according to our prisoner, they are both expanding without directly challenging each other. That threat to Knoxville only gives them more incentive to raid us.

"I also want a ranger organization set up. We must model it on the scouts that the Jessup and Early clans have set up to protect their farms outside of town. They have young men and women assigned to camp out in the forest at high vantage points, keeping a lookout. They have fires they can light to signal if any groups are approaching. We benefit from this early warning system and we should join them and help to expand it.

"We know that there are threats also from Charlotte. FEMA has joined the local mafia to help them control the city. The mafia suppresses rival gangs and keeps the killing and looting down. In return FEMA leaves them alone. It seems FEMA is more focused on the port cities, Wilmington, Charleston and others for now.

"Where am I going with this? Joe Stansky owed allegiance to the mob in Charlotte. Only he didn't make any payments after the EMP attack. They well might want to come get what they think is their share of the loot.

"So we should start a ranger corps with our young people, along with the clans. I propose we call it the Bird Rangers after Bird Early. He was the young man from Clayton's clan who died fighting Joe's gang."

There was a rustling in the audience with a few murmurs of "hear, hear."

"And lastly, I'm going to go rescue Rodney and Billy. We're not paying the ransom as that will only lead to Knoxville attacking us."

Jason looked around. The storm was about to start. "The floor is open for discussion."

The questions came fast and furious. Some were supportive, some critical, some dismissive.

"Won't your solo mission actually jeopardize our city? Won't it trigger an attack? Why shouldn't we try to pay the ransom and leave it at that?" This came from Dr. Morgan. Jason was a bit surprised but understood the motive behind the questions. Dr. Morgan, like most citizens didn't want another hot conflict. They just wanted to be left alone. The problem with that desire was that the outside world was not going to leave Hillsboro alone.

After fielding so many questions revolving around this theme, Jason offered his analysis. He knew many would reject it, but hoped the leadership would understand before it was too late.

"We've grown comfortable since getting rid of Stansky. I have as well. We haven't had any attacks. Our outreach to the surrounding towns—Hickory and others—while not completely successful have been positive. We have electricity. Even if it's limited it has made an enormous difference. We now have enough food for everyone. Our chemists, thank God for good chemistry teachers," this brought a supportive chuckle from the audience, "have made progress in anesthesia. Our dental care has improved with electricity and anesthetics. All this has made life seem pretty normal.

"But look outside of the city. There is no state government, there's limited outreach from a federal government. We hear rumors of the military splitting up. We hear about accommodations with gangsters in the name of civil order. We've walled ourselves in as have other cities and now we hear about other cities becoming city-states or regional powers. Let's face it, the country is balkanized and may be a generation or more in coming back together.

"We have to live with this reality." He paused for effect. "And we ignore it at our peril.

"I can only report what I learned from our messenger and draw my conclusion from my experiences. This Chairman will not stop with one hundred pounds of loot. He wants all we have...and we're fools if we don't prepare for that.

"So, no, I don't think my mission will change Knoxville's plans for Hillsboro. I think it can give them a reason to think twice about attacking us. And I think that if we do what I've proposed today, we can be ready for them.

"You want to turn us into a militarized community." Raymond Culver stood up and spoke as Jason paused.

"According to the models I mentioned earlier, yes."

"What if we don't want to live that way? We've walled ourselves in. We reject the refugees that come to us. I know we help them, give them some food, tend to their medical needs, but we don't let them in unless they have a specific skill, ability or expertise that can help us. We send them on their way...to where? That's discrimination. Some of us don't want us to become that kind of a community." There was a smattering of applause as he sat down.

"As you point out, we help them as we can, but if we are to open our borders to all, let everyone in, think about where we would wind up? We'd be overrun and then what the refugees seek would no longer be here. Remember what happened those first two springs and summers after the EMP attack. That would still happen, only a bit slower now. And what about the criminal element that would be let in? Do you want to add that to our troubles?"

Raymond tried to respond but Jason continued. "You bring this issue up again and again, but the council has supported my position repeatedly. We have to be selective. We can help those in need, but must limit who we let in. We have our own growing population of aging people who can't contribute that we are committed to support. No one wants to change that, but we certainly don't need to voluntarily take on more burdens."

At this point Charlie Cook stood up. "I'd like to say a few things. I know Dr. Culver. I know what he did during the Stansky era. He was allowed to remain in a cushy job, being the school administrator. Not even running the school. That seemed to be too much work. Instead he was allowed to delegate that work and sit in his office making up nice reports to send to Frank Mason. Frank encouraged the arrangement since it helped to have Dr. Culver be a supportive voice. I don't recall his speaking out against the atrocities that were going on.

"I can say this because I was on the inside. I was compromised in a larger way, but I can say unequivocally that Dr. Culver was compromised. That said, we all were compromised to some extent except for a few brave people, Steve Warner and the technicians who formed the resistance group."

Raymond Culver gave Charlie an angry look but didn't rebut his statement. For the moment the fight seemed to have gone out of him with Charlie's reminder of his passive acceptance of Stansky's regime.

The discussion went on for two more hours, but in a more supportive tone. Finally, Kevin spoke up.

"I agree that we should not buy off this Chairman, but I think you may be on a suicide mission. I would personally hate to see you killed."

Suddenly Anne stood up. "Jason is not going to get killed. He's going to come back from this mission. I know that because he promised me he would." There were smiles on the council and in the audience. Anne now had a fierce look in her eyes as she continued. "Don't think I'm being a silly-headed female. I've seen my husband in battle, I've seen him defeat Big Jacks' gang. It was eight valley residents, only two of them with any combat experience, against thirty gang members. And we prevailed. I've seen how our own family defeated a dozen gang members...just the four of us. I don't doubt my husband's abilities and neither should you. He will do what he says he'll do."

She looked around at each member of the council, her face still set hard. "And don't forget, he was the catalyst that saved this town. And he's going to risk his life again to do that for you."

With that Anne sat down. There was an uncomfortable silence.

Finally, Jason spoke up. "I'll make that the last word. I'm not asking for any vote on my mission. What we need to vote on today is to appoint Steve Warner as acting mayor until elections can be scheduled."

The voice vote was unanimous in support of Steve Warner with one abstention from Raymond Culver. Jason gaveled the meeting to a close and the crowd began to approach Jason, many expressing support, concern, or offering advice.

Anne stood by Jason's side and Catherine joined them. "I still don't understand what you did," Catherine said, "but I've seen this in you before, your dark side. Where you go before a battle."

"And you have shown that as well. It's not the healthiest trait to have, but necessary to do what has to be done. I'm happy if I can keep that away from all of us."

"But we have to be prepared, right?" Catherine said.

Jason nodded. He turned to Kevin, "I'd like to go over my plans and equipment this afternoon. I have to leave no later than the day after tomorrow."

"Why so soon?" Anne asked.

"Knoxville will expect their messenger back soon, probably within a week. I have to arrive before they put some alternate plan into action, or harm Rodney and Billy. Speed is essential in this situation." He kissed her. "I'll be home later tonight, after Kevin and I do some planning."

Chapter 5

W hat weapons are you going to take?" Kevin asked as they sat in his office.

"I'll need the M110, if I'm going to do any damage long range. That would sow some panic and confusion. For close up, I'd need an M16."

"Two rifles would be a bit of a load, especially with different ammo requirements."

"I know. I'm going to take just the M110. The group controlling Knoxville is probably using M16s. They've probably gotten them from a National Guard armory. I can grab one of theirs and use it if I need a close combat rifle."

Jason leaned towards Kevin. "What I really could use is a small caliber, silenced hand gun."

Kevin gave him a questioning look. "Like an assassin weapon?"

"Exactly."

Kevin smiled. "You're in luck. Wilkes found some interesting weapons in Leo's collection after the battle. He had a silenced .22 Walther PPK along with a couple of hundred sub-sonic rounds. We tested it and it's hardly louder than a sneeze."

"That's perfect." Jason smiled for the first time in two days.

The next day, as Jason was sorting his gear and loading his pack, Clayton showed up at the door.

"Clayton, What brings you here?"

"Heard you was going to free Billy and Rodney."

"You heard right, leaving tomorrow. Come in, sit down."

Clayton shook his head. Can't stay long." He motioned for Jason to come out onto the porch. They sat down in chairs.

"So you came here to tell me something, what is it?"

"I'm going with you," Clayton responded.

Jason looked at the mountain man. He was the leader of the Jessup and Early clans. They had come out of the deep Appalachian woods to help defeat Stansky's gang and settled onto abandoned farms near the city.

"Why would you want to do that? You have two clans to lead. You've got to be pretty busy."

"Billy's kin." Clayton said it as if that was enough reason.

"What about your wife, and boys?"

"Lisbeth be fine, boys be fine. They know I got to help kinfolk."

"This is dangerous, could be fatal, people are going to get killed."

"What we did here was dangerous. Clan boys got killed—"

"Yeah, Bird Early. I haven't forgotten."

"More'n Bird. Others were killed as well. We got to free Billy and Rodney. We got to make them fear us, so they don't come down this way."

Jason sighed and leaned back. "I can't argue with you." He knew when Clayton had made up his mind there was no changing it. Clayton was a man of few words and intense loyalties. If you were part of his group, there was nothing he wouldn't do for you. If you were an enemy, he was to be feared, implacable, fearless and deadly.

"I'd love to have you. I could use a good fighter alongside me. Kevin can't go; he's got to protect the town. We're really one big tribe now. My group has grown from myself, to my family, to the valley, to you and your clan, and now to the town."

"Not sure about the town, but you be part of our tribe now."

"Let's head over to see Kevin. See if we can get you a rifle that shoots faster than your bolt action .30-06."

"It's a good piece."

"It is, but it's not the right piece for the job. "I'm taking my M110 for long range use. It shoots the 7.62 mm round. Maybe we can find you an automatic that shoots the same round."

"Don't want to lug around a machine gun."

"No, I'm talking about a rifle, but one with auto fire option. If we have to put a lot of shots out there, you can't beat it."

"This be different from hunting in the woods."

Jason nodded. "Yeah it's going to be different." He got up. "Let's go see Kevin."

Later in Kevin's office, they talked about options. "We really only have the M16 for a rifle with automatic fire option, unless you want to take an M60."

Jason shook his head. "Nah. Too heavy and the belt feed will just be a problem. We've got to be lighter, faster."

Clayton didn't say anything. Jason could see he understood he was in a different world with military hardware. *Still he'll be an asset with any weapon.*

Kevin opened the door and shouted out for Lieutenant Tommy Wilkes to come into his office. Tommy had been promoted from his rank as specialist in the army to lieutenant in the militia after the battle. He had acquitted himself well during the fight and played a large part in securing weapons and ammunition from Stansky's warehouse, thereby limiting the gang's firepower.

"Wilkes, what do we have in 7.62 caliber rifles? I need something that can fire on automatic."

Wilkes looked thoughtful. He turned to Jason. "I heard about your mission. I just want to say that I'll keep a close eye out on your family while you're gone."

Jason smiled back. Tommy Wilkes was in love with Jason's step-daughter, Sarah. She was seventeen now and Wilkes was about eight years older than her. Jason figured it would only be a year or two more and they would be telling him and Anne they were getting married.

"Thank you. I'm sure you'll do a good job in that area. But let's get back to the question at hand."

Tommy Wilkes smiled. "I think I've got just what is needed. We found some AK47s in the warehouse. Apparently they were from Joe Stansky's gang days, before he robbed the armories."

"Are they in decent shape?" Kevin asked.

"We can go through them. There's six if I remember correctly. I think we can find a good one. We test fired a couple and they surprised me. They don't kick that hard. Pretty easy to control on automatic, unlike some other rifles."

"You mean like the old M14." Jason said.

Tommy Wilkes nodded. "I understand they took the auto function off of it because it was uncontrollable. This AK seems much more controllable. And it hits harder than the M16."

"Sounds like what you want," Kevin said. "Let's go have a look." The four men headed out of the office in the police headquarters to walk over to the warehouse.

After a half hour of selecting three rifles they went to the rifle range that had been set up near a section of the town's wall and tried them out. Clayton quickly figured out how to control the rifle on automatic.

"That's a lot of bullets fired. Seems wasteful," he said.

"Sometimes it's better to send a lot of rounds down range than pick a target carefully. But helps to try to aim the weapon, not fire blindly," Jason replied.

Clayton nodded. "Still seems odd."

The two men agreed to meet up at dawn by the north entrance gate into the city. Jason got out a map and traced the route. "We'll go along Interstate 40 for most of the way. The walking will be easier."

"Unless we get ambushed."

"There is that risk. We'll have to be vigilant. If we have to take to the woods, we'll do fine. It'll just take longer."

"How we gonna sneak into town?" Clayton asked.

"Got a map from the messenger. We'll have to play that by ear. He marked where he thinks Rodney and Billy are being kept, but he's not completely sure."

Clayton nodded, shook hands and left the group to head out of the city to his farm. He had over an hour walk, but he was used to walking. Everyone was used to walking.

As the other three headed back to the police station, Jason made a suggestion. "I'm going to tell you to execute Bud if I'm not back in a week. I want you to agree to that in Bud's hearing. It will keep him helpful, trying to please you."

"What do we do while waiting for your return?" Kevin asked.

"Work on defenses. If I'm not back in a week, you should accelerate those preparations. Hell, you should accelerate them now. If you don't see us in two weeks, you can assume we're dead or captured. In any case, you have to assume this Chairman is coming. Keep the scouts out far enough to give you time to get everyone to the walls.

"We've got about 30,000 people in town, maybe more, so if you get ten percent armed and ready, that gives you a lot of defenders."

"And we've got mortars and M2s we can set up along the walls," Kevin said.

"Yeah. Unlike Stansky, you've got the ability to defend the full perimeter. Don't let them into the city."

Chapter 6

T he next morning Jason and Clayton set out hiking west along I40. Their route would first take them west and then near Lake Junaluska, in Tennessee, the interstate turned north on its way to Knoxville. If they could keep to the highway and encountered no trouble the walk would take them about a week.

The spring morning was invigorating. In spite of the dangerous nature of their mission, Jason couldn't suppress some joy at being out in the open. Was it the quest? He chuckled softly. That was a part of it he had to admit to himself.

"What's funny?" Clayton asked.

"Nothing really. Just found myself enjoying the morning, even though we're heading into trouble."

"Don't pay to not enjoy things when you can. Trouble comes soon enough."

"You're right about that."

"I think this hiking on the road's going to get hard on the feet. The woods be softer walking."

"I agree but this is faster. Think of it as a clear path, all graded and smoothed out for us."

"And paved so it hurts the feet."

The highway was littered with vehicles that had stopped when the EMP burst had struck. The cars never moved again. There was evidence of wrecks as cars had become uncontrollable at sixty to seventy miles an hour. Jason thought about all the people who had left those cars. Where had they gone? Had they survived? At some of the wreck sites, they could see the skeletal remains of the victims. There was no question about their fate. The density of the cars increased and decreased like frozen waves of traffic.

"We're still stuck with walking. It would take a massive effort to clear these roads."

"Maybe helps keep others from moving around and bothering us."

"Yeah. It probably slows the feds down, but I sense we're on borrowed time. They're going to come around someday."

"That's why you put out sentries," Clayton replied.

That night they slept along the highway. Jason chose an abandoned car, while Clayton bedded down on the side of the highway. The next morning after breakfasting on some dried fruit and water, they again headed west, the sun at their backs.

The air was cool but Jason could feel the warmth of the sun on his shoulders. Nothing much was said as they plodded along. Both men carried backpacks loaded with fifty pounds of gear. They wore tactical vests. Their rifles were slung over their shoulders. Jason had dismounted his scope from the M110 and had carefully packed it in a cushioned case and put it in his pack. He would rely on the iron sights until he had to do some sniping. He was feeling the soreness from the first day. Muscles being called into action in a way they hadn't been for a long time.

"You feeling a bit sore this morning?" he asked turning to Clayton as they tramped along.

Clayton grinned. "Yeah. But only admit it to you. I s'pect it'll pass."

"I give it another day. If not, I'm going to be feeling old."

An hour later, Jason blinked. A flash of light had hit his eyes. Without breaking stride he scanned ahead to find the source. Something had reflected the sun into his eyes.

There it was again. A third of a mile ahead was an overpass. The flash came from there, just above the concrete retaining wall. A quick look along the overpass revealed nothing. There were ramps on either side of the interstate to connect to the crossing road. They ran uphill. Jason could not see if any vehicles were on the far, downhill side of the ramps. There could be a vehicle parked on either side of the interstate, on the downhill slope, nicely out of sight. But one thing was sure; someone was on the overpass observing them with binoculars, or a rifle scope.

Jason stopped at the next vehicle. It was a truck with a large front bumper. He un-shouldered his rifle and backpack and sat down on the bumper, facing the distant overpass.

"What's up?" Clayton asked.

"Something in my boot," Jason replied. He began to take off his boot.

Clayton leaned his rifle against the front of the truck and took his pack off as well. "Glad to set that down for a bit."

"Clayton, don't turn around and keep looking at me. Stay relaxed but don't turn around."

Clayton gave him a quizzical look.

"Don't react to what I'm about to say."

"I hear you," Clayton said. "But what you got to say?"

"Someone is observing us. With binoculars or through a rifle scope. *Don't turn around!"*

Clayton caught himself just in time. "Where are they?" he asked.

"On the overpass ahead."

"How you know?"

"The sun reflected off their binoculars or scope. It flashed in my eyes."

"So what you think we should do?"

"I'm trying to figure that out. They're probably armed but it's a pretty long shot to take right now. I suspect they're just waiting for us to get closer."

"Bandits!" Clayton said that with a note of disgust in his voice.

"They can see we got packs and rifles. We may not look easy, but I'll bet we look inviting. So the easiest thing would be to shoot us from ambush and then just come down and take everything." Jason stretched and then bent down to rub his foot. "Let's try to keep them off guard as long as we can."

He looked around casually. To his right the ground sloped gently upward to a line of trees. They were near a channel dug into the slope and filled with rocks. It spread out in a V shape at the top of the rise, gathering water to run off the hillside in the rocky channel, thereby limiting the erosion.

"We should try to make it to the tree line to our right. If we use the channel, we'll have cover from the shooter, but it will be tough going in those rocks." Jason reached over and took out a map from his backpack. "Let's pretend we're discussing an alternate route. The interstate starts going north soon, so we could be discussing cutting to the right, over the hill as a short cut. Come on over and look at the map with me."

He pantomimed a discussion between him and Clayton about cutting across country, pointing to the slope and woods.

"We make it to the woods, what then? We go after them?" Clayton asked.

"The crossroad ahead cuts through that hillside, so we'll intersect it part of the way up. I'm betting they'll hop in a vehicle if they have one and try to hit us as we come up out of the woods."

"If they got something to drive. If not, we can just go on, bypass them."

"That would be best, but we'd better be ready for the worst."

"They know we'll hear them if they start an engine."

"Yeah. We'll see what they do. If we don't hear anything, we should still assume they've found a way to get up the road quietly."

"So we just amble up the slope? Seems like inviting them to shoot."

"Getting into those rocks would give us some cover but it would be tough going, climbing and keeping below the rim."

"Plus they'll know we seen them."

Jason nodded and with another stretch, he put the map away and pulled on his boot and laced it up. He stood up and pointed up hill like he was finalizing their route.

"Let's just walk it casually, but stay apart. I don't think they can make that long a shot. They'll think they got a better chance to catch us at the road further up the slope."

"Hope you right. Makes my back itch to leave myself open like this."

Jason looked at Clayton. "I don't like it either. Don't like betting on someone else's shooting ability, but I don't see any other choice."

The two men shouldered their packs and rifles and casually set out towards the slope, climbing over the guard rail. As they walked uphill Jason had to force himself to not keep looking over to his left, towards the overpass. *Be casual, be methodical, you're just climbing a hill.*

After five minutes that seemed like an hour, they reached the trees and pushed through the dense brush at the edge of the forest. Both men sighed. Clayton's eyes were alight. The forest was his element. Jason also felt comfort amongst the trees.

"Let's move quickly up the hill. We'll stop about fifty yards from the road. I think we'll be able to see it by the gap of light where it cuts through the trees."

"We fan out and wait?"

"Yeah. We'll assume they're coming. We stay in sight of each other. They'll get antsy and probably come into the woods to investigate."

"That's when we take them down," Clayton said.

The two men moved up the hill silently. They continued until they could see the cut of the road above.

"Let's wait here."

Clayton nodded. Jason lay down behind two tree trunks that had fallen some years ago. They presented an uneven line that would hide his head and rifle. Clayton moved to his left behind a granite boulder that was next to a large oak tree. The notch between them gave him a good shooting position.

They heard the growl of an engine but it soon stopped. Jason couldn't tell if the sound had been coming closer before it ended. *Did they drive part of the way and are now walking?* He didn't know. The answer was to wait. He knew Clayton understood this. Patience...and stealth rewarded the hunter. Whether you hunted men or game animals. It would take some time for the bandits to become tired of waiting. Their impatience would be their demise. It was worth the wait. If the ambushers didn't show, Jason figured they would creep to the road and confirm the fact they weren't there, and keep moving up through the woods, cutting off part of the interstate.

About fifteen minutes later Jason heard it; the scuffling of feet up the hill, on the road. He looked over at Clayton who was looking intently up the slope. He'd heard it as well.

Now we know. Now we let them come to us.

Chapter 7

I t was another ten minutes before the bandits on the road got impatient as Jason expected. They wanted to find their quarry. He figured the promise of what might be in the packs was too attractive to ignore. Two of the three men started down into the woods from the road. They separated from each other by about thirty yards. *At least they are smart enough to do that.*

Jason caught Clayton's eye and pantomimed to him to wait one minute. He indicated he would take out the man on the right and Clayton should target the man to the left. The key was to take them down quickly and then get to any other bandits on the road before they could disappear. Who knew how many others were in reserve? Neither he nor Clayton wanted a full out gunfight with six or more armed men.

Jason's target was about thirty yards away. He had settled his rifle on him and was just about to shoot when Clayton fired. The man in Jason's sights turned as Jason stroked the trigger. His shot slammed into his left shoulder, throwing the man to the ground.

Jason stood up and ran to him. He was writhing in pain, his upper arm was torn open, probably broken. It looked like the bullet had penetrated his side after going through his arm. Jason threw the man's rifle away from him, he was not going to be moving very far, and ran towards the road. He slipped once and fell to his knees, catching himself with his left hand. Cursing, he got up and charged to the road.

On reaching the road, he saw the third bandit running back down the road towards the interchange and their pickup truck parked about two hundred yards away. The man was about seventy yards and getting more distant every second. Jason flopped to the pavement, sucked in a breath and blew it out slowly. Part of the way through exhaling, he paused, settled the iron sights on the man's back and fired. The M110 gave a satisfying kick and the man was flung forward, landing face down on the pavement. He squirmed around for a moment and then lay still.

"That's some shot," Clayton said. He had arrived at the road just as Jason had dropped to the prone position.

"Big target, moving straight ahead, no need to lead him, not too hard. The man I shot in the woods is still alive, let's go talk to him, find out who else is out there."

"Man I shot is dead," Clayton replied.

They went back down into the woods. The young man was lying on the ground groaning in pain. Jason squatted down so the man could see him.

"How many more of you are there?" he asked.

The wounded bandit looked young. Jason guessed he couldn't be more than twenty. He was breathing raggedly, seeming to struggle for breath.

"It hurts bad," he said at last.

"I understand that. I have some pain medication in my pack. I can give you something for the pain, but I need you to answer some questions first."

"I'll get our packs," Clayton said.

"You want something for the pain?" Jason asked.

The young man nodded.

"Tell me how many more of you are out there?"

"Just one more besides us three. They're all brothers. I joined them couple months ago. It hurts bad, hard to talk."

Clayton came back lugging the packs. Jason took his pack and dug through it to find the morphine autoinjectors he had packed. He pulled one out and stuck it into the man's thigh. "This should help."

Within a minute the man relaxed and calmed down.

"Now tell me about this gang, especially this fourth person."

"I joined them couple of months ago. I was on my own. My family all died after the power went out. Our whole town was wiped out, first by people dying, then by some gang raids. Me and a high school buddy, we survived by hiding in the woods. Later we took to robbing people. We set up at a bridge and charged tolls to cross. Didn't take everything, just some things to get along. Then a group came along and fought back. Bobby was killed and I was alone. That's when I came across the brothers."

He coughed. Jason could see blood in what came out. The bullet had probably lodged in his chest, coming through his side after shattering his arm.

"I'm all stove up," the young man complained. "This ain't good." He looked up at Jason. "Am I gonna make it?"

"Maybe. Can't say for sure. The bullet shattered your left arm and entered your side." The man's arm was bleeding profusely. Jason realized that if he wanted information, he'd better stop the bleeding. "I'll get something to bind that arm, stop the blood flow."

"I'll do it," Clayton said. "You keep talking to him."

Jason nodded. "Go on," he said to the man.

"Well the brothers, Aaron, Clem and Hank, don't know their last names. They ain't that nice. They'd take everything when they robbed people. Killed them sometimes. Sometimes they took girls or women and tied them up in the house. Raped them."

"The house. Where is it?"

"It's about a mile from the overpass, on the south side. We been working this area, but it's slim pickings. I think they was planning to move somewhere else, maybe some small towns nearby."

"They got any captives now?"

"Only one now. The rest died or they killed them when they got tired or angry. 'There's always more' they said."

Just then Clayton came back with a shirt he'd taken off the man he had shot. Jason cut it up with his knife and tied it tight around the man's arms. "What's your name?"

"Ronnie," the young man replied.

"The house is on this road?"

Ronnie nodded.

"And the third brother is at the house?" Clayton asked.

Ronnie nodded again. "He's the meanest one. Big. He hears about his brothers no telling what he'll do. Probably kill the woman he's got."

"She's a prisoner?"

Ronnie nodded again. "Tied to a bed. They let her up to eat and take a dump or piss, then she's tied back on the bed. They take her anytime they want."

"You do that?"

Ronnie shook his head vigorously which caused another bout of coughing up blood. "No," he gasped when he could get his breath back. "She's about forty, not bad looking, but she's too much like a mom. Seemed creepy to me."

"How'd they capture her?"

"She was traveling with her husband, heading east when we stopped them. We took all the food they had, the husband tried to resist, so Clem shot him. Then Hank, the big one, grabbed her and dragged her to the house. She's been there about two weeks."

He moaned and rolled over, his face to the ground. "This ain't good. You got any more of that drug? It's starting to hurt bad again."

Now Clayton spoke up. "What's your last name?"

"Clancy."

"I knew some Clancys, didn't know they was outlaws."

"We ain't. It's just I didn't know what else to do. And I never hurt nobody. Mister, can you give me some more stuff for the pain?"

Clayton continued, "You're hurt bad, you know that."

Ronnie nodded. "Broke up for sure. Don't think I'll make it."

"Probably not," Clayton replied.

Ronnie reached out to Jason. "Maybe you can do one thing. Maybe you can free that woman. Then I won't die feeling so bad. I'll feel like maybe I helped do one thing right. Seems like I didn't do anything right after the power went out. Didn't mean to be bad."

"You ran with a bad group," Clayton said. "Got on the wrong side of things, but it's a choice you make."

"Didn't know what else to do."

"Don't matter now."

"Can you help her?" Ronnie asked looking up at Jason.

Jason looked over at Clayton who gave him a perceptible nod.

"Yeah, we'll free her, and kill Hank."

"That's a good thing I done then. The house is the first one on the left after the overpass." He sagged back. "I'm done in. You bury me when I'm gone? Not leave me to the animals?"

"We'll check on you after getting this woman free." Jason stood up. "Got to go now." He grabbed his pack and Clayton and he walked back up to the road.

"What we gonna do?" Clayton asked.

"We should free the woman and kill this guy Hank."

"Don't have a problem 'bout that, but we can't take her with us."

"I know. But she's better off free and with Hank dead than if we just head off to Knoxville."

"Just so we understand."

Jason nodded. "Let's go do this," he said and they started down the road.

They passed the body of the third bandit and stopped at the pickup. "We should drive this part of the way,"

Jason said. "The engine will be a familiar sound to Hank. He won't suspect anything when he hears it."

"Can't just drive up though."

"No. We'll have to stop before we're seen from the house and go on foot. The key is to take the guy out quickly before he creates a hostage situation."

They got into the truck and started down the road.

They caught a glimpse of the house before reaching the driveway and stopped the truck on the road. They got out and moved up through the woods until they came to edge of the trees where the yard started. The house had wood siding that needed painting. It was one story with a small porch covered by a low-hanging extension of the roof. One corner post supporting the overhang was broken and the roof was starting to sag, giving in to the inexorable pull of gravity. A few ragged curtains hung in the windows.

There was a separate garage leaning to one side that looked in danger of collapsing. Judging from the tire tracks and mud, it looked like cars and trucks were just driven up on the front yard and parked wherever was convenient.

"We can't just walk up. It be too open. He can just shoot away at us," Clayton said.

"How about we separate and each come up alongside of the house. His instinct will be to look out the front. If we get to a window, we can try to locate him before we enter."

"Just don't shoot each other."

Jason smiled. "Yeah, that wouldn't be good. Maybe you go in from the rear. Then we're not shooting across from each other if we have to fire. The house probably has a kitchen and dining-living room. Those are probably up front. I'm guessing there are two bedrooms in the back. I'll go for the front side window. See if I can't locate the target."

"I'll try to get in from the back. I can keep him away from the woman."

"Set your AK for automatic fire."

Clayton looked at him.

"Just short bursts. It makes it less necessary to take time to aim accurately. You put a short burst down a hallway, if someone's in it, you're going to hit them."

Clayton nodded and flipped the selector on the rifle.

Jason felt a surge of adrenaline as they readied for the attack. Taking out a bad guy, freeing up a captive, energized him.

"You know a robin call?" Clayton said. Jason nodded. "I'll make one when I'm in place. You go then."

They both moved to the right. Jason stopped when they were facing the side of the house and Clayton continued on to the rear.

When he heard the chirp of a robin, he took a deep breath and stepped out of the woods. It was against his sniper training, but this was close-quarter fighting. They had to advance on the enemy and take him down before he could harm them or the hostage.

Jason walked over the open area, only twenty yards, to the house. It seemed nineteen yards too long. He looked through the window and saw Hank. The man was large. He must have been over six feet tall and weighed well over two hundred pounds. Hank looked over at the window as Jason raised his rifle. Hank dove for the floor as Jason fired. It looked like Jason's shot caught him in the shoulder. The man didn't hesitate but ran down the hall out of Jason's sight. Jason heard a short burst from the AK. Then all was quiet.

Jason went to the front door and flung it open, rifle at ready. Hank was lying in the hallway near the back door.

"Good suggestion," Clayton said in a calm voice from the back door.

They went into the bedroom behind the front room where Hank had been sitting. There, on the bed was the woman. She was naked, tied spread eagle with a pillow stuffed under her buttocks raising her pelvis in an obscene manner. Both men quickly looked away.

Jason went back out in the hall. There was a small closet. Opening it, he found some sheets. He grabbed one and took it into the room. He covered the woman. She stared at the men with wild, fearful eyes, turning her head from side to side.

"It's okay ma'am. We're here to rescue you. All the men who captured you are dead. You're safe now.

Chapter8

Jason cut the woman's bonds and the two men left the room. They closed the door to give the woman some privacy, to let her get dressed and calm down. While waiting, they dragged Hank outside. Both men were panting with the effort.

"He's a heavy one," Clayton said after they got the body into the woods.

"The animals will be around tonight. Could get noisy."

"Right about that."

Back inside Jason knocked on the bedroom door. "Can you come out now? We need to talk."

"No, go away. Don't hurt me." The woman sounded nearly hysteric.

Jason looked over at Clayton. He saw a questioning look in Clayton's eyes.

"Ma'am," Jason said, "I don't think it's a good idea for us to go away. At least not until we've talked. You're safe now with us. We're not here to hurt you. That big guy, Hank is dead. He can't hurt you."

"How do you know his name?" Her voice was now beginning to sound calmer, if still suspicious.

"One of his gang members told us."

"How did you know about this house, to come here?"

Jason felt his frustration rise. "Look I'm not going to talk through this door. We just rescued you at danger to ourselves. We don't want anything from you, so if you don't want to come out, we'll be on our way."

There was a moment of silence, then the woman said, "No, no. Don't go, I'll come out." The door opened and she stared at Jason.

He took a step back so as to not scare her. "My name is Jason Richards. My companion is Clayton Jessup. We're from Hillsboro." The woman looked at him as if he were an alien. She still seemed disoriented to Jason. She was dressed in jeans and a sweatshirt. She had no shoes on her feet. She was rubbing her wrist which looked chaffed from the ropes that had held her to the bed.

"My name is Helen," she finally said.

"I'm glad to meet you, Helen. Let's go into the front room and sit down. Do you want some water or something to eat?"

"Some water...please."

The men went into the living room. Helen followed. Jason and Clayton sat on a couch; the woman sat in a stuffed chair well out of reach of the men.

"How did you know about this house," Helen asked again.

Clayton sat quiet, studying the woman. Jason answered. "The gang made a mistake. They tried to ambush us. Now they're all dead. The young kid, Ronnie, told us about you and asked us to help you out."

She stared at him as if it were hard to believe what he had just said. "All dead? All of them?"

"Yes, ma'am. Well, to be accurate, Ronnie's probably not dead yet, but he won't last long with his wounds. Seems like he got a dose of remorse at the end and wanted to help save you."

She nodded. "He didn't do anything to me. He was nicer than the others." She shuddered at the thoughts that seemed to rise in her mind.

Clayton spoke up. "He took up with bad men and paid for it. Got to know where you stand now days. Good side or bad side."

"You're not from Hillsboro," Helen said as she turned to Clayton.

"No ma'am. From north of there. Way up in the mountains. But we come to Hillsboro to take up on the abandoned farms."

"I see," she said. Then she shook her head. "No I don't see." Her voice was sharp and angry. "I don't see what's happened, why the world has gone to hell, why people are killing each other, raping and killing." She choked back a sob. "Why did they have to kill Martin? He couldn't hurt them. Why take everything? We were just trying to survive like them, but we didn't rob, kill and rape to do it." She broke down in angry sobs.

They sat in an uncomfortable silence. The men nodded their heads in unspoken agreement, not knowing what more to say.

"You were headed to east? Were you going to Hillsboro?"

The woman nodded.

"Do you still want to get there?" Jason asked.

"Can I go with you two? Where are you going?"

"We're going into battle, in Knoxville, to rescue two friends."

"I don't mind. I won't be afraid."

"No, you don't understand. You can't come with us. We're going into great danger and we may not come back."

"But I won't slow you down. And I can help. I'm a nurse. Surely that would be useful if there's a fight."

Both men shook their heads.

Suddenly Helen stood up. "How can you be so cruel? You rescue me and then leave me here alone? That's heartless." She continued ranting and then ended up pleading, "Let me come with you, please."

Jason waited for her to calm down. She just stood there with a mixture of sadness and anger showing in her face.

"We're not cruel. We just set you free from a pretty horrible situation. I know you've been traumatized but you're better off now than you were an hour ago."

"Not if you abandon me. I'll just wind up a slave again...or dead."

"They's ways to avoid that," Clayton said.

Helen looked at him. "I'd like to know how." She looked and sounded skeptical.

"They's some rifles, here, in this house, and with the men outside. Rifles and ammunition. You take them and defend yourself."

"I don't know how to shoot. I don't think I could shoot anyone."

Clayton's face showed disdain but spoke calmly, "If you had the chance could you shoot Hank? If you knew you would kill him and end it, would you shoot him?"

Helen now looked confused. "Maybe...if I knew how to shoot and if I knew it wouldn't just hurt him and make him mad at me. When he got mad, he hurt me. I had to keep him from getting mad...do anything to keep him from..." Jason could see her eyes fill with tears. He guessed her mind was going back to those dark, desperate moments that had made up her life for the past two weeks. The sobs came again. She sat back down.

"Well he can't hurt you now," Jason said. "And we can show you how to use a gun so no one else can hurt you as well."

"I won't be a burden," Helen said quietly.

They talked off and on, with long silences in between as Helen began to recover and come to grips with the fact that her nightmare was over.

"Can we go find Martin? Bury him properly?"

Clayton shook his head. "Been two weeks? Best not to go there, animals and all."

That brought another round of sobbing as Helen absorbed this additional insult.

"We can make up a marker, a cross if you like, at the overpass. We can carve his name on it." Jason offered.

"That would be nice...thank you."

Jason stood up. "The bandits are gone. We'll stay here for the night. I'll see to some food." He turned to Clayton, "How about you going back up the road and collect the guns and ammo from the others?"

Clayton nodded and headed for the door.

"You want to help with the food, or ride with Clayton?"

"I'd rather stay here. But I don't know if I want to spend the night in this house."

"That's your call, but we'll be sleeping here. If you're not going with Clayton, come help me get some food together."

"I'm not very hungry."

Jason caught Clayton's grin as he stepped out through the front door. Jason turned back to Helen. "I'm not asking if you're hungry or not. I'm asking, no, let me be clear, I'm telling you to help me get some food together."

Helen looked startled. Fear began to creep back into her eyes. "Are you going to abuse me now? Make me do things?"

Jason swore in exasperation. "Look, Helen. Can I call you Helen?" She nodded watching him warily. "I'm not going to abuse you. We just saved your life. We just fought a gun battle and have been on the move since morning. We're tired and hungry. I would think you might just want to pitch in and help me get a meal together. On top of that practical consideration, it might help you to do something normal like prepare a meal. It's a very human thing to do, prepare food and eat together. It's almost an antidote to the savagery you've seen and experienced."

He started for the kitchen, then turned back to Helen. "And don't think you're the only one who's been savagely treated. I've seen worse done to friends of mine. You're lucky, you survived." With that he went into the kitchen.

Chapter 9

A few minutes later Helen walked quietly into the kitchen. Jason was looking through the cabinets.

"Let me do that. I know where the food is. They made me fix meals for them. After…" her voice trailed off, but she kept herself under control. She got a box of pasta out of a cupboard. In another one she grabbed a can of tomato sauce and some canned meat. "We can boil the pasta and heat up this sauce with the meat."

"That sounds like a winner. Better than army MREs."

"Why did you ask if we were going to Hillsboro?"

"If you were headed east, that would be the next big town on the way, so I assumed that might be your destination."

"Well it was. We heard that Hillsboro had resources. And after gangs raided our small town, we headed in that direction. We were two weeks on the road. We were pretty much alone through the Smokey's. We always hid when we noticed anyone else. Then we got here—"

"And things went bad for you."

She nodded, unable to speak.

"Can't I go with you? I won't be a problem. I'll cook, I can treat wounds, injuries. I can be really helpful." She was now looking at Jason, her eyes full of a desperate pleading.

"We're going back to where you came from." He shook his head. "You don't want to be a part of what we're going to do."

"It's cruel to leave me alone, here, like this. I'm scared I'll get captured again."

Jason didn't answer. They concentrated on heating the food in silence. Helen got out bowls and plates.

Clayton returned carrying three AR15 type rifles. He laid them in a corner of the living room. "They's lots of ammunition in the pickup."

"Come in the kitchen, we got some food ready," Jason called out.

"That pump work?" Clayton asked looking through the window at the hand pump in the side yard.

"Yes. The water's good, everyone drank it," Helen responded.

"I'm gonna wash up," Clayton said and went into the hall and grabbed a towel from the closet.

"I'll join you," Jason said.

When the two men came back in, Helen had set the food out on the kitchen table. She seemed to Jason to be much calmer.

"Thank you for getting this together," Jason said.

"Mighty hungry. Thanks," Clayton added.

Helen sat at the table while the men ate with gusto. Jason didn't realize how hungry he was. After eating they all went into the living room. Jason could feel a deep fatigue starting to settle in on him.

"I can't sleep in that bed," Helen announced. "I don't know if I can sleep in this house."

"Can't blame you," Clayton said. "You could sleep on the couch. Jason and I can sleep in the two bedrooms."

"I think I'm afraid to sleep out here...alone."

"One of us can sleep here, on the floor if that will help," Jason said.

"I think I'm afraid to have anyone in the room." She paused and looked around with fearful eyes. "I think I'm afraid to sleep, period."

"Can't keep that up for long," Clayton said.

Jason got up and went into the kitchen. He came back a minute later with a bottle of whiskey and three glasses.

"It's amazing they had any bottled whiskey left. Here's dessert." He held up the bottle.

"Oh no!' Helen said cowering in her chair. Don't get drunk. You'll hurt me."

"That what they did?" Clayton asked.

She nodded, staring at the bottle, like it was something malignant.

"Don't worry. We're not the type to get drunk, and keep reminding yourself it's us who rescued you." Jason said. He poured two glasses, one for himself and one for Clayton.

"You might find it helps you sleep. Up to you," Clayton said with a shrug.

"We need to talk about tomorrow," Jason said.

"Do we have to?" Helen asked.

"Yes. I know this is hard for you. I know staying here is hard and leaving is hard. You need time to recover from this trauma. But the plain truth is you don't have the time."

"We got friends...one of 'em kin, that we got to get to before they get killed," Clayton said.

Helen just sat in her chair, looking fearful and confused.

"I'm going to tell you what you need to do. You don't have to do what I say. You're free to do whatever you want—"

"Except go with you."

"Correct. What you can do is take a rifle we'll choose for you. We'll show you how to use it. You can practice in the morning. Hillsboro is only about sixty to eighty miles away. At twenty miles an hour you can be there tomorrow. You take the pickup. There's enough gas in it to get you that far. I'll write a note that will get you into town. You go see Dr. Morgan at the hospital, she'll help you get settled in. You'll be safe there."

Jason could tell Helen was listening, but she was also shaking.

"You be tough, you get to town. You be soft, you don't go anywhere. Things only gonna get worse here," Clayton said.

"I don't know how—"

"You have to do it," Jason said, interrupting her. "Steel your mind to it. You'll have time to grieve and recover when you're safe in Hillsboro. But now, you have to be strong."

"And strong-minded," Clayton said.

Helen nodded and sighed. "I guess I can do it. I don't know what else to do. You won't stay with me or let me come with you." She seemed to gather her courage. "But I want to burn this house down tomorrow before I go."

"That ain't a good idea. You catch the woods on fire, it'll spread over miles. That's no good," Clayton said.

"How about we drag the bed out in the morning," Jason said, "while there's no breeze, and you light it up. You burn it in the yard. It'll be a symbol of your victory over those who captured you. Then we all set out. Us for Knoxville, you for Hillsboro."

"Okay." Helen looked up at Jason. "Can I drive all the way to Hillsboro?"

"I think so. The interstate was more crowded on the west-bound lanes. You're going east so it should be easier. Just drive down the side of the road when you come to jam ups. I think you'll be able to get most of the way there."

"Will I meet any bad men along the way?"

"That's what you got the rifle for," Clayton said.

"We didn't on our way here. This was the first ambush we encountered. Chances are you'll be fine."

Helen nodded. "Would you mind, each of you, sleeping near the living room tonight? Maybe in the hall or kitchen? I'd feel better."

"We most likely stand guard all night," Clayton said.

"Take shifts," Jason added.

"We can bring a mattress out to the hall and sleep there when we're not on guard. Best to stand guard outside. Hear better," Clayton said.

With the arrangements set and Helen calmed down, Clayton headed outside with his AK to take the first shift. Jason dragged a mattress into the front hall and Helen put a sheet and blanket on the couch.

The night passed uneventfully. Helen must have had bad dreams as she cried out in her sleep. She woke each time Jason and Clayton changed over on guard duty. Each time the men had to calm her down.

At first light Clayton was up. Jason joined him in the kitchen as they scrounged up something to eat. It was a can of beans and a can of corn heated on the propane stove. Helen got up and went outside to wash her face from the pump. When she came in they persuaded her to eat some of the heated food.

"Big day. Got to fuel it," Clayton said.

"Take some of the canned food with you. Even cold it will provide nourishment. We can't pack canned goods," Jason said.

"Take some water as well," Clayton added.

After Helen had assembled food and water, Jason led her to the living room.

"Let's pick a weapon for you," he said.

He chose a civilian, semi-automatic Colt AR15. The action worked smoothly and it seemed to be in the best shape. There were nearly two hundred rounds of ammunition.

"We're going to have you fire this so you can get a little comfortable with it. It doesn't kick hard. But pack up what you're going to take first. We're going to make a lot of noise and after that, you're going to burn that bed. That's a lot of noise and smoke, so we'll want to leave right after that."

"We be attracting some attention for sure," Clayton said. "Not sure this be a good idea."

Helen started back to the house to gather her clothes and supplies.

"I know," Jason said. "But Helen needs to try the rifle and she needs to burn this bed. Maybe it will help her feel like she's had a victory over these scum."

Helen packed up her things and came back into the yard. She loaded them into the pickup. Clayton set out some kitchen pans, on a bush at the edge of the front yard. He put the targets about twenty-five yards away.

"If you can hit these, you can put someone down. You let 'em get this close and then open up. Be hard to miss."

Jason showed her how to line up the front and rear sights and place them on the target.

Helen's first shots were way off target, high and wide. "It's loud," she said.

"Keep at it," Jason said. "Hold the gun tight to your shoulder. Line up the sights, put them on the target, and squeeze. Don't jerk the trigger."

By the time she had run through the twenty-round magazine, she could hit the pans.

While she was shooting, Clayton went into the bedroom where Helen had been tied and came back out dragging the mattress. He threw it in the middle of the front yard. Jason followed with the box springs. Then both men went back into the bedroom and kicked apart the cheap, wooden bed frame. Minutes later they carried two armfuls of splintered wood outside and threw it on the pile. Next Clayton found a garden hose and cut a length of it. He stuck it down into the gas tank of the pickup and siphoned out a quart of gasoline into a cooking pot.

Handing the pot to Helen, he said, "You pour this all on the pile. You're gonna burn up your nightmare."

Helen poured out the gas.

Jason took a rolled up magazine, went into the kitchen and lit it from the propane stove. He brought it out to Helen. "It's for you to burn this down. Burn away the evil that was done to you."

Helen nodded. "This is for Martin, this is for me. This bed goes to ashes and the men go to hell." She put the torch to the pile and the flames rose up. The morning was still and the sparks and smoke rose straight into the air. The pile would soon be ashes. Helen stared at the flames.

Clayton looked around nervously. "Time to go," he said. "We doin' too much announcing."

Helen turned to both men. "What about the ones you shot yesterday?"

"What about them?" Jason asked.

"Do you just leave them?"

Clayton looked at Jason and spoke, "As I recall, you promised to bury Ronnie."

"I guess I did," Jason replied. He turned towards the old shed. "I'll get a shovel. We'll do it on our way."

When he returned with two shovels, he and Clayton hoisted their backpacks and slung their rifles over their shoulders.

At the pickup Helen turned to the men. She put her hands out and reached up to touch each man on his shoulder. "Thank you both for saving my life."

"You're welcome," they said.

"One last word of advice," Jason said. "If you run late, do not use your headlights. That's too visible and could attract unwelcome company. Just find a cluster of vehicles you can park with, don't use your flashlight, nothing to attract attention. Sleep with your rifle ready, a round loaded in the chamber and the safety on and keep the doors locked."

Helen started to look at fearful.

"Don't be afraid, this is just being cautious. It's what we all have to do now. If you don't make it today, you'll finish your drive the next morning. You probably won't have to stop, but if you do, follow my advice and you'll be fine."

She looked at him gravely, nodded, and turned to get into the cab. She started the truck and eased down the driveway.

"Turn right at the interstate." Jason shouted after her. Her arm reached out of the window and waved.

"She's gonna be all right. Gonna get there before nightfall," Clayton said.

"Probably. She's got wheels. It's shank's mare for us, so we better get going."

Clayton looked at him oddly. "Shank's mare?"

"Our own two feet. We better go, don't want to be late."

"We bury the kid?"

Jason grumbled under his breath. "Pain in the ass, but we did promise."

"You sort of promised," Clayton replied.

"Yeah, I did. And I appreciate your help. Let's do it quick and get going."

The two men walked down the drive way and headed towards the interstate.

Chapter 10

The hike was uneventful for the next two days. As they got closer to Knoxville, however, they saw more people, many of them going south on the other lanes. The travelers eyed the two men warily, keeping as far from them as they could. In some of the stalled vehicles, there were bodies, now heavily decayed. They must have died in the cars, or been shot.

That night Clayton insisted on hiking into the woods to camp.

"It be too open here on the highway. Better if we go into the woods. We can find a spot that ain't exposed, make a fire, keep watch easier. Hard to sneak up on us in the woods. Most people make too much noise."

As soon as they reached the woods, Jason recognized the value of Clayton's advice. They moved quietly and with confidence. Clayton was born a woodsman and Jason realized he had become one himself. They were in their element. It didn't take long to find a place to set up camp.

That night they spread their ground cloths up against a rock outcropping that shielded them from the direction of the road. Clayton set some snares and they sat around the small campfire eating their MRE meals.

"You brought snares." Jason remarked.

"Sure. Don't weigh much, don't take up any room, might get us a fresh meal."

"Can't argue with that." Jason was coming to appreciate his companion's readiness and ability to adapt.

"You got any plan for when we get to Knoxville," Clayton asked.

Jason shook his head. "Not yet."

"Ain't good to get there without a plan."

"I've been thinking about it. Don't know exactly what to do. We need to learn more about what's going on in Knoxville. Need to stop somewhere to get information. And we have to try to do that without raising too much suspicion."

"Maybe people think we be looking to join this Chairman."

"That might work. But we want to probably be coy about that. Not make it too obvious."

"So we go into one of the small towns outside of Knoxville. If any still got people in 'em."

"Hopefully one with some people and not Knoxville officials."

Clayton gave Jason a sharp look. "You think they have officials in the towns?"

"Could have. Maybe some sort of administrator, representative...or some small police presence. If the guy's trying to exert his influence on the surrounding territory, he's got to plant some of his people in the surrounding towns."

"That going to make it harder."

"Trickier, that's for sure."

The men sat quietly, thinking, listening to the sounds of the night forest. There was an occasional hoot of an owl far off; the sudden swish of wings as the flying predator dove for an unfortunate creature. In the distance they heard howls and some barking cries. Jason looked over at Clayton.

"Wolves?"

"Coyotes more'n likely."

"Could be trouble for us?"

"We're far enough away and don't have any kill to attract them."

The night's quiet was disturbed again. This time by a cry that sounded like a cross between a baby and a woman in distress. Again, Jason looked at Clayton.

"Bobcat. More of 'em around now. More game in general." He put another couple of sticks on the fire. "Wild dogs be the worst. The one's that survived start running in packs. Plenty of deer for them, but they'd go after humans as well. Coyotes, not so much. They still try to avoid people. Got to be careful of dogs though."

Down the slope from where they were camped the ground grew marshy as a stream drained into a small pond nestled between the hills. A whip-o-will started up with its rhythmic call. It was a signature call of the night. Jason relaxed upon hearing it. The sound brought him back to the days of hiking alone in the mountains before he found Anne and the girls. The memories were both good and bad. Good with hope for the future and the feeling of peace he had found in the forest and bad for the sense of loneliness that had stalked his trek.

He shook off the memory. *Remember the good parts. That's the key.* He made a silent promise to himself that he would get back to his family. He and Clayton would find a way to rescue Rodney and Billy; make the tribe whole again.

"Next inhabited place we come to, let's stop and talk to them. Start learning more about what we're up against," Jason said.

"Let's try not to get shot."

"We'll try." He rolled himself in his blanket and stretched out on the ground cloth. "You taking the first watch?"

Clayton nodded.

"Wake me when you get tired," he said to Clayton.

In the morning, after heating some water for tea, Clayton set out to check his snares. He came back grinning with a rabbit in his hand. "We got us breakfast."

He set about gutting and skinning the rabbit and then skewered it on a stick and propped it over the fire. Soon the aroma of roasting meat wafted through the air.

"This is a whole lot better than sleeping on the side of the road," he declared.

He pulled the rabbit off the stick and handed Jason a leg. They both dug into the meat with relish and the meal quickly disappeared into their stomachs.

"That beats MREs," Jason remarked as he wiped his face on his sleeve.

"And canned meat and beans," Clayton added.

The interstate followed the Pigeon River. They were heading north in the general direction of Douglas Lake. It was late afternoon when they came to a cluster of houses and service buildings. There was a collection of road tractors and trailers parked in a dirt yard packed down from decades of spilled oil and tires compressing it. The compound was on the west side of the highway with a local gravel road leading to the compound. There were enclosed van trailers and numerous open ones that looked like they had been used for sand or gravel hauling. They were sitting in the yard, unhooked, waiting to be called upon...for what, Jason couldn't guess.

"Maybe there's someone in those houses," Jason said. "The place looks inhabited. Let's check it out."

"Carefully," replied Clayton.

The two men walked across the median and the southbound lanes and climbed over the boundary fence. Once on the far side, they stopped to survey the compound. Everything was still. There was no sound, no movement.

"They's tire tracks. Vehicles been moving around, not long ago," Clayton said.

"Some older cars work. Maybe it's the same with older trucks. That means there could be someone at home."

"Let's go slow. If we're being watched we want them to have time to figure out we're not a threat."

The two men started across the truck yard. There were large, metal garage buildings to their left on the side of the dirt yard. Across the yard, ahead of them was a field that had once been a lawn with beaten paths through the tall grass. The paths led to two houses. They could see no one in the windows. When they got to the edge of field, Jason put out his arm for them to stop.

He put his hands to his mouth and called out, "Hello in the house!" There was no answer. He called out again. They stood in the open waiting to see if they would get a response.

From the repair garage, to their side and now a bit behind them, came a response. "Stand where you are. Don't move or you'll be shot."

Both men stood still but swung their heads to the left. Standing in a doorway stood a bearded man with long, wild hair. He held a shotgun pointed at them. Jason estimated they were thirty yards away, close enough for a twelve gauge to be lethal.

"Should'a seen that coming," he muttered. "We don't mean any harm," he called out. "We're passing through and wanted to ask about how things are around here. We're a bit nervous about getting closer to Knoxville."

"I'll be the judge about whether you harmful or not. Enoch!' he shouted to the house. "Come on out here."

The front door opened and another, younger man stepped out and started walking towards Jason and Clayton. He was dressed in jeans, a tee shirt with holes in it and work boots. He carried what looked like a bolt action .30-06, similar to the rifle Billy had carried.

"We have to fight our way out, drop to the ground at an angle and bring up your AK on full auto," Jason whispered to Clayton.

"Already set it before we climbed the fence from the highway."

The younger man also stopped about thirty yards away. He was careful to not position himself directly across from the older man. If shots were fired, the two of them wouldn't hit each other.

"I got the younger guy," Jason whispered. "You take out the shotgun."

Raising his voice, Jason said again, "We aren't looking to rob or hurt anyone. We're just looking for information."

"Like I said, we'll be the judge of that," the older man said. "Where you from?"

"East of here," Jason answered.

"Where exactly is that?"

"Near Hillsboro."

"Heard about Hillsboro. Heard they're doin' all right. Bet you got some goods on you."

"Look we don't have any goods. Just some camping gear. We're hiking west."

"Maybe we relieve them of some of their load," the young man, Enoch, said. He grinned at them.

"If you're thinking of robbing us, we ain't going down without a fight."

"You make a move, we'll kill you on the spot," Enoch said.

"Maybe, maybe not. At least one of you'll get shot, bad, maybe killed. You willing to chance it? Could be either of you." Jason needed to sow a seed of doubt. It would slow them down.

"Let's shoot them now and be done with it," Enoch said. His voice now carried a slight note of anxiety in it.

Enoch raised his rifle to his shoulder. Just then the front door of the house opened again. A woman came out on the front stoop.

"George Nutter, you and Enoch stop this instant! No one's gonna shoot anyone that comes to our house in peace. Not while I'm still walking this earth! George you put down that shotgun. Enoch you do the same. Just wait 'till Joshua gets back. Your brother's not gonna be happy about this."

"Emilia, we don't know what these men are up to. And they're armed."

The woman was now marching across the high grass, cutting a swath through it with a forceful stride. She had a homespun blouse on and a long skirt that reached her ankles. Her hair was graying and pulled back in a bun.

"I can see that, I ain't blind. I also see my son aiming his rifle at them and talking about robbing them. Since when did we become bandits?" She was closing in on Enoch. "And since when do robbers stand out in the open and announce themselves?"

Enoch had lowered his rifle by that point. When the woman reached him, she cuffed him on his ear, knocking his head to one side.

"Ow, you don't have to do that, Ma."

"Seems like I do, since you don't seem to be using any manners I taught you. Get on back to the house. Me and your uncle will deal with these men."

The young man turned back to the house.

She put her hands on her hips. "Now, what're you doing here," the woman said to Jason and Clayton. Her tone was as fierce as her face.

"We're just passing through, heading west. We thought someone might be living here so we came over to ask about how things are around here. Can't be too careful," Jason answered.

"Fore we talk more, put your weapons on the ground and take off your packs. No one's going to shoot you. Ain't that right George?"

"No, Emilia. Wasn't planning on it in the first place."

"Could a fooled me...and you certainly fooled Enoch. You should a corrected him right away, not waited for me to come down here."

She turned back to Jason and Clayton as the put their gear on the ground. "Now where you from?"

"Hillsboro," Jason replied.

"That in North Carolina?" the woman asked.

"Yes, ma'am," Jason replied.

"And you," she said looking at Clayton.

"Hillsboro. But really from north, up near Linville Falls."

The woman eyed him carefully. "Yeah, you don't sound like you come from Hillsboro, or any town. What's your name?"

"Clayton Jessup. We Jessup's and Early's moved down to Hillsboro area this past year."

"You're old family," she said.

"Yes'm."

"You related to Jubal Early?"

"Yes'm. My wife's an Early. But we's the poor side of the family. Side no one wants to talk about."

She now smiled and stuck out her hand. "I'm Emilia Nutter. This is George, my brother-in-law. My son is Enoch. He's nicer than he showed you today. Come up to the house." She paused before turning away. George put the men's packs rifles in the garage for safe keeping."

Jason stiffened. He knew it showed. The woman looked at him.

"Don't you worry, we ain't gonna rob you, I already told you that. You'll get your stuff back, but I don't want it in my house." She looked Jason up and down. "You probably got another gun, a pistol hidden somewhere on you anyway."

With that the woman turned away. "Come on. I got some tea and biscuits in the kitchen."

Chapter 11

Jason and Clayton sat in Emilia's kitchen. It was clearly her domain. She directed Enoch and George on what to do and where to sit, as she did the two travelers. Jason took a liking to her immediately and not just because her intervention in the yard had saved everyone from a shootout. He could tell Clayton felt the same. They were eating some biscuits covered with honey while sipping lemon grass tea.

"Now, you told us where you're from, where are you headed? From what we've heard, Hillsboro's doing all right," Emilia said.

"We're heading west," Jason said.

"We could see that. We watched you come up the highway," George said. Emilia gave him a glance but didn't say anything.

"Why so vague?" Emilia asked.

Jason paused for a moment. "We've found it best to say little. It only seems to invite trouble."

"Well, you say that, but you also say you came onto our property to seek information. Seems like what's good for the goose is good for the gander."

Clayton looked over at Jason. "She got a point."

"It don't make no difference to me, but it might get you more information in return. There's not much trust around anywhere these days, we all know that. But that don't mean we shouldn't try to reach out to people we think we can trust." Emilia got up to pour them more tea. It's late. Why don't you stay for supper? My husband,

Joshua, will be back shortly. He knows more about what's going on than most. We can talk while we eat."

Jason looked at Clayton. His face was impassive. "I guess we can stay. Thank you for the invitation. It beats eating camp food or MREs."

"If you want to freshen up, there's a pump in the side yard. Enoch, go get two towels for our guests." The young man got up and disappeared into the hallway.

"I want to apologize for my son. He thinks we have to shoot first in order to survive. George should have set a better example." She gave George a sharp look. "They did the right thing to start. You can't be too careful and we've had a lot of problems as you can imagine, being so close to the highway."

"We're just glad you came out when you did. Things looked like they were going bad."

"You seem like a nice fellow. What did you do before the power went out?"

"I ran a gym in Hillsboro."

She shook her head. "A gym? Where people paid you to work and sweat?"

"Yep."

"Never understood that. We do enough hard work and sweatin' without having to go to a gym and pay someone for the privilege."

"Some people just sit at a desk all day. That isn't good for being healthy."

"Don't have to worry much about that nowadays," George said.

"Seems like we didn't have to worry much about that anytime," Emilia said.

Just then Enoch came back with two towels. "Here you go," he said, dropping them on the table.

"Enoch." Emilia's voice carried a threat in it. "I expect you to show some manners. You been brought up better than that. I'll not have you embarrassing me in front of guests. You park that look and that tone of voice right now, you hear me?"

"Yes'm."

"I want you to apologize to Mr. Jessup and Mr. Richards for threatening to rob them."

"I didn't threaten to rob them," Enoch said in almost a whine.

"Don't argue with me. I can hear just fine and I heard what you said, 'maybe relieve them of their load'." That sounds like robbing to me."

Enoch looked down at the table. "I'm sorry."

"Look 'em in the eye, boy!" Emilia barked at him. "You was wrong, now be a man and admit it."

Enoch took a deep breath and looked up. He looked at both men. "I'm sorry. It was wrong of me to talk like that. We needed to cover you, but not threaten to rob you."

"I accept your apology," Jason said. Clayton nodded in agreement. "It makes sense to be careful. That's why we called out. We didn't want to look like bad guys."

Just then they heard the clatter of a diesel engine coming up the drive, the pistons hammering against the high compression. Emilia looked out of the kitchen window.

"Here comes Joshua." Her voice expressed her enthusiasm for her husband's return.

Jason watched out of the window from his seat. An ancient looking road tractor pulled into the yard, the exhaust stack belching black smoke. The driver maneuvered the tractor-trailer rig and deftly backed it into an open slot along with the other trailers. There was a loud hiss of compressed air, creating a dust cloud, as the brakes were set and the engine shut down. A tall, lanky man stepped down from the cab. He had on work boots, jeans and a long sleeve shirt with a leather vest. He headed straight for the house with long strides.

"I'm home," he called as he opened the front door.

"We're in the kitchen," Emilia called out. "We've got some visitors."

The man came into the kitchen. He stopped and stared at Jason and Clayton. Before he could speak, Emilia introduced the two.

"This is Jason Richards and Clayton Jessup. He's related to some Earlys. They've come from Hillsboro, on their way west."

Jason and Clayton slowly stood up and shook Joshua's hand. "I'm Joshua," the man said. He gripped them with a strong, meaty hand.

"These men came over from the highway to gather some information about the area. I've invited them to supper. I figure they might have a lot they can tell us as well. It's so hard to know what's going on outside of our own small area."

"Yeah, we can share information." Joshua said. "I need to wash up. What are we having for supper tonight?"

"I'm going to fry up the catfish Enoch caught yesterday. Got some hushpuppies to go along with it and some greens from the garden."

"Ah, that sounds great!" Joshua got up. "I just have to get my towel."

"Our guests will join you. I told them to wash up. Supper'll be ready in about a half hour."

The men went out to the pump and washed up.

"You've got quite a nice set up here," Clayton remarked. "It's too close to the highway for me, though."

"It's home and business. We decided to stay after the power went out. Got the river for fishing," he gestured over his shoulder, "and good bottom land for farming, and we got the business. I realized my older tractors could still work and figured there might be a need for that, so I've kept the business going even after the big outage. George has been my partner all along. He keeps the machines running, can fix just about anything."

They walked around the property as they talked.

"Fishing good in the river?" Clayton asked.

"Comes and goes according to the levels, but we can generally rely on catfish and bass. It's a nice change from the deer, squirrel and rabbit. 'Course we got a cow and she's got some good years left in her...and some chickens, so we do well."

"I imagine you had to defend all of this," Jason said. "It'd be pretty attractive to gangs."

"Yeah. We had our challenges."

Soon they heard Emilia call out for dinner and the men headed back to the house.

They came back into the kitchen where Emilia explained to her husband what had happened in the yard, leaving out Enoch's transgressions since she had already dealt with them.

"Now what do you want to know that caused you to stop by and almost get shot?" Joshua asked.

"Since we're headed towards Knoxville and we've heard about this Chairman, we'd like to know more of what's going on there. Has he or his men been in the area?"

"We've seen a few military vehicles which belong to his militia," Joshua said. "Just north of us is Newport and he's got a representative there. The man works with the local council to coordinate security and collect taxes...tribute I call it. I got to deal with him in my work. But tell us a bit about Hillsboro. If things are good there, why'd you leave?"

Jason sighed. "Seems as though a lot of people have heard about Hillsboro. You're right, it does have good resources and that worries us."

"But you left—"

"Yeah. Clayton and I left. I was the interim mayor. We got rid of a gangster who ran the city and were able to make some reforms. By everyone working together, we have been able to improve things a lot there. Clayton and I, left to find two of our people. And that's where the story gets hard to tell."

"But you'll need to tell it if you want information," Joshua said. He looked at Jason, his brow knit in thought. "I'm bettin' they're in some kind of trouble, something to do with Knoxville. So you want to know what you're getting into."

"You're close," Jason admitted. "How powerful is this Chairman?"

"He's powerful enough. He's getting a currency going again. Gold based. I think he's melted down a ton of gold jewelry and is minting coins." Joshua stood up and took one out of his pocket. "Has an impression of the city and 'Knoxville' stamped on it."

"How do that work?" Clayton asked as he fingered the coin. "How's he set the value?"

"He's got the coins in one, ten and twenty values, 'Knoxes' he calls them." They just decide that a bushel of grain, gallon of gas or diesel, ten rounds of ammunition are worth so many of the coins. So a trader could take the coin, knowing he'd be able to exchange it for an equivalent value in merchandise. It's easier than direct trading. The coins allow exchanges to happen more quickly."

"But what if someone says his ammunition is worth more?"

"He gets reported to the authorities. He barred from trading for a while. If he gets fussed up about it, they take away his goods. He loses everything."

"Pretty harsh," Jason said.

"Yep. But it makes for compliance. Once a month a group sits down and decides if the values need to be adjusted. There may be more gas around, someone found a tanker that hadn't been emptied, or there was a good grain harvest. The values change and that's posted. Everyone can see what is going on."

He put the coin back in his pocket. "I get paid like this although I can often negotiate a strait barter."

"What do you do?"

"I truck supplies for Knoxville."

"You work for the Chairman?" Clayton asked. His voice betrayed his alarm.

"I'm not employed by him, if that's what you mean. I *do* work for him. I'm an independent contractor."

"What do you haul?" Jason asked.

"Sand, gravel. We have a quarry nearby. It's really a sand and gravel hillside we're digging away. Been at it for years. Remember I said George could fix anything?" The two men nodded. "After the outage, he got our trucks working, the old ones. Then he got an ancient front loader working over at the gravel site. Now it seems Knoxville wants sand and gravel. They're making concrete. I think it's to reinforce barriers into town."

Jason just stared at Joshua. "I never thought a place would get something like that going so soon, a currency and an industry."

"It's been forced on us, but it ain't all bad. 'Course, like I said, when I haul fuel, I take a cut on my own. Officials don't mind since it saves the coins. The city pays for my fuel, but I can put aside some. Got a good stash built up for a rainy day."

Joshua leaned forward towards Jason. "Now I've told you my little secret, suppose you tell me why you're really heading to Knoxville."

There was a silence around the table.

"Not sure it would be good for you to know. We don't want to put you in an awkward position, if someone were to question you."

"Don't worry about us. We don't have much to do with Knoxville or the militia, except for Joshua doing hauling for them," Emilia said.

Jason looked over at Clayton who shrugged as if to say, "what's to lose?"

He took a deep breath and recounted the story. He left out the part of cutting off the messenger's finger. When he was done the table remained silent for some time.

Finally George spoke. "That's gonna be a suicide mission."

Emilia got up and began to clear the table.

"Sure ain't going to be easy." Joshua said.

"Now you know why we need to know as much as possible about this chairman," Jason said.

Chapter 12

The Chairman, don't know his name, has been taking over territory outside Knoxville," Joshua said. "Seems like he wants to build his own empire. He claims to have been given a vision that he will unite the central south, Tennessee, Kentucky, Alabama, Mississippi. Word is his first challenge is Nashville. All the cities seem to want to grow in power. So far neither one has attacked the other. Guess they figure that's too costly. Instead they go around grabbing up resources from smaller towns."

"They're stripping houses, stores of gold, jewelry, food, clothing, anything they can find," George added.

"There doesn't seem to be any state government so it's every city for itself," Joshua said.

"That's why I don't want anything to do with them," Emilia said. "I worry about the work you do right now. They stay away from us, leave us alone, we be all right."

"You mean you don't want to move to the big city?" Joshua asked with a grin on his face. Enoch grinned as well.

"I'd as soon be stuck in hell with my back broke," Emilia replied. "You know that."

"Yeah, but we just wanted to hear you say it, Ma," Enoch said, grinning.

Turning back to Jason, Joshua continued. "Word has it that the Chairman is going to take over Johnson City."

"We heard from the messenger. That's what worries me. We're about as far southeast of Knoxville as Johnson

City is to the northeast. I don't see much holding him back from coming at us."

"Maybe you're more organized, got more firepower," George said. "He may think Johnson City is an easier target."

"Run by a crazy man," Clayton said.

"Those rifles you boys're carrying, they're pretty serious." George went on. "That one looks like an AK47, the other one looks military too. That a sniper rifle? You a sniper?"

Jason looked at George. "Was. Army sniper. Served in Iraq."

"Can you help me sight my .30-06 in?" Enoch asked. "I got a scope but it don't seem to help."

"I can help, sure. But can you spare the rounds? And can you shoot them so near the road?"

"We got plenty of ammo. And shooting around here only helps to keep the wanderers out. Be worth spending the ammo to make it easier to hit deer."

"You can do that later," Joshua said. "I'm thinking Jason here would like a little more information on Knoxville."

"That's right. I've got a map in my pack. I'm hoping you can show me where the Chairman has his operations, where he stays, and where our boys might be held." Jason wanted to confirm what the messenger had told him.

"I can do that. George, can you go out with Jason so he can get his pack?" George nodded and the two men got up and went out the front door.

When they came back, Emilia had tea out with biscuits and jam. "It's something sweet to finish the meal."

Jason spread the map out on the table. Joshua grabbed a pencil and looked at it carefully. The other men crowded around him and Jason.

"Mind if I mark on it?" Joshua asked.

"No, go ahead."

Joshua proceeded to outline a section of downtown bordered by West Summit Drive on the north, Henley Street on the west, the Tennessee River on the south and

James White Parkway on the east. "This is his main area. His activities are actually concentrated on the south part of this downtown, around the courthouse and city-county building. It's where he runs everything. A lot of the militia are housed in the building across from the city-county building. It's a high rise."

"Where are the checkpoints coming into the city?" Jason asked.

Joshua marked the map. "On the north, they blocked off the I40 and I270 interchange. It's a massive intersection with lots of ramps. That's what I've been helping with. They're making concrete barriers and rock piles to slow or stop any vehicles. They funnel them all down a ramp that's heavily guarded. Same on the south where the James White Parkway joins another road running along the river. Only three bridges are open, James White Parkway, Henley Street and one on the west that dumps you onto the university campus. They all heavily guarded."

"So how does a hiker, someone passing through, get into town? Is that even allowed?"

"Don't know for sure. Probably is, but there's probably a toll. I know they collect tolls for people going past the city on I40." Joshua looked at Jason and Clayton. "You boys look too well armed not to arouse suspicion. They'd think you might be a danger. Or they might want to draft you into the militia, without your permission, if you know what I mean."

"So where do you think our boys are?"

"They're most likely in the holding cells for the courthouse, right here." He marked the map. "Be right in the middle of it all, with the Chairman and his men next door almost in the city-county building. Don't see how you'll pull this off, let alone get out of town after."

"We be working on that," Clayton said. There was no smile on his face. Jason knew what he was thinking. This was going to be nearly impossible, but Jason knew Clayton

would not shirk from the challenge; neither of them
would.

The room was silent as everyone considered the
enormity of the task.

"Can you show me how to sight in my rifle? Before it
gets dark?" Enoch asked finally.

"Sure," Jason answered. He got up. "Let's go look at it."

They walked outside. Enoch gave Jason the .30-06. It
was serviceable. The scope moved slightly which would
have to be fixed.

They walked to the workshop so Jason could dismantle
the weapon and check it thoroughly. After going through
it and tightening the scope on its mount, they went back
outside.

"How far do you usually shoot for a deer?"

"I don't know. It's hard to estimate the distance."

"Show me."

Enoch pointed to a far fence about seventy yards away.
"Bout that far, I guess."

Jason figured he was overestimating the distance. One
usually didn't get a seventy yard shot at a deer in the woods,
especially in the denser parts. "All right. Go put something
the size of a deer up against that fence. Enoch went back
inside the shed and came out with a piece of plywood.

"Okay if we shoot holes in that?" Jason asked. The boy
nodded and walked it down to the fence.

Jason grabbed a small box from the workshop and lay
down on the ground. He rested the rifle on the box and
aimed from the prone position. With the cross hairs
centered, he squeezed off a shot. The bullet hit the dirt in
front of the board. Jason turned the elevation dial and
then tried another shot. By this time everyone had come
out to watch the show.

This time the shot clipped the top of the board.
"Bracketing it," he said with a grin at Clayton. "I'll get it
this time."

Another adjustment to the elevation and the next shot hit near the middle, but off to the right. Jason dialed in a sideways correction and his fourth shot hit the center of the board.

"Wow, you hit it dead center!" Enoch exclaimed.

Jason didn't answer. He zeroed the dials on the scope. "Now see the marks? They're set at zero. You are zeroed in for this distance. If you want to shoot longer you have to set the rifle some clicks higher, like this." He demonstrated to Enoch. "If you shoot a shorter distance, which is probably what you'll be doing. I don't see many deer shots in the woods at that distance. Am I right Clayton?"

Clayton nodded. "That's way further than most shots, less you get them out in a field."

"So, you turn the scope this way to lower the aim for shorter distance."

"How many clicks does it take?"

"Depends on how much you change the distance from your zero setting. You can test this here in the yard. Just keep notes so you know how far to go from your zero setting."

"I didn't know it was so involved." Enoch replied.

"It gets even more involved when you start shooting out five hundred yards or more."

"So, you kill anyone?" Enoch asked.

"Enoch!" Emilia said sternly. "That's not a polite question to ask."

"You ma's right. Ain't none of our business," Joshua said.

Jason looked Enoch in the eye. Jason felt his face go hard. "I have killed way more men here in the U.S. since the EMP attack, than ever in Iraq. There are very bad people out there who will harm you and your family. If you want to protect them, you better learn how to shoot properly, how to take care of your weapon." He paused. "And how to tell friend from foe and not put yourself in a foolish situation for no reason." Jason kept his eyes locked on Enoch as he let the message sink in. "You understand what I'm saying?"

Enoch looked away. "Yes sir."

Jason looked up and smiled at everyone. "You'll be all right then."

Chapter 13

As the evening deepened the talk turned to the Chairman. Joshua didn't know much about him. He had never talked with him and only seen him a couple of times.

"What's he look like?" Jason asked.

"Nothing special. Tall and thin with white hair. I've been told he can talk up a crowd. They say he moves fast and makes decisions quick."

"So how we gonna recognize him?" Clayton asked.

"He always wears a white navy dress cap. I've seen it. Got lots of gold braid on the bill and all white on top. Nobody else wears anything like that."

"Does he wear a dress uniform?" Jason asked.

"No. Fatigues or battle uniform they call it. The hat stands out. Everyone knows it's the Chairman when they see that coming."

"You know where he lives?" Jason asked.

Joshua shook his head. I wouldn't try anything like kidnapping him. He's well-guarded."

"Not planning anything like that. But it might be helpful to have a private meeting with him at his home rather than his office."

"Can't help you there."

"Well you've been a big help. I'm glad we stopped and I'm very appreciative of your hospitality. We probably should be going now."

"Since it's late, why don't you bunk down in the shed next to the workshop?" Emilia asked. "I can feed you a good breakfast tomorrow before you go."

"You're welcome to spend the night, if you like," Joshua said.

Clayton nodded to Jason. "Thank you. We'll take you up on your offer," Jason said.

The next morning after ham and eggs, biscuits and jam, Jason and Clayton stepped out the front door and shouldered their packs and rifles.

"I'd get off the interstate from here," Joshua said. "You should head west. Keep close to the National Park. Head for Gatlinburg. You'll have less chance of running into the militia down there. From Gatlinburg go north, off the road. You'll probably want to skirt Pigeon Forge. Just increases your chances of getting stopped. Look out for the Mountaineer Motel on the south side of town. The militia allow it to operate but it's a dangerous place."

"Full of lowlifes and farmers who should know better than to spend time in such a place," Emilia said with disdain.

"The man who runs is pretty tough and seems to be connected. I stopped once to ask him about the work I had been offered and he gave me a pretty good take on what I was getting into."

"You didn't go in there, did you?" Emilia asked.

"No. Just stopped the truck in the lot and asked some questions. The truck was enough of a novelty, everyone came out to look."

"Well I'm glad of that. No telling what a body could catch in a place like that." She sniffed her disapproval.

"After Pigeon Forge, head northwest, cross-country and you'll run into Knoxville." The two shouldered their packs. "Good luck to you all," Joshua said.

"Thanks, and good luck to you," Jason said. They waved and headed north out of the truck yard to the highway.

"We should head west, soon as we can," Clayton said.

They walked up the local road bordering the Pigeon River instead of the interstate.

"If we see a shallow section, let's cross the river where we can. From the map we have to head not just west, but a little south of west to get to Gatlinburg."

Clayton shook his head. "Don't see no reason to aim for Gatlinburg, just head to Pigeon Forge. It be shorter."

"You thinking what I'm thinking?" Jason asked.

"Depends."

"Well I'm thinking that this guy that runs the Mountaineer Motel might be someone we want to talk with."

"Could be. Could be dangerous, we give away what we're up to and he passes that around."

"That's true, but it might be worth a stop. We could just say we're on our way to Missouri. I expect that's what Rodney and Billy would have said."

"If they come by there."

They hiked in fields when they could, used the woods for cover to stay out of sight when they saw farmhouses. The going was slower than on the highway but less depressing to Jason. There wasn't the constant reminder of the breakdown of society from the littered interstate. At night they made camp as deep into the woods as they could go. If they were too close to any houses, they would cold-camp, not risking a fire.

The nights were filled with the increased sounds of night predators. Since so many people had died out, the wildlife had moved in closer to the towns, many of which had been abandoned. Jason wondered if the die-off had been over seventy percent. Certainly Hillsboro was greatly reduced in population. People who had managed to keep farm livestock, had to work harder to protect them from the increased boldness of predators. He shivered as he thought of the wild dogs being added to that mix. They didn't come with a fear of humans which made them more dangerous.

Two nights out the rain came in late in the afternoon. Clayton and Jason rigged their tarp as best they could and started a fire started before the rain got too heavy. They spent the night feeding it and huddling in their rain ponchos trying to stay warm and dry without much success.

It took two days of careful hiking to reach the road heading into Pigeon Forge. They walked north, in the woods, paralleling Route 321. Late in the afternoon, they saw the Mountaineer Motel. Jason picked an observation spot across the highway from the motel, about a third of a mile away. They were up on the hillside, looking down with good cover. They could watch through the binoculars undetected and, later move deeper into the woods to sleep.

The motel consisted of a central lobby which Joshua said had been converted into a bar with a stage at one end. Food could be had but the attraction was alcohol, a band, and strippers. From the lobby two rows of rooms branched out forming a ninety degree angle to one another. The rooms were on two levels.

"Figure the best thing is to watch for a while. See what goes on."

Clayton nodded. The two men got as comfortable as they could and began their vigil.

As the evening progressed, people arrived on foot, entering the lobby of the motel. A band started up. Clayton and Jessup could hear the sound through the stillness of the night. There were electric lights, a generator ran in the background. The growing intensity of the crowd noise coming from the lobby confirmed that much alcohol was being consumed. Along with the growing male shouts there were the occasional screams from a woman. The general noise brought back bad memories for Jason of his rescue of Judy from the gang that had captured her.

Around one in the morning people started funneling out. Some staggered under the influence. Some headed to the rooms, some wandered up the road.

"Them be easy prey for dogs if they're about," Clayton said.

"I wonder how many don't make it back home."

"Weapons won't help if they too drunk to use 'em."

There were women joining some of the men headed to the rooms.

"They got a regular industry going," Jason said.

After things quieted down, the lights were turned off. The two could see some of the women making their way back to the lobby from different rooms. Clayton and Jason headed farther back into the woods to sleep the rest of the night away.

"Not sure they's any reason to go in there tomorrow. Could bring more trouble than it's worth."

"Let's talk about it tomorrow."

Chapter 14

The next morning after some cold jerky, dried fruit and water, the two men crawled back to their overlook. The motel was quiet. It looked empty, like a relic of the world before the EMP attack. But closer inspection showed signs of human activity, a trash pile on the side of the building, tire tracks in the dirt and within an hour, smoke rose from the chimney.

The two men waited for another hour, then shouldered their packs and rifles and headed out of the woods, down the slope and across the highway. They walked across the dirt parking lot and opened the door to the lobby. It was dark inside. The windows had been painted black. A strong smell of booze and sweat permeated the air. A coat check area was immediately to their left. From there the room opened up. There was a dark, worn carpet on the floor. Jason couldn't make out the color in the dark of the room. A bar ran along the left wall. It looked transplanted from another place. The large room was cluttered with small tables and accompanying chairs. At the far end of the room was a stage with some sound equipment on it. On each side of the stage were platforms with poles in the center of them.

"Anyone here?" Jason called out. "Hello."

A door on the left, near the front of the bar swung open. A man came out wiping his hands. Jason could see a kitchen behind him before the door closed. "We ain't open yet."

The man stopped part of the way towards them. He eyed them warily. "You ain't from around here," he declared.

"No, we're not," Jason replied. "We saw the smoke and thought we stop by. Not many people about to talk to."

The man stood only about five foot eight inches tall but seemed as wide as he was tall. He presented a fireplug of a figure, solid and tough. He had large hands and bulging forearms.

"You the owner?" Clayton asked.

"I'm the cook. Carl's my name. They call me "Cookie". The owner ain't up yet. His name's Bubba Garrett. Don't know him by any other name than Bubba."

"Well, Cookie, can we wait for him? We'd like to ask him about things in these parts. We're passing through. It pays to know what's going on in each area."

"Where're you headed?"

"West to Missouri, maybe further."

"Don't know why anyone wants to travel. Seems to me things gonna be about the same everywhere. You can wait, but I got to warn you, Bubba don't like nobody bothering him first thing when he gets up."

"We'll be careful. Don't want to offend anyone," Jason replied.

Cookie looked at both men. "Looks like you two can handle yourselves. Got some stout weapons there. You some kind of militia?"

Jason shook his head. "No, but we know the importance of being well armed nowadays."

"You got that right," Cookie said. "Can I get you breakfast or something? I got eggs and some bread."

"We don't have any money to pay you. No one uses money back east."

"You can pay in ammo. That works."

Clayton shook his head. Jason said, "No we best hold on to our ammunition."

Cookie shrugged. "Suit yourself. I'll stand you to a cup of coffee, on the house."

"You have coffee?" Jason said in surprise.

"Yep. Boss gets it. He's got connections. Comes from Central America. We get it up from New Orleans. 'Course we cut it with chicory to make it go further, but it's still better'n nothing."

"We be thanking you," Clayton said.

Cookie looked at him. "You're from the mountains. Don't hear that much around here."

He turned and disappeared back into the kitchen. Jason and Clayton went over to a table on the right side of the room which gave them a view of the kitchen and the front door. They had their backs to the wall. They put their packs on the floor and propped their rifles next to them.

Cookie came out with two mugs of steaming coffee. "Here you go. I got to get back into the kitchen. The boss'll be here soon and the whores'll be up. They'll be wanting me to feed them. Those girls sure like to eat. Must burn a lot of calories dancing and screwing." He leered at the two men and headed back into the kitchen.

Jason and Clayton nursed their coffees, enjoying the rare drink. A half hour later a large man came into the lobby. He stopped and looked over at the two sitting along the wall. The man stood about six feet tall. He had a large face. His cheeks showed scars from what Jason guessed were years of boxing. His ears were disfigured from scar tissue which only convinced Jason of his guess. He was portly, but still solidly built. Jason guessed he weighed a good two hundred-fifty pounds. *Not a man to be trifled with.*

"Cookie," the man shouted out in a deep, gravelly voice. The cook came running out of the kitchen. "Who're these?" he said jerking his thumb at Jason and Clayton.

"Travelers. Passing through. They stopped and wanted to talk with you." Cookie looked at his boss with concern.

"I told them they could wait...thought you might want to talk to them."

"Not first thing in the morning," the man said. So far he had ignored both men, talking only to Cookie. He walked towards the kitchen. "I'm gonna get something to eat first." This last seemingly directed at Jason and Clayton.

Ten minutes later, the man came out from the kitchen with a large mug of coffee. The rich aroma preceded him as he walked over to the two at the table.

"So who are you and what do you want?"

"My name's Jason and this is Clayton. We're heading west and someone mentioned this place. We thought it might be a good place to stop and get some information on the territory. Can't be too careful."

The large man just stood in front of them, looking down. Jason was unsure if he should get up or remain seated. He didn't want to do anything that could be interpreted as aggressive.

"You look like army." The man said to Jason. Turning to Clayton he said, "You look country...no, more like mountain, hillbilly. Where're you two from?"

"Back east," Jason answered.

"Back east where?" the man asked.

"North Carolina," Clayton said.

The man turned to him. "North Carolina, *where*?" He spoke more pointedly this time.

"Linville Falls," Clayton said.

"Where the hell is that?"

"North of Hillsboro, up towards Johnson City."

"That so, and how about you?" he asked turning back to Jason.

"Hidden Valley. It's north of Hillsboro as well."

"You ain't in the army? You look like it and that rifle is army issue for sure."

"Was in the army. Bought this one after getting out."

"Where the hell did you get an AK47?" he asked Clayton.

"From a man that tried to kill me," came the reply.

The man finally seemed satisfied with the explanations. Jason was happy to not be pinned down about Hillsboro. He didn't want anyone to make that connection.

"I assume you're Mr. Garrett?" Jason asked looking up at the man still towering over them.

"Ain't no Mister. Call me Bubba." He pulled a chair away from the table, turned it around, and sat down in it, his arms over the back, holding the coffee cup. "Now what you want to know, mystery travelers?"

"Well, we're getting closer to Knoxville and we've heard about this Chairman, so we'd like to know what the situation is. Should we be expecting trouble?"

"Not unless you're looking for it. The Chairman has organized the city, got electricity going, started a currency." He swept one arm around the room. "That's why this can exist. We still take some barter, but I couldn't run a bar and strip club without currency. I get paid in gold, I can buy supplies, pay people. It's how I make a living...and employ others to make a living. People are beginning to do better. When they do, things get better for me."

Just then a group of six females shuffled into the lobby and sat down at the far end of the bar. They were dressed in a mix of jeans and sweat shirts, bath robes or house coats. None of them looked very old. Jason was shocked to see a couple of them that appeared to be in their teens.

"Them girls," Bubba continued. Jason realized he had noticed his glance over to the girls. "I give 'em a place to work, place to sleep. It's safe and they get to earn a living."

"Some of them look pretty young," Jason said.

"At least they ain't starving out on the streets."

"They all come here looking for a job?" Clayton asked.

Bubba gave him a long look, seeming to measure him. "How I recruit and hire ain't none of your business." His voice held a hint of danger.

"Back to this Chairman," Jason said. He still wanted more information. "He won't make any trouble for us as we pass through?"

"He's too busy to be worried about you two. Got big plans for the area. 'Course his militia may want to talk to you about coming to work for them. I could use a couple of men like you, for security. You interested?"

Jason shook his head. "I don't think so."

"Well the militia may have a serious interest in you. If you don't want that, you best go well south of town and avoid any patrols."

"He taken over much of the territory?" Clayton asked.

"More and more. Seems like all the cities are doing it. Nashville and Memphis. I even heard about Hillsboro, 'course you'd know more about that." He stopped to look at both men. "So what's going on in Hillsboro?"

"Don't really know. We ain't from there," Clayton said.

"Well, the word is they're pretty well off since eliminating Joe Stansky's gang. The Chairman doesn't like to hear about that. Makes him nervous I think." Bubba grinned. He stood up. I got things to do. You want to hang around, you got to buy something, food, booze, a girl. Can't sit around for free." He turned away and shouted over to another man who had come in while they were talking. "Mack, show these men to the door if they ain't ordering."

With that Bubba disappeared into the kitchen. The girls at the end of the bar now looked over at the two as Mack approached. Mack was obviously the bouncer, tight shirt, big muscles and a large pistol strapped to his side. He stopped out of reach and crossed his arms.

"You want to order now, or you want to leave?"

"We'll be going. Tell Cookie thanks for the coffee," Jason said. The two men picked up their packs and rifles and walked to the door with Mack following.

Chapter 15

J ason and Clayton aimed northwest from the motel, heading straight for Knoxville. They skirted the highest ridges but kept to the forests. They would avoid Seymour, southeast of the city, not wanting to further announce their presence.

"You figure that guy'll pass the word about us?" Clayton asked.

"I expect he will. I don't think he bought our stories about not having anything to do with Hillsboro. We need to not be seen from here on out."

Clayton nodded. Both men were in fast hiking mode, wanting to cover the ground quickly in case the militia was alerted to their presence. The hours passed with little talk as they concentrated on their pace. The packs weighed heavily. To Jason it reminded him of the training hikes during Basic. Only now he was older. Still he kept at the pace, huffing like a steam engine, but not slowing down.

They stopped briefly in the early afternoon to eat some dried fruit and meat and drink some water. Then it was back on pace, pushing themselves hard. As they approached Seymour to their west the woods gave way to flat farmland. It was easier going but more exposed. With no way to move unobserved, they finally decided to just walk the back roads as fast as they could. If seen, they hoped people just dismiss them as travelers with a destination and not any threat.

North of Seymour, they gained some forest cover again but that gave out as they approached the suburbs of South Knoxville. These were heavily treed neighborhoods that, like Hillsboro were mostly empty with an occasional house from which a light shone. They easily avoided these and continued to work their way towards the river and the center of the city.

Finally, they saw a major multi-lane highway, which swept over the river in a massive bridge.

Jason consulted his map. "The courthouse complex is on the north side of the river and to the west. We need to get across this highway and work our way in that direction. Bud indicated there are some tall buildings on this side of the river. Good place to reconnoiter."

The men worked their way slowly north near the parkway until they came to another large road that went over it. The overpass would provide cover for them to cross the parkway to head west. After watching for some time and seeing no activity the two ran across a feeder road, jumped the fence, and dropped into the tall grass.

"We can crawl to the overpass and then use it for cover to cross the highway," Jason said.

They worked their way through the grass on their bellies. Half an hour later they were at the overpass. It was now dusk which helped. They crept out and slipped under the roadway. Leaning up against one of the support beams, they rested. Again, after listening and watching, they made their way across the north-bound lanes. The few cars that were abandoned helped provide cover. They stopped in the median, watching and listening, before crossing the south-bound lanes. They heard an engine coming from their right, the direction of the river and the massive bridge. It was one of the ones that Joshua said were kept open.

"That's a diesel engine," whispered Jason. "Could be a Humvee."

"Militia," Clayton replied. "Going on patrol or relieving an outpost. Don't figure they just drive around. Use too much fuel."

The men waited another ten minutes after the engine sound crossed over them and faded out of earshot to the south. They then crossed the last lanes. On the west side of the parkway they could now see the lights from a low-rise apartment complex to their left. Jason took out his map.

In the dim light Jason marked their position on the map. "If we can get through these apartment blocks, we'll reach some woods," he said. "At least I think they're woods. There's no roads shown on the map. It's just south of the tall buildings near the river, so we can safely approach them through the empty area."

Clayton nodded. "We got people on our left in those apartment buildings and probably some houses with people in them ahead. Ain't gonna be easy."

"We go from house-to-house. The night is to our advantage now."

The men set out. Someone in the apartment complex to their left must have had a dog that they had kept alive as it began to bark when it got their scent. Both men looked at each other.

"That ain't good," Clayton said.

"I doubt anyone's going to come out looking though. Let's keep moving. We'll get out of the dog's scent range soon."

They kept up their cautious traverse of the neighborhood. Ahead they caught a gleam of candlelight through a window. They slipped between two dark houses on their right and moved through the backyards. They could see a small, dense patch of woods ahead and to the right. It would shield them from the inhabited house.

Jason pointed it out and Clayton nodded. They made it to the woods. It was getting darker now. Jason rummaged in his pack and pulled out two pair of night vision goggles. These gave them an advantage in the night. With the increased visibility they managed to keep moving forward with little sound.

Coming to the edge of the woods, they saw in front of them another low-rise housing complex, obviously inhabited. They stopped inside the line of trees to study the buildings. It was a U-shaped complex made up of three buildings. The arms of the U ran away from where they were hiding. There was an open parking area in front of the apartments. To the left of the complex were more individual houses with few trees for cover and then a street. To the right were more houses but with a narrow strip of trees, now very much overgrown. That could provide cover for them to get close to the neighborhood street giving them the best chance to cross. Beyond the street were more woods. If they could reach that, they'd get safely past the apartments.

"If they got dogs, they'll smell us," Clayton whispered. "Breeze is slight but coming from our right. We'll be upwind."

"Gotta go to the right. Other way is too open."

Clayton nodded. They began to move through the narrow tree line. As they reached the road a dog began to bark furiously back in the complex.

"Let's go," Jason said. The two men bolted out into the street.

"Who's there?" someone shouted. "Hey there," came another shout. Jason sensed they had been seen.

"Get the others," another shouted, "there may be bandits."

When they reached the trees on the other side the two men didn't stop but crashed through the trees as fast as they could go. The shouts from the complex filled the air. It sounded like some men were coming up the road they had just crossed bringing the dog with them.

"Get over to the other road, we'll cut them off there!" The shout came from the chasing group.

It was a footrace now. Jason and Clayton ran as fast as they could with their heavy packs. Their rifles were in their hands as they ran. They crossed a school yard and on the other side, Jason pulled up.

"Stop," he called to Clayton. "If they got a dog, they can just track us."

"We got to get rid of the dog."

"I don't like doing that." Jason thought for a moment. "Maybe we can talk to them. We aren't a threat."

"Doubt it'll help."

"Let me try anyway," Jason responded.

Jason slipped off his backpack. He cupped his hands to his face and shouted to their pursuers, "I don't want to shoot your dog. Put a leash on him." He waited a moment. "We're not interested in you. We're just passing through. Stop chasing us."

"Get the dog!" Someone shouted.

"I doubt you can shoot the dog," another yelled out.

"Don't. I'm a trained sniper. We don't want trouble so stop now and we'll be on our way."

"How do we know that? How do we know you won't sneak back later?"

"Did we come at your apartments or did we just walk past them? Don't be stupid. We're not interested in you."

Jason and Clayton could hear murmuring amongst the men across the school yard. The dog was barking but seemed to be under control.

"Shut Max up," someone shouted.

"Let me turn him loose. They're bluffing. They can't hit Max, he's too fast."

"Did you hear? Someone else said, "he's a trained sniper."

"I don't believe it."

Jason decided to take a chance. He lay down with his M110 resting on his backpack, aimed at the open yard. Siting through the scope with his goggles wasn't ideal, but it would work. He shouted at the men. "Hey, throw out a fist sized rock out on the ground."

The corner of the building was about fifty yards away across a blacktop playground surface. There was a hesitation and then a rock came flying out to roll onto the pavement. Before it stopped Jason squeezed off a round and the rock shattered.

"Not bluffing," he shouted.

"Damn," someone said.

"We got a deal? You go back to your apartments and we go on our way?"

While the men were discussing what to do, Jason stood up and he and Clayton slipped quietly away. Once across the next street they began to run again. This time they went to their left, away from the buildings they were heading towards. They were aiming for a large empty space on the map that they now could see was a dense wood, maybe five or more acres in size.

"We can't go straight to the buildings. If they follow with the dog, they just track us to the buildings and we be sitting in a trap."

When they were deeper into the wood, Jason stopped and pulled out his map. He held a small flashlight with his fingers over the lens to block most of the light. "Let's cross the woods and check out what's on this road. If it's industrial at all, maybe we can find some chemicals to cover our scent."

Clayton looked at him. "How we do that?"

"Bleach, or some other strong chemical. Put it on our shoes and spread it over our trail. It could put off a dog."

"Better'n nothing."

They started west again, away from the housing complex.

Chapter 16

A t the far side of the woods was a secondary road with businesses running along it. One of them looked like it had been a repair shop.

"Let's check there," Jason pointed to the building. There may be some chemicals inside."

The door was ajar, indicating the shop had probably been looted for anything of value. It was pitch dark inside. They slipped on their goggles and the impenetrable darkness was partially relieved in a dim green light.

"Look around in the corners where a jug may have been overlooked. Almost anything other than paint might work," Jason said.

After ten minutes of rummaging around with Jason growing increasingly uneasy, worried about possible pursuit, Clayton came over with a plastic jug of solvent used to clean auto parts. It was old and had partially broken down and lost some of its volatility.

"Might work," Jason said.

He soaked a rag in the chemical and laid it on the floor.

"Hope it don't melt your boots," Clayton said as Jason stepped on the rag.

"Now you," he said after finishing. "Boots seem okay."

After treating their boots, the two exited the building and headed up the road towards the river and their observation position.

The building they had chosen was unfinished. The construction had been caught by the EMP event and abandoned. It was a seven-story apartment building overlooking the Tennessee River with a view to the City-County building and courthouse on the opposite bank. They made their way carefully to the roof in the dark.

"This would be a great place to snipe from," Jason remarked when they had settled in on the rooftop.

"Only if you didn't want to live long," Clayton said.

Jason looked at him.

"If anyone pinpointed you, they'd be here in a heartbeat and you'd be trapped."

"You're right...if they pinpointed me. The idea would be to take my shot, maybe take out the Chairman, and then get the hell out before anyone figured out where the shot came from. This wouldn't be a position to try to hold."

Jason used his night vision goggles to observe the City-County building through his scope. He could see well enough to identify guards at the door. After watching for two hours he observed a change in guard.

"They just changed the guard. I'll keep watching to time the shifts."

"I can help," Clayton responded, "With the spotting scope."

Between the two of them, they watched for the next four hours. After learning the timing of the shifts, they put their gear away. They wrapped their ground cloths around them to ward off the night chill and dew and settled down to try to get some sleep.

The next day the two men watched the activity across the river, Jason through his rifle scope and Clayton using the spotting scope. Men were coming and going at the City-County building. Some wore a type of uniform similar to the National Guard. Jason thought they might have been taken from an armory and modified. Others were dressed as civilians but had a distinct armband, probably indicating they were in the militia.

Clayton finally spoke up. "You're the military man. What's the plan? We can't just walk in there."

Jason pulled back from his scope. "I want to identify this Chairman. If he's headquartered in the City-County building, we should be able to see him come and go from here."

"What if he lives in the building? He don't have to come and go."

"Yeah. That would be a problem, but he's got to go out sometime. He can't just stay holed up in an office."

"We could be here a while. Hope our boys are okay."

"We can't move until we know where the Chairman is."

"He that important?"

"I figure if we can get to him, we can convince him to let our guys go."

"Just 'cause we ask nice?"

"I'm working on that. Something to convince him it's in his best interests."

"Good luck with that."

Jason didn't answer. The problem had been plaguing him since they started on this rescue. He didn't doubt they could infiltrate the Chairman's compound. He didn't doubt he could execute the Chairman with a well-placed shot. But the problem of finding Rodney and Billy and getting them out of town seemed impossible to solve. It would take something drastic.

He turned to Clayton. "Why don't you watch the street we came down? I can watch across the river. If anyone is going to come after us, best to know soon so we can get down to the main floor."

"More options then."

Jason nodded and turned back to the river.

Around eight in the morning Jason announced, "Here he comes."

"The Chairman?"

"Yep."

Clayton came over and aimed the spotting scope across the river. They saw a tall figure wearing a white navy bill cap. He got out of a Humvee that had pulled up near to the front door. There were two men with him that looked like bodyguards. The deference of the door sentries was obvious, even from a distance.

"So, he doesn't sleep in his office. Let's watch through the day to see when he goes home, wherever that is," Jason said.

"How do we get to him?"

"Maybe we can get into the building at night and wait in his office."

"Just need to know where his office is and how we'll deal with the two guards."

Jason grunted in agreement.

"Can see now we couldn't do this with a large group," Clayton continued. "We can move quiet enough but I'm trying to figure out how this ain't a suicide mission, for us and Rodney and Billy."

"We'll need a hostage," Jason said.

"Only hostage that will work is the Chairman."

"What I'm thinking."

Clayton stared at Jason for a long moment. "How we gonna get across the river?" He asked.

Both men swept their eyes across the bridges. Many blocks to the east was a freeway bridge that had checkpoints on either side of it. The nearest bridge to their right was closed. The one on their left was open but also with checkpoints and guards. Beyond that bridge was a railroad bridge. It was unused since the EMP attack and looked unguarded since no vehicular or pedestrian traffic could traverse it.

"Bet we could make our way across the railroad bridge," Clayton said.

Jason nodded in agreement. "Beats swimming across the river."

"Don't want to do that."

The men spent the day alternating between watching and sleeping. They were going to be up most of the night. When it got dark, they packed up to make their way across the river.

"Before we go, let's talk about what we're going to do," Clayton said.

Jason nodded. "We get across the river, we can work our way through the trees almost to the City-County building." The landscaped areas of the city had long been neglected and were overgrown, providing good cover for an infiltrator. "We wait until the last watch change at night. Then we capture the guard and make him lead us inside to the Chairman's office."

"He'll be missed when the morning guard comes."

"Yeah. That's around 8:00 in the morning. We'll have four hours to set up. The guards won't know what's happened, only that someone deserted their post. The Chairman shows up between eight and nine so there'll be little time to sort things out."

"We wait for the Chairman in his office?"

Jason nodded. "We'll have to neutralize the guards. We want to do that without shooting if we can. If we can't, I have a .22 with a suppressor which makes hardly any noise."

"Then what?"

"If we get control of this guy, we can make him bring Rodney and Billy to his office. Maybe under the guise of us checking them out before we negotiate a ransom payment."

"And how do we get out?"

"I haven't got that fully figured out yet, but I got a couple of ideas."

"You want to share? I'd like to know if we got more options than a shootout in the Chairman's office."

"We take him hostage and walk out with him."

"They never gonna let us do that."

"I'm going to make it so they have to. Kind of like mutually assured destruction. Me and the Chairman."

Clayton gave Jason a sharp look.

"I think I can set up a situation where if we're attacked, or I'm shot, the Chairman dies—automatically."

"Like a grenade? We didn't bring any."

"Kind of like that."

"The rest of us will die as well."

Jason sighed. "You're probably right, but it's our best chance to pull this off."

Clayton looked hard at Jason. "You always been honest with me. You fight well. I didn't know if we'd come back from this alive but I agreed with you that paying the ransom would only bring trouble to Hillsboro and my people. We got to make them understand the people in Hillsboro are tough. If we gonna die, we want to make them think twice about attacking our people."

Jason put his hand on Clayton's shoulder. He looked into his eyes which were clear and unwavering. The man had said more than usual for him, but he was direct and unflinching in his honesty.

"We got a chance to make this work. If this Chairman is sane and has some sane people working with him, we'll get out alive."

They made their way down the stairwell of the building and out into the dirt yard. The road to the west of them continued over the river and was one of the manned entry points. They had to retrace their path back away from the river, staying in the cover of buildings until they were far enough to not be seen or heard. The night vision goggles gave them an advantage but they couldn't assume those at the checkpoints weren't similarly equipped.

They picked a spot where there were buildings close to the road on either side, minimizing their exposure in the open roadway.

"When we get across the road and reach the railroad tracks. They'll be a lot of cover on each side to shield us."

"Let's hope for no more dogs."

"Amen to that."

After crossing the road, they got into a large patch of woods and moved west. The woods continued until they reached the tracks. Jason breathed a sigh of relief.

"Should be a bit easier from here."

They walked in the ditch down beside the tracks which were built up on a gravel bed. It was quieter going and they were more shielded. Thankfully the growth on either side of the right of way was thick.

They reached a street crossing just before the train bridge. The tracks went over with the street running underneath in a single lane passage. They stopped at the edge of the clearing and scanned to their right, towards the working bridge. They could see the barriers set up to slalom any vehicles through, slowing them before the checkpoint.

Without a word, Jason moved back and, using the cover of the trees, crossed the tracks to the far side. Clayton followed and the two men crouched low and began to move forward. When they reached the bridge, they took off their packs and began to crawl on their hands and knees, keeping below the railing.

After three minutes of crawling, they reached the cover of the trees on the far side.

"River bridge is next. We'll be in good cover until we get there," Jason said.

They could see the train bridge two hundred yards ahead.

"Then more crawling. A lot more."

Jason nodded.

The bridge had little in the way of sides to shield them. Its virtue was that it was unguarded and, hopefully, unwatched.

"Figure it take about an hour if we crawling," Clayton said.

"About that," Jason said.

It was an iron truss structure built on concrete piers about thirty feet off of the water with the trusses set below the rails. It was rusted and heading into serious decay to the point where it might not hold the weight of a loaded freight train. Near the downtown shore the trusses went up above the tracks, giving a greater clearance for commercial river traffic below.

The two men started out moving in a crouch and when their muscles grew cramped, they went on hands and knees. It was a bit disorienting to see the water below, through the cross ties. They carefully placed hands and knees on each tie which were about eighteen inches apart with nothing but water showing in between.

Part of the way, Jason stretched himself out on the ties. Clayton was behind him and did the same.

"Not very comfortable," Clayton said.

"We just have to be patient." After a minute of stretching, Jason rolled over and began to crawl again, hands and knees fashion.

"This easier than trying to walk in a crouch," Clayton said.

"Hard on the knees though."

"We survive it."

When they neared the side of the river, they stopped and scanned the bank with their night vision goggles. As they had hoped, there was no one on this side either. The guards seemed to be assigned to the checkpoints only.

Ten minutes more of crawling and they slipped down the embankment from the tracks and into the trees. To the east, the manned bridge was elevated higher than the train bridge and the checkpoint was set up further back into the local streets.

"We should be able to make our way underneath without coming into view of the checkpoint," Jason said.

"Hopefully we can get close to the City-County building without going further into the city," Clayton said.

"Yeah. Moving further in increases the odds of someone seeing us."

Jason checked his watch. "We have an hour and a half. We want to be in position before 4:00 am when the guard changes over."

They started moving east, keeping the trees between them and the apartment buildings facing the river. They couldn't be seen from anyone across the river since they were up against the tree cover. If they didn't make any sounds, no guard at any of the apartments would know they were passing by.

Going under the road bridge proved easy but on the east side, the tree cover ended. There were just overgrown fields that had once been mowed grass bordering the road.

"Crawling time again," Clayton whispered.

"We're doing well on time, so let's not rush this part."

They crawled through the grass, pushing their packs ahead of them. Jason stopped to listen every twenty yards. It took an hour to move the two blocks. Finally, a massive concrete and glass building loomed ahead, just off to their left, beyond an intersection.

"We need to get behind this building. Time to move in a block," Jason whispered.

"Lead the way," Clayton said.

They moved up the street, keeping close to the overgrown vegetation. At the next block a street ran off to their right between the City-County building and the large building facing the river. Without a sound they moved through the once attractive grounds surrounding the building, now filled with tall grass and brush. Even in the inhabited parts of the city no effort was expended to keep the grounds from reverting to their natural habitat. It created an odd mix of civilization and apocalypse in one setting.

They came to an elevated walkway that connected the two buildings together. Passing under it they went to the left and slowly approached the stairs leading to the main doors. The guard stood at the base of the stairs.

Chapter 17

They stopped outside of earshot of the guard.

"I'll work my way to the bushes at the side of the stairs. You leave your backpack and weapon here and just walk up. Act like you're drunk or confused. Get the guard's attention. When he passes by me, I'll take him down."

Jason set out crawling towards the guard. He had to move slow. He was close enough the guard would be able to hear any scraping sounds.

Clayton watched his progress. When Jason got to the bushes, Clayton stepped out and staggered forward.

"Who's there?" the guard shouted.

"I need help," mumbled Clayton. He kept going forward.

"Stop where you are. You're not supposed to be here."

"Can you help me?"

As the guard approached, he passed Jason's hiding place. Jason stepped out and threw his left arm around his chest and, with his right arm, pressed his knife to his throat.

"No sound or you're dead," he whispered into the man's ear.

The guard froze.

"You'll live if you follow my directions. Understand?"

The man nodded slightly with the knife still at his throat. "What do—"

He stopped as he felt the knife blade push against his neck, starting to cut into his flesh.

"No talking," Jason whispered.

Clayton came up, bringing their backpacks and they marched the guard up the stairs to the main entrance.

"Unlock the door," Jason said.

"I don't have a key," the guard responded.

Jason put his face close to the guard's so the man could clearly see him in the dark. "Don't lie to me. It will get you killed. Yesterday I watched you hand a set of keys to the guard who relieved you. Now pull out those keys and use them."

The guard was a young man. He looked to be barely out of his teens. He was shorter than Jason and Clayton and not built as solid. He was now very afraid. He put his hand into his pocket and pulled out a ring with numerous keys on it.

"Open the door," Jason said.

He unlocked the door and Clayton pushed him inside, locking the door behind them.

"Now you're going to take us to the Chairman's office. Don't bother to tell me you don't know where it is. You'll only piss me off."

They trudged up the stairs. The building was built in the shape of a triangle with two straight sides and the third side flowing in a graceful curve from one leg to the other. They went up two flights of stairs and walked back along one of the legs. It was pitch black inside. Jason used his flashlight with his hand covering most of the lens to allow only the most meager light to escape.

It wasn't the tallest building in the center-city compound but Jason could understand why the Chairman had picked it. It was like a fortress with few windows. When they stopped at the Chairman's office the man took out another key and opened the door. Inside was a receptionist area with chairs for those waiting to see the man in the inner office. The inner office had windows but only on one side. They faced a block-long building across a street. When things got hot, that would be where the snipers would be set up.

Jason closed the blinds. He told the guard to sit on the floor. Clayton watched him while Jason took some zip ties from his backpack and tied the man's wrists behind his back. With the man secured he asked Clayton to go into the adjacent offices and pull down any blinds to layer over the ones in the office.

"We need to make sure no one can see inside. If they can't see us, they can't shoot."

"What about infrared? Or something like those night vision goggles?" Clayton asked.

"If they have infrared, it will only show the heat signature from bodies. They won't be able to tell who is who."

Jason squatted down in front of the guard whose eyes were wide with fear. "You'll be okay through what's going to happen as long as you don't try to interfere with our plans. Now I need to ask you some questions. Is there a receptionist?"

The man nodded.

"Good. Are there guards stationed on this floor during the day?"

The man nodded again.

"How many?"

"I'm not sure—"

"Be careful. Remember what I said. Don't lie and don't tell me you don't know anything."

"I don't know for sure. There's probably six men. It's a plumb job but it only goes to those closest to the Chairman."

"That's better. Now who's the second in charge? Who backs up the Chairman?"

"There's a militia general. That what you mean?"

"No. Who's the next man in line to give orders for the Chairman? Someone the general would have to listen to."

"That would be Phillip Cordell."

"His office in the building?"

The man nodded. "Next office down the hall. But he spends most of his time outside. I think he's the eyes and ears for the Chairman."

Just then Clayton came back with an arm full of drapes. He set about hooking them to the existing ones. When he was done, there were three layers of cloth covering the windows.

Jason turned back to the young guard. "Now the two men who come with the Chairman, they the same ones each day?"

The kid nodded.

"They come up to the office with him?"

"I don't know," he said fearfully. "I swear I'm not lying. I don't go in with them. They're part of the Chairman's guards so I guess they come up here. I'm told the guards have their own room here in the building. Sort of on call for the Chairman, or Mr. Cordell."

Jason allowed a slight grin to escape. "You're doing okay...so far."

"What are you gonna do? When everyone finds out you're here, you'll never get out. If you want to join up, or talk to the Chairman about a problem, there's better ways of doing it than this."

"You're probably right," Jason said. "But never mind what we want."

Clayton was sitting on the desk. "What do we do with him?"

The boy turned to look at Clayton. He could barely make him out in the dark; just a shadow on the desk.

"Please don't kill me. I didn't do anything. I did what you asked. I told you everything I know."

Jason stood up. "We'll find a place to stash him. Some place out of the way."

"Can't let him sound an alarm."

"You're right. We'll tape his mouth so he can't make any noise."

"If he tries, we'll just have to shoot him," Clayton said.

"I'll be quiet. Quiet as a mouse. You don't have to shoot me. Just put me in a closet somewhere." The boy was unnerved by Clayton's matter-of-fact statement.

Jason clicked on the flashlight again and swept the shrouded beam around the room. There was a closet in the far right corner, built into a dividing wall between the offices. Next to the closet was an inset with a wet bar.

"We'll put him in there," Jason said pointing with the light.

"So now we wait," Clayton said.

"Yep. There's always a lot of waiting in these kinds of ops."

"We in the middle of the hornet's nest now. They're asleep but things will happen fast when they wake up."

"Let's talk about that."

"First, let's put the kid in the closet. Make it so he can't hear or speak."

Jason cut some cloth from the kid's shirt sleeve and stuffed a wad in each ear. Then he taped over his ears. Next, he put a strip of duct tape over the boy's mouth. When he finished, he walked him to the closet and zip tied his feet and pulled them up to his wrists in a hog-tied manner.

"You'll be uncomfortable, but safe. You'll survive and no one will blame you for what happens. Especially after they find you trussed up like this."

Jason closed the closet door.

"He can't hear or speak and he can't kick at the door to warn anyone. I doubt if he would try that anyway."

"Never hurts to be sure," Clayton said. "Now how do we control this when things erupt?"

"We have to neutralize the two guards if they come into the office with the Chairman. We have to take control of him. He's our hostage, our leverage. They'll do what he tells them to do. The Chairman needs to understand that we are willing to go down, taking him with us, if he doesn't do what we say."

"The others need to think that as well for this to work."

"True enough. I'm betting the Chairman can make that point for us. We just need to make it to him."

"If the guards come in with him?"

"I'll eliminate them with the .22. It's quiet enough it may not create a general alarm. The receptionist could be a problem, though. We may need to get control over her as well."

"Shoot the guards?"

Jason nodded sharply enough so Clayton could see him in the dark. "Can't have them around to worry about. Remember these are the enemy."

"I got no problem with that. Just think the fewer we kill the easier it will be for us to get what we came for. Don't want to incite a harder response than we have to. We got the general to think about."

"Yeah. I'm worried about him as well. I hope the Chairman or Cordell can control him."

"Make the Chairman's life depend on it," Clayton said.

The two men sat back against the office wall and stretched out their legs. They rested. It would be three more hours until the change of the guard. When that happened things would move fast.

Jason's thoughts drifted back to Hillsboro and his family. He was a father now. Would he see his son and wife again? Would he see his two teenage step-daughters? He wondered about his decision to attempt this rescue. *Yes*, he thought to himself. *You have to stop evil before it can grow and metastasize.* But how much of a price did they have to pay to live in peace and try to rebuild their lives? And why did evil always rear its vicious head when society broke down? Are we all that corrupt...or most of us?

Jason clamped down on his thoughts. He refused to allow himself to second guess his presence in Knoxville. He had made a choice. One Anne had not been happy with. But he was here, trying to rescue two men who were a part of his tribe. Hard times made for hard choices.

Jason looked over at Clayton who sat quietly seeming to stare ahead into the dark of the office. *Probably wondering the same things. This could be the end of our run.* He shook his head. *No, we have to survive this. We can't let our families and Hillsboro down.*

He sat still now, a hard, dark center growing inside of him. *No mercy, no weakness.* As Clayton had said, "They must fear us."

Chapter 18

T he sun came up. Both Jason and Clayton got up and stretched. The Chairman would be coming soon if he kept to his pattern.

"I'll put myself behind the door, you wait behind the couch," Jason said. There was a couch along the side wall. "You can back me up. I'll grab the Chairman. You cover the guards if they come in with him."

"Shoot if they resist? It'll be noisy."

"Can't be helped. We'll have the Chairman. If we have to shoot, things will happen faster, but the outcome will be the same. We'll be in control of the Chairman so we'll have the leverage."

Both men drank some water and ate some rations from their backpacks. Jason went over to the desk and checked for any weapons in the drawers. He removed a 9mm semi-automatic and put it in his backpack. Then they took up their positions and waited.

They heard the door to the outer office open. There was the muffled sound of conversation and the door closed. Then the inner office door opened and a thin man stepped through the entrance.

Jason threw his left arm around him and put his .22 pistol to his head. Clayton stood up with his AR16 and swung around to check the outer office. It was empty.

He closed the door.

"Don't yell and you'll be okay. Yell and you'll get hurt," Jason said.

"What do you want? Do you know who I am?" The man asked. He had a vibrant voice but pitched high with tension.

Clayton pulled up a straight chair and Jason pushed the man into it. He took another one and pulled it in front of the man while Clayton secured his hands behind his back with zip ties.

The man looked to be in his fifties. He had had a full head of shocking white hair. His eyes were fiercely blue. They shone brightly now with agitation.

"I asked you, do you know who I am?"

"We know who you are," Jason replied.

"Then you know you're in a lot of trouble. You can avoid making it worse by stopping right now. If you have a complaint, a problem, I'll listen. You'll get some punishment, I can't let this pass, but I may be able to help with whatever drove you to do something so stupid as this."

"As a matter of fact, you can help us out with a problem," Jason said.

"I'll listen, but first you have to untie me and put down your weapons. I can't help you otherwise."

Jason studied the man. It was important that the Chairman see how committed they were, even desperate. "You'll listen and you won't be untied."

"My secretary will be in here shortly. She'll alert the guards and then you're screwed."

"Thanks for the heads up." Jason turned to Clayton, "Maybe you should wait for her in the outer office. She can be helpful."

Clayton nodded and headed to the door.

"Make sure she goes through her normal routine before bringing her in," Jason said as he left.

"Now Mr. Chairman," Jason said, turning back to his prisoner, "what is your real name?"

The man didn't respond.

Jason held up the Walther PPK. "This is a silenced small-bore pistol. It doesn't make much noise. Probably can't be heard in the outer office. If you don't cooperate and answer my questions, I can begin shooting you, starting with your feet and working my way up. It's painful and you'll be crippled for the rest of your life if you don't die, medicine being what it is now days. I suggest you answer me."

Jason looked at the man coldly. He knew his face reflected an unconcern about which option the man chose. The Chairman's eyes changed. They lost some of their fierceness as he stared at Jason. Doubt now crept into his face.

"My name is not important but if you must know, it's Tom Horner."

"Okay Tom. Now you asked me what we wanted, so I'll tell you. We're from Hillsboro. We've come to take our kin back home with us."

"Did you bring the ransom? Where's my courier?"

"No, we didn't bring the ransom...or your courier."

"You're not kin to those men. One of them is black."

"True enough, but they're members of our tribe. See we take personal relationships seriously in Hillsboro. Fighting alongside one another for your survival develops strong bonds. So they're both family to us."

"I told the courier to inform you we'd release them when you paid the ransom."

"That's just the problem. You shouldn't have taken them in the first place."

"How do you know? They broke our laws. I had to arrest them."

"So you say. But I know they were passing through, headed west. They had no interest in Knoxville. If they broke any of your laws, especially made up ones they were unaware of, it was not their intent."

"Ignorance of the law is no excuse. You should know that."

Jason gave Tom a cold smile. "I'm not here to discuss your laws. I'm here to take my men back."

"You can't get away, you're in the middle of my territory. I suggest we talk about how to limit the damage for you and your partner."

Just then they heard the outer office door open. Jason jumped up and put the pistol to Tom's thigh.

"Not a sound, or I'll shoot," he whispered.

There was a scuffling sound a muffled cry and then Clayton entered the inner office with a woman. He had one arm around her torso and one hand over her mouth. The woman's eyes were wide with fright. They got even wider when she saw the Chairman in the chair with his wrists bound. Clayton shuffled the woman over to the couch and pulled her down.

Jason put a finger to his lips and looked at the woman until she nodded. Clayton slowly withdrew his hand.

"You can remain ungagged if you keep quiet, like you boss here. Understand?" The woman nodded. "What's your name?"

"Mary."

"Okay Mary. You're going to be fine. Just do what we say when we tell you. It will be pretty simple for you, if you don't try anything stupid."

Mary starred at Jason, her mouth open, fear showing on her face.

"Got it Mary?" Jason said in a stern voice.

The woman flinched and nodded her head.

"Let's get on with it," Clayton said. "Times a wasting."

Jason turned back to Tom. "You're going to call your second in command and tell him to come to your office. You've got a busy day and something unusual just came up. If he asks, tell him it has to do with the Hillsboro prisoners.

Tom just looked at him.

"Repeat that back to me."

The Chairman repeated what Jason had said.

Jason turned to the woman. "Your part is to play the hostage. That means you just sit there with your mouth shut. Can you do that?"

Mary nodded.

"When's the assistant come in?" Jason asked her.

"He'll be here shortly. He likes to let the Chairman get his day started, coffee, maybe a snack, work out his agenda or to-do list, before they meet."

"Do you usually call him?"

Mary shook her head. "He just comes to the office."

"He stops in his office first?"

"Yes," she said.

Jason turned to the Chairman. I'm going to untie you so you can sit at your desk. Mary will sit on the couch with my partner. I'll sit in this chair. I'll have my jacket on my lap. My pistol will be under it. How you act, what you do will determine whether or not your assistant gets killed."

"This is crazy. You can't get away. Stop this now before someone gets hurt. Mary shouldn't be a part of this."

"You need to understand that if you don't follow directions, you'll die. Even if we die, we're capable of taking out a lot of people, starting with you and your assistant. Mary might die also. It's on you if you don't play along."

"If you die, your friends will also."

Clayton spoke up from the couch. "Could be. They's fighters. They know the score. But you'll die for sure."

"All your dreams of empire, gone," Jason added. "We'll snuff them out in a heartbeat if you don't cooperate. I've got no sympathy or patience with someone who'd kidnap my people and try to ransom them."

The Chairman was now staring at Jason. His burst of anger now gone.

"Here's your first test," Jason said as he got up and crossed over to the Chairman. He took out his knife and sliced through the zip ties. The man massaged his wrists.

"Now go sit at your desk," Jason said. "Your phones work. Call your assistant. Keep it on speaker and tell him what I told you to say."

The Chairman did as he was told. A few minutes later the assistant entered the room. He stopped when he saw Jason. Turning to the right he saw Mary and Clayton sitting on the couch. Clayton had hidden his AK47 but the man could see how frightened Mary looked. He stopped at the door.

"Close the door, Mr. Cordell," Jason said.

He looked back to Jason, then to his boss, sitting behind his desk. Jason could tell he was sizing up the situation. It looked normal, but Mary didn't look right and he probably noticed an odd look on the Chairman's face.

Jason looked over at Tom. "Mr. Cordell should be involved in our discussions. I suggest he sit down."

The Chairman nodded and pointed to the other chair in the middle of the room.

Phillip Cordell walked over to the chair and sat down facing the desk. "What's going on Tom?"

"These men want to negotiate the release of our Hillsboro captives."

"How did they get in?"

"We slipped in last night. Broke in, if you want to call it that. Figured that was the best way to get in front of the Chairman, seeing as how strangers don't seem to be well treated here."

Phillip turned back to Tom. "What do they want? Do they know how dangerous this is, what they're doing?"

"We know," Jason replied. "You need to know how dangerous this is for you and the Chairman, here."

Phillip turned to Jason. "I'm talking to my boss."

"No, you're talking to me and I'm talking to both of you." He paused for a moment as Phillip digested what he said. "We're willing to negotiate for the release of our two men, but we need to see them. Call it proof of life or proof they haven't been abused. Your job, Phillip," Jason dropped the mister, "is to get them here so we can see what shape they're in."

"I can't do that," Phillip's voice was firm.

"Yes you can," Jason turned back to Tom, "Can't he Mr. Chairman."

"You want me to get those men out of their cells and bring them here?" Phillip's question was directed to Tom but Jason answered him.

"You can and you will, if you want this to end well and no one gets hurt. We have a tense situation here, we all need to realize that. Mary could be in danger. But there's no need for that if you bring the men here. Then we can get on with our negotiations."

"What negotiations?" Phillip asked. "You pay the ransom, you get the men."

"Well, that's what we have to talk about. There may be a payment or something else of value to exchange." Jason stood up. His coat dropped to the floor. Phillip looked directly at his pistol. "You come back with our men and knock on the outer door. Don't open it until you hear us shout to come in. There must be no one with you but our two men if you don't want to get yourself shot. Now go. Everyone is depending on you."

Cordell looked over at Tom who nodded in a guarded way. He turned to go.

"And Phillip," the man stopped as Jason called his name, "don't do anything stupid. I expect you to alert the guards but if anyone tries to storm this office, people will get killed. If my partner and I feel threatened, the Chairman and Mary won't survive. Am I clear?"

Phillip nodded and left the office.

Chapter 19

"Now we wait. I hope for everyone's sake Cordell doesn't do anything stupid," Jason said.

"He'll bring the men," Tom replied. "But it won't change your situation. You can't get them or yourselves out."

He was beginning to feel confident he could wait out the situation without getting hurt and his men would handle the rest once Jason's team tried to leave.

"We may have an offer you won't want to refuse, something of great value. Let's wait to see how our guys are doing."

Clayton grabbed his carbine and went to a corner of the window and pulled back an inch of curtain. "We got men collecting outside where we came in."

"What I figured. They probably got some snipers set up in the building across the walkway. Don't expose yourself."

"Can't see them. All the windows are open but dark inside. Expect you're right though. Good place to shoot from."

His matter of fact tone was unnerving to Tom. *What role did these men play in Hillsboro that they'd be so suicidal?*

"Are you someone important in Hillsboro?" He asked Jason. You know about the courier and you seem to be in charge. You've obviously got some training. Did the mayor send you? Are you in the army?"

"Was in the army and yes, the mayor did send me in a way. I insisted since I felt connected to the two men."

"And you're willing to die for them?"

Jason looked directly in Tom's eyes. There was no warmth, only a deadly look coming from him. Tom suppressed a shiver.

He responded, "I'm willing to kill you for those two men...and Phillip...and Mary even. Sorry Mary, but this is a deadly serious game we're playing here."

Jason kept his focus on Tom until the Chairman turned away. "But you'll die as well."

"Like I said, maybe we will. But you definitely will die. We'll take our chances after that."

"And you?" Tom turned to Clayton. "You willing to die for this crazy plan? I notice this man seems to be doing all the talking."

"We be together on this. You best understand if you want to live." Everyone could hear the deadly intent, the fatalism in Clayton's voice.

A half hour later there was a knock on the outer door. Clayton slipped out to the receptionist's office and crouched behind the desk, to one side of the door. If any shooters came through, he would be out of their line of fire. They would be focused on the inner office door and he would have a moment of surprise to take them down. He only hoped Billy and Rodney would not be in the way.

When Clayton was in position, Jason crouched behind Tom with his pistol to Tom's head and called out to come in. The door swung open and Rodney and Billy stepped through it. They were handcuffed and in waist and ankle chains. Phillip Cordell followed them. There was no one else in sight.

"Close the door, lock it, and bring them in here," Jason called out.

When they passed through the outer office, Clayton stood and grabbed a chair and jammed it against the outer office door. He followed the three into Tom's office and closed that door as well.

"They probably got the hall filled with militia," Clayton said.

Both Rodney and Billy looked at Jason and Clayton in astonishment.

"How did you get here?" Rodney asked.

"We came to take you two home," Jason responded. He came around the desk and gave each man a hug.

Clayton came up to Billy. "You doing all right? They didn't hurt you?"

Billy was smiling and shook his head. "I'm okay. Boy I'm sure glad to see you. Glad to see both of you."

"Rodney. Looks like you got beat up," Jason said. He stepped back behind Tom.

"I got roughed up a bit at first. The Chairman's militia seems to be a bit racist." Rodney gave Tom a sharp look.

"Clayton better check our Mr. Cordell for weapons. Don't want him to smuggle anything in that could trigger people getting shot."

After checking Phillip for weapons, Jason had him sit on the floor between the two chairs. Rodney and Billy sat in the chairs facing Cordell.

"Now unchain these men," Jason ordered.

"Not until we have something worked out."

Clayton walked up behind him and smacked him on his head with his open hand. The blow knocked the man on his side.

"Don't have time to waste," Clayton said. "Do as he says."

Cordell looked over at Tom.

Clayton grabbed Cordell by his hair and turned his head back and up, until he was looking at him. "If one of us tells you to do it, you do it. I can knock you silly and then find the key, or you can get it out of your pocket now and do what you're told."

Cordell reached into his pocket and pulled out the key. He went to each of the men and unlocked them.

"You've seen the men, they're unharmed. They're unlocked. Now what is this offer you say you're going to make?" Tom asked.

"First we play a game of musical chairs. We're going to all get up and move around each other, grab a partner and turn in circles a few times, then move on to another. I'll stand by the couch and watch. If either Tom or Phillip try anything, I'll shoot them."

"What's this all about?" Rodney asked.

"Heat signatures. If they're using infrared scopes, they won't know who is who and won't be able to fire. When we're done, no one will sit behind the desk."

When they finished shuffling around, everyone sat on the floor in the middle of the room.

Jason leaned forward towards the Chairman. "We're going to trade your life for the lives of these two men and ourselves. I figure you're so important a one for four trade will seem a small price."

"Why would I agree to that?"

Jason looked at the Chairman. "Are you stupid? You agree so you get to live and keep your little kingdom going."

"You'll never get away," Cordell said.

Clayton whacked him again. "Shut up. We've heard that before. It don't mean nothin' to us."

The Chairman now seemed more assured of himself. He appeared to Jason to understand bargaining. "How do you propose we proceed?"

Jason took a piece of paper and pen from the Chairman's desk. He wrote down a list on it and handed it to the Chairman.

"You have a Humvee brought up the side street with a full tank of fuel. I want three M14 or M16 carbines and six extra clips, all loaded. I also want one 12-gauge tactical shotgun. A Mossberg A1. You probably have some from raiding the armories. Bring it with a box of shells."

"You won't—"

"Enough!" Jason shouted putting his face to the Chairman. Cordell stirred but Clayton put a hand on his shoulder.

Just then the phone rang. Tom reached for it but Jason grabbed his hand. He pulled the phone off the desk and set it on the floor.

"You can answer but only on speaker. If it's your general, you relay our list to him and get him to send an unarmed man up with the weapons in a bag. You try to give him any other orders, you get shot. Understand?"

Tom nodded and punched the speaker button.

"Tom here," he said.

"Tom, what's going on? Are you all right?"

"Yes. I'm all right. Mary and Phillip are here as well. No one's hurt. I've got a list of things I need you to bring here and we can get this resolved."

"I've got men surrounding the building and snipers—"

"General you're on speaker. Everyone can hear you."

"Shit," the man exclaimed.

"It's okay. They suspected snipers would be in place. Here's the list. Let's get this over with a quickly as we can with no one getting hurt."

He read the list to the general.

"I can't arm these men, Tom. They're terrorists."

"Mike, they're already armed. I assume they want these for their escape and journey home."

"I don't know. It doesn't seem right. Not the way hostage negotiations should go."

Tom raised his voice. "Just do it. I've got this under control. They get what they want and they'll leave. I've got Phillip and Mary here and I don't want any casualties. They're leaving after we give them the weapons and the Humvee."

"It's against my better judgement and advice."

"Just do it and be quick. I want to get this over with."
Jason hung up the phone.

"What's his name?" Jason asked.

"Mike McKenzie," Tom answered.

"He got any military experience?"

"He's a veteran. Was a major in the army before retiring."

"Passed over for Lieutenant Colonel?"

The Chairman shrugged.

Now Rodney spoke up. "Is he loyal? Follow your orders?"

Tom nodded. "He's a solid man, reliable."

"He follows Phillip's orders when you're not around?" Jason asked.

Tom looked at him questioningly. "I'm always around," he finally said.

Jason tried again. "When you're busy, does Phillip ever give out orders?"

"Yes. We are well organized. We've brought peace and stability to this town. Everyone supports us."

"But they don't get to choose. There ain't any elections," Clayton said.

Tom looked over at him. "The time isn't ripe for something like that. Not for a while, yet."

"Spoken like a true dictator," Jason said.

"And you're doing it better in Hillsboro?" Phillip asked.

"We are. And we're not kidnapping people and holding them for ransom."

No one spoke for a moment.

"What happens next?" Tom finally asked.

"We collect the weapons, we confirm the Humvee is in place, we leave," Jason said.

Both Rodney and Billy looked at Jason with doubt in their faces.

"Just like that?" Tom said.

"Just like that."

"Then you'll free us? All of us including Mary?"

"If you cooperate, we will. No one gets hurt, like I said before. Isn't that what you want?"

"Yeah. We don't need to get anyone hurt," Tom said.

The group lapsed into silence while they waited. Occasionally there was a whimper from Mary who sat on the floor with the men.

After ten minutes, there was a knock on the outer door. Jason gave Rodney his .22 and took out the 9mm. "Watch these two," he said. He and Clayton got up and went into the outer office. Clayton took up his position behind the desk and Jason, went to the door. He took out the chair wedge and unlocked the door.

Crouching down he told the person outside to open the door, drop a large bag inside, and close it again. When the door closed Jason locked it and put the chair back under the doorknob. He brought the bag into the inner office and opened it. All the items were in the bag.

"Call the general and tell him to back the Humvee up to the stairs."

Tom did as he was told.

"Okay. You can leave now?" Tom asked when the Humvee pulled up outside.

"Just one last thing. You're going to come with us to ensure we get out alive," Jason said.

Tom's eyes grew wide. Jason guessed he didn't figure on being dragged along.

"That's right. It could get dangerous for you. If anyone tries to take us out, sniper fire, one of us will kill you. In fact, we'll make sure that happens."

He went over to his backpack and took out a roll of duct tape. Then he grabbed the shotgun and checked it for rounds. It was loaded but no shell was in the chamber.

"When this is gun is live, it's dangerous to mess with. Clayton, take Mr. Cordell over to the couch and keep him there. Use my .22 to shoot him if he moves. It's quiet and no one outside will know he's shot. Rodney, Billy, hold the Chairman from either side."

"What are you going to do? I followed your instructions. You said this wouldn't escalate, no one would get hurt." Tom's voice rose in fear. Billy and Rodney gripped him from both sides. He couldn't move.

Jason zip tied his hands again behind his back, then crouched in front of him. "Your militia likes you, don't they? The general and other officers?"

Tom nodded.

"This is going to ensure that no one gets hurt while we leave, especially us. You'll be fine if your men don't act stupid. It'll be uncomfortable but that's a small price to pay for our security."

Jason stuck the shotgun up to Tom's neck on his right side.

"Rodney hold the shotgun there. Don't move Tom, it could go off."

Tom's face was white, his eyes wide with fear.

Jason took the roll of duct tape and, starting with the barrel of the shotgun, pressed up against Tom's neck, he began to wind duct tape around the man's neck and the barrel, securing the shotgun to his neck.

"Swallowing may be a little difficult, but you won't gag. Stay calm."

When he was done, the shotgun was firmly attached to Tom's neck. Rodney held it but if he had let go, the weapon would have just dangled from the Chairman's neck.

"Tom," Jason said, leaning close to him. "This is called a dead man's switch. We're going to be in this together. So, I'm hoping just as hard as you that nothing goes wrong."

He took control of the shotgun from Rodney.

"Everyone stand up," Jason ordered. "We're going to shuffle again and then stand in a group in the middle here."

When they had finished shuffling, with Jason walking along side Tom and holding the shotgun, he told Rodney to grab the tape.

"I'm going to put my right hand on the grip with my finger on the trigger. I need you to tape my hand to the gun. Then you have to tape my index finger so it can't come off the trigger. Keep enough slack so that if I'm shot, the gun will go off when I collapse and fall. My drop has to pull the trigger."

The Chairman stiffened.

"Oh my God," Mary whispered from the back of the group.

"It'll be okay. Rodney just needs to be careful and Tom and I just need to walk carefully together. If I stumble, his head gets blown off."

Tom started shaking and breathing hard.

"He's hyperventilating. Billy cup your hands over his mouth."

Billy's eyes were as wide as Tom's, but he did as he was told.

"Steady, steady," Jason said in a calm voice. Tom's breathing began to slow.

"You're going to be all right. I'm in this with you and I don't want to get killed. You can trust that fact. We're going to help each other so neither of us gets hurt. Do you understand me?" Jason looked close into Tom's face. He nodded but fear was still evident in his face.

"Rodney, let's do this," Jason said. "Tom, if it helps, close your eyes. Rodney's going to be careful."

"You can't be doing this," Phillip said.

Clayton leaned over to him. "You want me to hurt you?" The man shook his head.

"Then keep your mouth shut."

"Phillip, your role will be to keep the general, Mike, in line," Jason said. We're going to release Tom when were clear of town and not being followed. We don't plan on taking him back to Hillsboro."

Phillip looked at Jason with his mouth open.

"You understand me?" Jason said forcefully.

Phillip nodded. "You're crazy."

"Maybe...and willing to die and take the Chairman with me, so don't screw this up. I know you'll follow, the general will insist on it. But if we see you, it will just delay releasing Tom. We do not want to see you after we leave."

While they were talking, Rodney finished taping Jason's hand and finger.

"Now we'll test it." Before anyone could react, Jason went limp and started to fall, his finger pulled hard on the trigger as the tape allowed the hand to slip down while the finger remained taped in a curl around the trigger.

There was a collective gasp from everyone in the room except Clayton, Rodney and Jason.

"It works. Now, just before we leave, Rodney, you'll put some duct tape over Tom's mouth. Not too hard, but just enough so he can't talk. Then I'll chamber a round."

Chapter 20

W e're going to call Mike and tell him what's going to take place," Jason said.

"He's not going to like it. He may not go along with it," Tom said.

"That's your job to convince him. Your life depends on it."

When Mike was contacted Tom told him about the situation. It elicited a string of curses which Tom waited out.

"Look, Mike. I'm in a difficult spot here. You have to cooperate or things will go sideways and I could die." Tom looked over his shoulder as best he could to Phillip. "Can you tell him, Phillip?"

Jason nodded and Phillip told Mike that the hostage-takers seemed to have no interest other than retrieving their men back and getting back to Hillsboro. They didn't want war, which was what Mike had been promising in lurid phrases. Both he and Tom thought Tom would be freed once they were clear of town.

The general finally agreed with strong threats about the hell he would wreak on the others if the Chairman was harmed.

"Now everyone stand up," Jason ordered. "It's time to go. Put the backpacks in the weapons bag. Each man take one of the M16s and extra clips. Hold them at low ready. My shotgun should be all we're gonna need."

He chambered a round with a loud, metallic click; Tom shivered.

"Phillip you'll go ahead and make sure everyone is calm. We don't want the Chairman or me to get killed. Tell them anyone shoots one of our team, I'll pull the trigger and the others will unload on you and anyone else in sight. It will be all over for you and the Chairman."

Phillip started for the door.

"Mary you stay here. After we're out of the office, you can release the guard. He's tied up in the closet," Jason said. "Phillip, tell them we're coming out and to stand down."

The Chairman started walking unsteadily alongside Jason.

"Steady Tom. If you trip it will set off the shotgun and we'll both die needlessly." Jason put his left arm around Tom's waist to help him. The shotgun hung from his neck like an obscene growth with Jason's right hand locked on to it.

When they entered the hallway there were militia troops on either side of the door. Many gasped as they saw the Chairman step out with the shotgun taped to his neck.

"Stand down, stand back!" Phillip shouted, waving his arm to direct the militia to fall back. "No one is to interfere. I've worked this out with General McKenzie and the Chairman. These men are leaving and will be releasing the Chairman when they go."

The men gave way and the procession made its way to the stairs.

"Careful now," Jason whispered to Tom. "Things will settle down when we're in the Humvee."

General McKenzie stood at the bottom of the stairs. He was flanked by various officers of the militia. The rest of the lobby was crowded with troops, all armed.

"General, tell your men to lower their weapons," Philip said. "We don't want anyone getting killed. You can see the situation. If you kill the terrorist, the shotgun will fire. His hand is taped to the trigger. It won't come off."

The general stared back at Phillip, his face contorted in rage. Jason guessed this seemed like an affront to his authority. If he reacted the wrong way, they were all going to die.

"General McKenzie," Jason called out. "This set up is to just ensure that we get to leave. We have no interest in harming the Chairman, just in getting our men back home. If anyone starts shooting, people will die. All of us, including Tom and Philip, and possibly you. That will cause chaos and anarchy for Knoxville. You don't want that."

The general looked hard at Jason, evaluating him. Jason stared back at him. This was the moment. There had to be no hint of a bluff involved. He hoped he had established that by taping himself to the shotgun, making himself both a target and the instrument of the Chairman's death.

"Lower your weapons," the general ordered. "Stand down and let them pass."

The group exited the building and went down the stairs to the Humvee.

"Everyone stand around the Chairman and me," Jason said as they reached the vehicle. "Phillip, General McKenzie, can you come over closer? Stand about ten feet away."

Jason spoke to both men after they had come closer. "Phillip, are the road checkpoints cleared? We'll be crossing the river on the parkway."

Phillip turned to McKenzie who was still bristling in anger.

"Are we cleared to go over the parkway bridge?" Jason asked him.

"Why do you have Tom's mouth taped? I'd like to hear from him that he's in agreement with what Phil wants me to do."

Jason turned to Tom, "You okay with the arrangements?" Tom nodded.

"There's your answer. We're trying to not die here, both me and the Chairman."

"Are you sure?" Mike asked, ignoring Jason's comments.

Tom nodded again with a muffled "uh huh."

"Now here's how this will proceed," Jason said to both Phillip and the general. "We'll release Tom somewhere down the road. I can't say where for obvious reasons. If we see any pursuit or following of us, it will only delay getting Tom released. You need to understand that point. We must not see you following us."

"We got it," Phillip replied.

"I want to be sure the General is in agreement. Do you agree General?"

Mike glared at Jason. "I agree. I also agree that I'll find you later and have you hanged."

Jason allowed a thin smile to cross his face. "Maybe. Your boss may just want to put this all behind him once we're gone. Now step back both of you. It's time to go."

"How about I lead until we're through the checkpoints on the bridge," Phillip said.

"I know the route, so don't try to mislead us," Jason said. "You stop when we're over the bridge. And understand, if I'm shot and the shotgun doesn't go off, one of my men will kill the Chairman."

Phillip nodded and he and McKenzie went off to another Humvee, this one with an emergency light rack on its top.

"Rodney, you drive," Jason said. "Clayton, you sit in front next to him. Both of you keep your weapons close. I'll get in the back with Tom, and Billy can squeeze in next to him. I don't want my trigger hand blocked in any way."

The men all nodded as they began to get in.

"You can't want me to let them go, can you?" Mike said after he and Phillip got into the lead Humvee.

"You see what that guy set up, mutually assured death, him and Tom. We don't have a choice."

"You trust them to let Tom go?"

"Right now, it's the only play we have."

"Consider that if I take them out, there's a chance Tom could survive and it sends a signal that no one can mess with Knoxville and get away with it."

Phillip gave the general a long, hard look. "You can't be serious. You heard what he said. One of the others will shoot Tom. We lose him, it could unravel all that Tom, you, and I built. You know how charismatic he is. The people look to him to save them from anarchy. His popularity is what allows us to rule without lots of force. With Tom gone, the whole population will be second guessing us. First, how did we let him get killed? And second, how can we continue to protect them from Nashville."

He shook his head. "And when Nashville hears, they'll start moving against us. We've kept them at bay so far while we get stronger. We need to keep to that plan."

"But you're letting them get away with this."

"I didn't say that. We're just letting them get out of town and release Tom. After that we can go to Hillsboro and teach them a lesson."

"We were going to do that anyway. They're pretty rich in resources."

"Right. Now we do it sooner rather than later."

"How do we keep track of them? If they see us, they'll hold on to Tom longer. We don't want them dragging him all the way back to Hillsboro."

"We've got communications with our area administrators. That's something they probably don't know about. I'll contact all of them and put them on alert. They can monitor the progress. They're using roads, they'll be passing through towns we control."

"When you contact them, find out if anyone saw them on their way into town. That will also help determine their route."

When they had crossed the bridge, Rodney pulled up next to Phillip's Humvee.

"This is where we part company," Jason said. "Like I promised, you don't follow and we'll release Tom. He'll be safe, on the road somewhere. You'll be able to find him."

"Better keep to that plan and make sure he's not harmed, or we'll be coming after you." Phillip looked at Tom. "We'll get you back, don't worry."

Tom tried to look at Phillip, but his neck didn't move much with the shotgun taped to it. He blinked and attempted to nod as Rodney drove off.

Chapter 21

"Wow!" Billy exclaimed as they passed beyond the last checkpoint and headed down the expressway. "I can't believe we made it out. You did it."

"We ain't home yet," Clayton responded. "Lots of ways this can go bad before we get to Hillsboro." He looked back at Jason. "You gonna stay taped to that shotgun? You be all right, not get too cramped?"

"It isn't very comfortable, for me or Tom, but I can't untape us until we drop Tom off. Too many possibilities for a counter attack. You can take the tape off his mouth, though."

Clayton reached back and carefully pulled the tape. It was more painful going slow, but safer considering the predicament Tom was in.

"Thanks," Tom said. "Can I have a drink of water? My throat's pretty dry."

"Scary, huh?" Billy asked. "Maybe you feel a little like we did when your goons grabbed us."

The Chairman didn't answer.

"Billy give him a drink. Be careful not to pour too much and choke him," Jason said. "I don't want an accident."

"This freeway is going to end soon, Rodney said. "You got a route planned out?" He looked at Jason in the mirror.

"Clayton can get the map out and you two figure out the best way. We probably go through Pigeon Forge and from there, pick a route. We'll drop the Chairman off somewhere after that."

"They going to be coming after us?" Billy asked.

"They'll follow."

"But you told them not to."

"They'll just be more careful so we don't see them. We have to assume they'll be on our trail and try to kill or capture us before we get to Hillsboro."

"Why drop him off? Why not just take him to Hillsboro with us?" Rodney asked.

Jason was silent for a moment.

"I don't want him to see our defenses, what we've got in store for anyone who tries to assault the town."

Clayton didn't say anything. Finally, Rodney spoke.

"You've got some new defenses?"

"Yep. Tell you about them later," Jason said.

"We stick to the roads?" Clayton asked.

"We've got some choices. Let's not talk much about our plans in front of our hostage here. He'll relay all of that back to his general."

They drove on in silence. Clayton handed out some trail food to Rodney and Billy. The two hadn't had much to eat during their confinement. When the freeway ended a few minutes later, they jogged right and then turned south on Route 441.

"Looks like this be the main road south towards Pigeon Forge. They'll assume we're on this road." Clayton sounded worried.

"Not much we can do about that. We'll have more options after Pigeon Forge," Jason said.

Finally, Tom spoke up. "You seem to be a man of much influence. Have you considered Hillsboro joining with Knoxville to create a regional organization?"

Jason shifted in his seat to look at Tom. He had been watching out of the righthand side window, looking for threats.

"No, the thought didn't cross my mind. Although we've learned that Knoxville is asserting control over smaller towns around it and may be going after Johnson City."

"We've brought protection to the smaller towns."

"And they pay for that?"

"Someone has to pay for the benefits. They aren't free. Men need to be fed, their families taken care of. We establish a tax levy. It's up to the local communities how they collect it."

"Sounds like a protection racket," Rodney said.

"We provide benefits. Do you know we've established a currency? That alone improves trade."

"How you figure?" Clayton asked.

"Makes it easier for people to do business. You just exchange the currency in each transaction. You don't have to always match the person who's got what you want with what you have to trade. It's easier to get to what you want in multiple steps instead of having to find just the right person to do it in one step."

"I heard it's a top-down system with your people setting the exchange rates, the values. That's never a good thing. The market can't adjust and find the right balance," Jason said.

"And people get punished for not following the rules," Clayton added.

"I don't know who you've been talking to, but it's working well so far. The system takes advantage of the gold we've collected so we can put that to good use." He paused. "Hillsboro's got a lot of gold resources from what we've heard. You could join us and find an outlet for all that wealth. I'm guessing right now it just sits there, not doing anything for you."

"That why you wanted to ransom these two?" Clayton asked.

The Chairman didn't answer.

Clayton continued. "You planning on taking over Johnson City?"

"Taking over is not the word I'd use. More like pacifying it, getting it under control. There's a man running it who's pretty crazy. From the information we have, the town's in a desperate situation, lots of violence and force being used by the authorities."

Clayton nodded but didn't say anything.

"We're trying to restore order. I'd like to work with Hillsboro in that process."

"You're worried about Nashville, aren't you." Rodney said.

"I won't deny it. They're looking to expand their influence. They've put a number of smaller towns under their control and maybe making an alliance with Memphis, although Memphis doesn't seem to be interested."

"Why don't you get with them?" Clayton asked.

"They want to set the rules, dominate us. I'm not going to put myself under their authority."

"That's the way Hillsboro thinks about it as well...thinks about you." Jason said.

"You make that decision for them? Are you in charge?" The Chairman's blue eyes lit up as he engaged in the discussion.

"No, but I know the sense of the town council. See we're organized differently from you. We fought a painful battle to get rid of the gangster that was running Hillsboro."

"Joe Stansky. We heard about him."

"That's right. When we succeeded, we decided to end martial law and institute civilian authority. That's something you haven't done."

"The people are fine with my leadership. They understand that I bring stability to their lives. Stability, that's what important. Keep things under control so people aren't afraid. They'll always support that."

"It about the price. It's also about what works in the long run," Jason said. "You've established a top down system. The rule of the strongman. It works at first. It can provide quick solutions and stability, but it doesn't work in the long run."

"It's working just fine. We're doing better than Hillsboro. We've got a currency going, Goods are being traded more efficiently because of that. We've got some electricity back. People are happy. Like I said, give them stability and they'll be happy." His voice grew stronger as he warmed to his theme.

"I'm establishing order out of chaos. Through me we'll organize the south into a strong regional power. They'll be peace, prosperity, order. People will have services restored. They'll be freed from fear of gangs and bandits."

He leaned forward, dragging the shotgun with him.

"The federal government is shattered. We won't see a return to a united country for some time. In place of that, we have to established regional structures, beyond city-states." He thumped his chest. "I can do that."

"But they didn't get to elect you. And they don't get to decide to try someone different. In fact, no dissenting opinions are allowed, I'll bet," Jason said.

"Why would anyone want to change? I've established a system that works. Opening up the process would only allow kooks or fools to step up and say they have a better idea. There's always someone out there that thinks they can do things better. It would only cause turmoil and make us weak."

He paused for a moment. "Can I have another drink of water?"

Jason nodded to Billy who carefully put a canteen to the Chairman's mouth.

"Thanks. As I was saying, we have to be strong and an authoritarian structure is the only thing that will work in these times. Cities that are on their own are going to be vulnerable. You should be worried about Charlotte. If the mob that runs it decides to come for Hillsboro's wealth, you'll wish you had joined with us." Jason could see his enthusiasm. He began to understand how the man could influence crowds.

"What you don't understand is that your system is too rigid," Jason replied. "People inevitably want freedom, want choices. Like your money system. One man, or a small group, can't fully understand the market and the relative value people place on their goods or labor. It changes all the time. You've forced an exchange on the system, which may seem good, but you don't have a mechanism to allow it to adjust naturally to market demands. Your 'evaluators', or whatever you call them, will always be a step behind. I wouldn't be surprised if there wasn't a black market already cropping up. Those always reflect the true market value of goods."

Jason continued, "We're allowing the relative values to develop over time. It will happen and a currency will evolve. We prefer to allow that to occur 'organically'. Another thing. The citizens all feel invested in Hillsboro. I doubt yours feel the same."

"I think they feel fine with what we're doing."

"So you say. Do you know where the word 'civilization' comes from?"

Tom looked at Jason and tried to shake his head but the shotgun wouldn't allow it.

"Don't try to turn your head," Jason said. "I'll tell you. The root of the word is 'citizen'. Civilization is formed from citizens, from civilians. When civilians run their affairs then you have civilization. When rulers are in power through force you have what used to be called barbarism. Now it's called a dictatorship.

"Since our citizens run things, they will support and defend what we do and who we are. Our town is run by a council, as I said. Nine members, three elected each year, so you get to serve three years. Membership is always turning over, yet there's always a group with some experience in place."

"What if someone is so popular, they're re-elected over and over?"

"You have to sit out for three years before you can stand again for election. So everyone has to go back to being a civilian and function under the rules they helped established."

"How long have you had that in place?"

"I admit," Jason said, "we haven't been at it that long, but the plan should prove more flexible than your structure. We're betting on citizen involvement and the creativity of our people."

Rodney broke into the conversation. "We're coming up on Sevierville. You got any suggestions?"

Jason thought for moment. "Let's go through Pigeon Forge. Sometime after that we can unload the Chairman and head off on our own."

"Which way do you suggest going?" Rodney asked.

"We'll discuss that after we drop off the Chairman."

"I don't think we're going to convince each other," Jason said, "but there's one thing you should know. We've organized ourselves like Switzerland."

"I don't understand," Tom answered.

"Every person in town over sixteen years of age is trained to use a rifle. Every household has at least one long gun in their possession. Most have two or three."

"My God. That's a recipe for anarchy if I ever heard one."

"Things are quite peaceful. But if Hillsboro is ever threatened, we have thousands of trained shooters to augment our militia. People feeling invested in the community makes them willing to put their lives on the line to defend the community against outside threats. The community acts like a clan with the same loyalties one has to the family. Bottom line is Hillsboro is united, armed and dangerous."

Jason turned away to look out the window again.

They passed through Pigeon Forge. Their passage was noted by the Chairman's administrator in town. He radioed back the news to General McKenzie. The route now joined with Route 321 heading south to Gatlinburg. Shortly after Pigeon Forge, they drove past the Mountaineer Motel whose owner also radioed their movement back to the General.

When they drew near to Gatlinburg, Jason called for a halt. "Someone get some cloth for a blindfold for the Chairman. It's time to unload him and continue on our own."

"Why blindfold me?" Tom asked.

"So you can't see where we go from here. You'll be all right. I expect it won't be too long before the militia comes along to pick you up. But we've got options from here on, so you won't know exactly which one we've chosen."

They stopped the Humvee. Jason and the Chairman got out slowly.

"Be careful. Don't want to ruin everything at this point," Jason said.

Clayton cut the tape away; Jason let out a sigh and massaged his right hand.

"That's a relief."

After the shotgun was removed from Tom's neck, he sighed as well and moved his neck to loosen it up.

"I suggest you consider what I've said before initiating any action against Hillsboro," Jason said. "We don't threaten you and we don't want to get into your fight with Nashville. You leave us alone and we'll leave you alone."

"Until the Feds come," Tom said. "Then which side will you be on? And if the Feds decide to make me the regional authority, what will you do then? I won't look kindly on all the crap you were spouting on about back there. You won't have a friend who will now have the federal government behind him."

"You can hope for that, but that's playing a long shot, from what I see. We'll leave you to your experiment. History is not on your side in the long run."

The men sat Tom down on the roadside and got in the Humvee and drove off.

Chapter 22

Head east towards I40. We may have to go on foot soon," Jason said.

"We just dump the Humvee?" Rodney asked?

"Let's put some miles between us and the Chairman. Then if we have to ditch it, we'll hide it so no one will know we're on foot."

"You think we'll be better off in the woods?" Rodney continued.

"The Humvee presents a target," Jason said.

"But we move faster with it," Rodney replied.

"We better off in the woods," Clayton said. "They don't know the woods like we do."

"I'm happy to go in the woods," Billy said. "Better'n staying on the interstate. Too open there."

"We get in the woods, no one will find us. They won't be able to track us. It be slower but we'll get back without any more trouble," Clayton said.

Rodney sighed. "Looks like I'm out-voted."

"You're in the company of woodsmen," Jason said. "You'll see. The Knoxville militia will be out of their element if they follow us into the forest."

Twenty minutes later, Jason directed Rodney to pull off on a side road, no more than a two-track trail. It wound south into the hills. They started up the trail, then stopped. Clayton and Billy got out and cut some branches to sweep the tracks away. When they were done, you couldn't see from the paved road that any vehicle had used the trail.

They proceeded in the Humvee deeper into the mountains. Forty minutes later, they pulled off, unloaded their gear, and pulled on their backpacks.

"Shank's mare from here," Clayton said with a smile.

Rodney looked at him, then Jason.

"Old joke," Jason said and headed into the woods going east from the trail.

When it got dark, they stopped and made a cold camp.

"No sense stumbling around in the dark," Clayton said. "We can go when the moon gets up."

"Did you really set up a Swiss-type citizen's militia already?" Rodney asked.

"I exaggerated a bit, but we're working on it. I'm hoping it will give the Chairman some concern about attacking us."

"And the special defenses?"

"I made that up. It's better he imagines how good our defenses are than to see how little we've prepared for any attack."

"Clever," Rodney replied.

"Let's hope it works."

There would be a three-quarter moon that night. If the sky remained clear, it would provide good light for the group to cover more precious miles. Everyone lay down in their blankets and ground cloths. On the far hillside they could hear the bark of a coyote which was answered by others, setting up a small chorus. In between, the night's stillness pressed down. For those accustomed to the forest the quiet was a comfort; for Rodney it still was a bit unnerving.

He got up and walked off to sit on a log. Jason stirred and saw him. He unwrapped himself from his gear and sat down next to the sergeant.

"You doing all right?" Jason asked.

"Yeah. Couldn't sleep. Maybe it's too quiet. Not used to the woods."

"You move through it okay."

"Army training. Didn't get that so much from Iraq or Afghanistan, more from Fort Benning. Lots of woods down there."

The two men sat for some time listening to the night, the soft breeze of rustling through the pine needles and oak leaves.

"Thank you for coming for us," Rodney said. "But why didn't you just send them the ransom? Be a whole lot less dangerous."

"The courier was unhelpful...pissed me off." He paused for a moment. "And I figured they'd just see it as a sign of weakness, that we'd rather pay than fight. I guessed they'd be back for more and more, so better to try to end it now."

"Still, took a lot of balls to walk into that hornet's nest. Did you know how you'd get out?"

"Not in detail. I knew I had to set up a mutually deadly scenario, one that was fail-safe. The idea crystalized in my mind as we got close to the target. As I expected it wasn't all that hard to get in. Getting out was going to be the problem."

"Well, thanks for that. We may not have made it back yet, but I'm feeling pretty hopeful now." Rodney patted Jason on the shoulder.

"You still want to go to Missouri? Going to start that trip all over again?"

Rodney sat quietly, staring out into the darkness.

"Yeah. It's still in my mind. 'Course I've got to adjust my timing. Not sure if Billy will still want to go now."

"Family. It's a strong draw. But Hillsboro is becoming family, or clan, maybe. That's what I'm hoping for anyway. We'll need that bond if we're going to survive."

"You got your family there, mixed in with the town. Mine are all in Missouri and I don't know what's become of them. I only have this sense that I can help...that I should help." He took a deep breath. "Wouldn't be right if

I stayed, not knowing if they need me. So many are struggling…"

"Let's get ourselves back, then you can wrestle over it. We're still not out of the woods yet."

"Literally as well as figuratively," Rodney said.

"Smart ass," Jason said. "I'm going to get another hour of rest in. You should to. The moon will soon be up and we can start hiking again." He got up and went back to his blanket and ground cloth.

An hour later, Clayton was jostling everyone awake.

"Time to go."

The men rolled up their gear, packed it away, and set out. They walked for the next four hours until the sky turned from black to blue with the light creeping over the mountains to the east.

The birds began to call out, claiming their territories. The men stopped, ate some rations, and drank some of the water.

"We'll have to refill our water supplies soon," Clayton said.

"Going to have to add to our food as well," Jason said.

"You thinking what I'm thinking?" Clayton asked.

"Stop at the Nutters?" Jason said.

"Yep. Quick stop'll get us some water and maybe some food for the trip. Later we can set snares again and maybe get some rabbits."

"Can we risk a fire?" Rodney asked as they walked along.

"Get far enough into the hills. Set up in a hollow. Yeah we can do that," Clayton said.

Chapter 23

I t was afternoon when the group came to a ridge. Below them was the Pigeon River and Interstate 40, which followed the river as it cut through the mountains. To their right and south the valley opened up. In the wider area, between the river and the ridges on each side stood a farm house and out buildings along with a dirt lot in which road tractors were parked along with some trailers.

"Looks like the Nutter place," Clayton said.

Jason nodded. Let's hike south on the ridge. We can cross the river when we get down to them. They look to be a couple of miles away."

The group backed away from the dense cover at the ridge. In the woods the hiking was easier. They set off to the south. A half-hour later they worked their way back to the ridge line and checked out the compound from the brush cover. The house and front dirt lot stood below them about 500 feet and about a half mile south of their position.

They could see multiple figures out in the yard. Jason got out his M110 and use the scope to better see what was going on. Clayton took out the spotter scope.

"Looks like some military types down there. Wonder what they up to," Clayton said.

"Probably asking about us. The Chairman might have radio communication with his administrators. He may have them out looking for signs of us passing through."

Suddenly Jason and Clayton could see rifles leveled at the Nutters. The boy, Enoch, started towards one of the men and was clubbed over the head. He collapsed to the ground. The two men started forward, but stopped as rifles were pointed at them.

"Uh oh. Something's going on. Don't look good," Clayton said.

"Are they arresting them?" Rodney asked. He couldn't see the details as well as Jason or Clayton.

"Don't know," Clayton replied.

"How far are they?" Jason asked.

"Twenty-nine hundred, forty feet. You going to take a shot?"

"Just want to be ready," Jason said.

He reached up and turned the elevation dial on his scope to set for the distance and drop.

Just then Emilia came storming out of the house with a shotgun in her hand. One of the men swung his rifle towards her. She was aiming the shotgun with her right hand while waving her left arm.

"She giving them hell, looks like," Clayton said.

"Things could get bad quick here," Jason said.

There were three men in the yard. Two of them were covering Joshua and George, the third had his weapon pointed at Emilia.

"It's a stand-off Clayton said.

The man pointing his rifle at Emilia finally turned and stuck his barrel against Enoch's head. Emilia paused and then laid down her shotgun. Now the man pulled Enoch's arms behind him and cuffed him. He stood up and motioned Emilia to come forward. The other two watched the men, keeping their rifles trained on them.

When Emilia approached the man, he swung his arm and hit her in the side of the head. She fell to the ground. Joshua started forward and the man covering him fired, hitting him in the shoulder and throwing him to the ground.

Jason flipped off his safety.

"What're you doing?" Clayton asked when he heard the metallic click. "You'll get them killed."

"Can you take them all out?" Rodney asked.

Jason didn't answer. He had already gone into sniper mode, slowing his breathing and heart rate. The scope settled on the head of the man who had cuffed Emilia. Jason felt the connection between him and the target, an old, familiar feeling. He caressed the trigger.

The rifle barked and the man's head exploded. The other two men looked across the river, startled by what had just happened. Without looking, Jason slid the rifle to the next man and squeezed off a second round. The man flew back as the bullet slammed into his chest. The next shot hit the third man as he was turning to find cover. The bullet hit him in his side, chest high, and threw him to the ground.

It was over in just under three seconds. Joshua ran to his wife and George jumped to Enoch. Both men tried to cover the two on the ground, but no more shots came from the ridge.

"Holy crap!" Billy exclaimed. "That's some shooting."

"What I was trained for," Jason replied. He stood up and waved his arms. The men noticed him on the ridge and pointed.

"We may as well go down and cross the river. No sense being stealthy now," Jason said.

"You took quite a chance there," Clayton remarked as they made their way down from the ridge. "Coulda' got them all killed."

"I knew what I was doing."

"Why'd you shoot? Why not let it play out?"

Jason turned to Clayton. They had reached the bank of the river.

"Didn't look like it was going to get any better. They club the boy, knock Emilia down, shoot Joshua. They weren't going to start acting nice after that. Maybe they kill them, maybe they take them away, in cuffs, like the boy. It wasn't going to get better for them."

Clayton only shook his head. He had fought with Jason to free Hillsboro and respected his abilities, but he had never seen his sniper skills up close.

The men found a shallow section and waded across the river. As they approached the compound, George came up to greet them.

"Did you do that?" He asked Jason.

Jason nodded. "Everyone okay?"

"They're all right. Shook up. We all are. Joshua's hurt. The bullet went through his shoulder."

"What'd they want?" Clayton asked.

"Wanted to know about you two. I guess it's because of these men?" George responded looking over at Rodney and Billy.

"Our friends. The ones we came to find."

"Well you sure stirred up a hornet's nest of trouble with whatever you did. Come on." He turned and led them back into the yard.

Emilia was up as was Enoch.

"That was some shooting," Joshua said. Enoch just stood there with his eyes opened wide. He had awoken on the ground and saw the man's head explode and the other two fall from the rapid shots that followed. It had all happened with no indication of who did the shooting; as if the bullets came flying out of nowhere.

"Well, you come back at the right time," Emilia said. She was looking at her husband's wound. "You make quite an entrance. Not sure if I want you coming around too often."

Jason just stood there. His face must have had a confused look on it. Emilia smiled.

"Thanks for that," she said.

"Man, I don't know how to thank you," Joshua said. "I don't know what they were going to do, but it didn't look good. Then they hit my wife..." his face got dark.

"I'm glad you weren't killed," Emilia said. "Now we're all alive...and they're dead. Thanks to Jason. Hell, that man didn't hurt me. I've been head butted by a horse harder than that."

"Emilia, Joshua, these are our friends, Rodney and Billy," Jason said pointing to the two men. "This is Emilia, her husband, Joshua, son Enoch, and brother George."

Billy nodded.

"Glad to meet you," Rodney said. He stuck out his hand and, after a moment's hesitation, Emilia took it. Rodney turned towards the bodies and the Jeep Wrangler the men drove up in. "We should hide the Jeep and the bodies before anyone else comes along.

Emilia gave him a hard look. Jason knew she was the one who gave the orders around their compound.

"He's right," she said. "Enoch, find the keys and drive the Jeep into the shed. George, you and these men take the bodies around behind the barn. We can bury them later."

"I'll help you tend to Joshua's wound," Jason said. "I have some familiarity with bullet wounds.

Emilia nodded. "Let's go inside." She turned to the other men, "Wash your hands before you come in. I don't want any stink from those low life's in my house." She took her husband's arm and walked back to the farm house, stooping to pick up her shotgun. Jason followed.

Rodney and Billy looked at George. "Let's do what she says," George told them. They got to work cleaning up the yard.

Chapter 24

After putting the Jeep away and digging shallow graves, the men washed up at the back-yard pump and came into the house. Emilia and Jason had bandaged Joshua's shoulder and put his arm in a sling. She was now setting out some tea, biscuits, and ham along with some glasses of water and some clear liquid in a large bottle.

The men sat down around the kitchen table.

"Pour yourselves a drink," she said pointing to the glass jug. "It's local brew and not too bad. Seems like we could all use a drink."

The men poured the moonshine into smaller glasses, Enoch included, and raised their glasses.

"To saving the day," Joshua said. The men nodded and took swallows. Enoch and Billy both coughed from the strong liquor.

"You don't like moonshine?" Joshua asked.

"Enjoy makin' it, but don't really like to drink it," Billy responded.

"You make moonshine?" Emilia asked.

"Yes ma'am. With my father 'fore he died.

"What's your name boy?"

"Billy Turner."

"You from Clayton's neck of the woods?"

"No ma'am. South of him, closer to Hillsboro."

"Billy and his family have lived for generations in a place called Hidden Valley," Jason said. "I got to know them when I met my wife who lived there. It's near Hillsboro."

Emilia nodded. Jason could see she like placing things and people in context, getting everything in its proper place.

"Everyone eat something. We got a lot to talk about and probably not much time to do it," Emilia said. The men filled their plates while Emilia looked on with a concerned face. She nibbled at a biscuit with butter and honey on it and sat quietly, waiting for the others to eat.

Finally, she spoke up. "What you did, stopping by before and now, shooting those men, has torn up our lives."

Everyone stopped to look at her. "I know you meant no harm and figured you were saving me, or the rest of us, but it has serious consequences."

Jason looked at her in confusion.

"It looked to me like you were going to get killed...or hauled off somewhere. We just rescued our friends from getting captured for no reason. This Chairman doesn't seem to respect people's rights."

"I understand that," Emilia said, "but killing these men now puts us in a dangerous situation." She leaned forward towards Jason. "Do you think no one knew they were coming here? How do we explain where they went? What do we tell them, even if they don't find the Jeep and bodies?"

"I'm sorry, Emilia. I thought you all were in grave danger."

"Don't be sorry. What's done is done. You didn't know. But now we have to figure out what to do."

"In Jason's defense," Joshua said, "things were looking pretty bad for us. You know Sam Floyd doesn't like us. He sent those men. He's been wanting to find an excuse to take our trucks and use them for himself. With his authority as an Area Administrator, who knows what accusation he could have come up with."

George nodded his agreement and said, "Sam's a snake, you know that, Emilia."

"I know it, but it still don't change what we're dealing with."

"What do you think we do about all this?" Joshua asked. "You saying we can't just keep on doing what we've been doing?"

"And how do we explain to Sam and others about these men disappearing?" Emilia asked. "We just say they came to talk to us and then left? And we don't know what the hell happened after that?"

Emilia gave out a disdainful harrumph. "That won't get us too far. People know Jason stopped here. Sam knows it and probably others. I reckon Sam planned to bring us in. Maybe take us to Knoxville to interrogation...or something."

"He wouldn't dare," George said jumping into the conversation.

"Wouldn't he?" Emilia asked. You said yourself he was a snake and had eyes on our trucks. He'd use this as an opportunity to get us out of the way and take what we got."

Jason jumped back into the conversation. "I don't want to be rude, but it sounds like I maybe did the right thing. This incident wasn't going to end well."

Emilia turned to him. Her worn face, lined with years of hard work in and out of the sun, still hadn't lost its strength and vigor. She would not be called an attractive woman, but her proud visage captured one's attention.

"You're probably right. We've been living on borrowed time. I've felt it," she turned to her husband, "and Joshua's felt it. More rules, more evidence of intimidation, pressure from the Chairman, we get the sense people are not to be allowed to make their own way."

"We had that, and worse in Hillsboro," Jason said.

Jason could see Emilia come to a decision. She sighed and looked at her husband.

"Joshua. It's time to go."

He looked back at her. Their eyes locked for a long time. He nodded. Jason could see the bond between them. They had faced adversity all their lives. Faced it together and had overcome and carried on. They were survivors. They might never have become successful and rich in the previous world, but their survival instincts and grit would give them success in this new world.

"What are you going to do, ma'am?" Rodney asked.

"We go back into the mountains. We have an old family place that's far away from the Chairman. No one will find us. We bring our animals and plants we'll do just fine. We got family there."

Clayton nodded. He understood family, clans and retreating into the mountains. "How we got along for years. Until this man," he pointed to Jason, "talked us into going to the flatland farms, one's that had been abandoned."

"How'd that work?" Joshua asked.

"Worked fine, once we got rid of the gangster running things. That's what the people here got to do."

"Let the people of Knoxville do it," Emilia said with a sharp voice. "I got no truck with city folk. They let this man run their lives, but he now wants to run our lives," she swept her hand around, "and the lives of everyone around these parts. We'll go where he ain't."

"You sad to go, Em?" Joshua asked.

Emilia looked at her husband. She smiled. "Not when I'm going with you. We faced harder than this before. Right after the power went out. We defended what we had, defended our lives. This'll be like going home. If I never hear about Knoxville and the Chairman again, I'll be a happy woman."

"Do we have to leave?" Enoch asked.

"Yes. We're decided," Emilia answered. "Can't stay here."

"When will you go?" Jason asked.

"Soon as we can. Maybe tomorrow. You stay the night. Maybe you can help us pack up since you helped make this move happen," Emilia answered.

"We can't get caught by the Chairman's men..." Jason paused as Emilia gave him a sharp look. "But you can't either." Jason looked over at Clayton and Rodney. "We can help. Then we'll have to move out ourselves."

"Faster we all get going, the better it be," Clayton said.

Emilia cleared the table and the men talked about what they needed to take and what could be left behind. The Jeep, being serviceable was going to go with the Nutters. They would pack up their chickens, load up their cow, dig out their garden plants, pack tools, seeds, and household items. It would all be loaded into one of Joshua's trucks to haul into the mountain retreat.

When they were done, Emilia grabbed her son.

"Enoch, you help me pack up the house for the trip. The men will get the rest loaded into the trucks."

"That's woman's work," he complained.

"Well I'm the only woman around here and I ain't doin' it myself, so you'll just have to give me a hand. Besides, there's no one gonna know you helped your mother and make you embarrassed."

She turned away. "Damn foolishness."

Chapter 25

Later that night, Jason went out on the porch. The moon was coming over the ridge to the east. The night's pale light grew stronger. Faint shadows showed on the ground. The crickets chirped away. In the distance he heard the occasional hoot of an owl.

Clayton and Rodney came out a few minutes later.

"You two couldn't sleep either?"

"Lots to think about," Clayton replied.

The men sat quietly for some time, savoring the peace of the night. In the distance there rose the distinct howl of a wolf.

"Been expecting that," Clayton said. "Deer increasing. Wolves got a ready source of food for themselves."

"Never heard that before," Rodney said. "I guess there were wolves here a long time ago."

"Yep. Hunted out hundreds of years ago."

"I understand there were buffalo here in the east as well," Jason said. He shifted in his chair to face the two men sitting next to him. "But you two didn't come out here to discuss the resurgence of wildlife in the Appalachian Mountains."

"We got to decide what we do next, how we travel," Clayton said. "We lost some time today. If the Chairman's men headed this way, the interstate is an easy route south towards Hillsboro, they'll be catching up to us. They could be here by tomorrow."

Jason sat back in his chair. "We don't want to fend them off here. Tough spot to defend."

"They can't take all the trucks, we could use one of them," Rodney said.

"Not enough room in the cab," Jason said. "They're big, but they only seat two."

"The forest still be the best choice," Clayton said. "They'll stick to the roads until they get too jammed up. We just hike the woods. They won't find us."

"What are we, three days out from Hillsboro?" Jason asked.

"Three or four's my guess," Clayton said.

"Well we have to expect some of the pursuit will come this way. They only had two choices at Gatlinburg, south, or east, over to I40, which brings them our way," Rodney said.

"Agreed," Jason replied. "Much as Emilia thinks I may have made things worse, we helped them. But now they have to leave and we have to get back into the woods."

"We help them off and get out of here. Hopefully before noon," Rodney said.

Jason stood up. The night's peace was now lost with the thoughts of the pursuit and the danger that it brought. "We better get some rest. I imagine Emilia will get things going very early."

The next morning Emilia roused everyone before the sun came up. After re-bandaging her husband's wound, she had started a huge breakfast and now would tolerate no one sleeping in. The men came into the kitchen in various states of wakefulness.

"You all get some food in you. I'm cleaning out the larder. Then we got to load our gear and get on the road." She turned to Jason, "I expect the Chairman is pursuing you?"

"We talked about that late last night. They had a choice at Gatlinburg, go south or head this way. We figure they split up."

"How many of them are there?" George asked.

Jason shook his head. "Don't know. Maybe fifty?"

"So maybe twenty-five headed our way?" Emilia said.

"That's a good guess. It wouldn't be good to be caught here with that many armed men coming for us."

"We fended off lots of the rabble and gangs after the power went out. But not that many at once and they weren't trained or well-armed," Joshua said.

"Well, eat up and let's get this show on the road," Emilia said. "Enoch and me will pack up the house things, you men get the rest packed."

"I'm going to bring my tools," George said.

"Bring whatever you want, but let's get moving," Emilia said.

"We'd like to be going by noon," Jason offered.

"After you eat, Joshua, you and George pack your clothes into a trunk or suitcase and then get outside. Enoch and I will handle the rest."

The men dug into the food and then set about getting the outside gear packed while Emilia and Enoch started putting household items in cloth bags.

After he was dropped off the Chairman sat impatiently, waiting for his men to arrive. He had no doubt they were following. It was just a matter of how far back they were and how long he'd have to wait.

Twenty minutes later General McKenzie showed up with a convoy of vehicles and sixty men.

"What took you so long?" Tom asked as they cut him free.

"Didn't want to risk getting you hurt so I kept back. I didn't know how fast they'd move."

"Well now you go get them. Bring them back dead or alive. They can't get away with this. It makes us look bad. Where's Cordell?"

"He's talking to everyone back in town. He wants to keep a lid on what happened."

"Fat chance. The best thing is to bring them back, like I said. I need to get back, but you keep going. They're a half hour ahead of you. At Gatlinburg they could only go two ways, so split your men and follow both routes. Push hard. They'll probably stay on the roads since it's faster. You should travel night and day."

"You think it will take days?"

"It's three days to Hillsboro at best from here. So, yes it might. The faster you move, the faster you catch up to them and get back to Knoxville."

After giving the Chairman a Humvee and driver, the general set off with his men towards Gatlinburg. There he split the team, choosing to go with the group that headed towards I40. They drove late into the night and only stopped when they came to a severely obstructed section of the road. Cars were interlocked, along with a jackknifed tractor-trailer that complicated efforts to clear the blockage.

"Could they have gotten past this?" one of McKenzie's men asked.

"In the Humvee, they could work their way around off the pavement, on the side slope. The troop truck won't handle that grade, so we'll have to wait for the morning to clear a way."

With daylight McKenzie was able to use his men to unlock the bumpers of cars. They used the truck to push them off the pavement. Then the truck was strapped to the trailer and pulled it straight, opening a lane through which they could pass. They were on their way again.

Chapter 26

Rodney collected the weapons and ammunition from the three men that had been shot. He assembled them in the dirt yard.

"You should take these," he said to Joshua.

"We got our own rifles," the man replied.

"These are better for defense."

"And hunting as well?"

Rodney shook his head. "Not so much. Your 30.06 rifles are better, but these shoot faster and will stop a man. Take them in case you get attacked."

Just then Enoch came out. "We keeping the guns?" He asked his father.

"Rodney says we should."

"How do they operate?" Enoch asked as he picked up one of the M16s.

"I can show you, but I better check with your mother," Rodney replied. He remembered Emilia had commandeered her son to help pack up the house.

"Mom won't mind," Enoch said.

"Just the same, we better ask." Rodney had no desire to get on Emilia's bad side. He turned and walked up to the house.

After getting Emilia's approval, Rodney went back out into the yard. He showed Enoch the parts of the rifle, demonstrating how to switch the firing from semi-auto mode to three-burst, auto mode. Then he began to show him how to break down the weapon and reassemble it.

While he was busy taking the rifle apart, Joshua and George gathered around him.

Suddenly Emilia came out of the front door. "The day ain't getting any younger," she called out. "You men get back to your packing. Let Rodney show Enoch. We can't all just sit around."

With that she went back into the house and slammed the door.

"You got the basics," Rodney said to the men. "I think you can figure the rest out on your own." He counted the magazines. "You've got full mags in the three rifles and six extra mags. If you save these for defense, not hunting, you'll have a good amount of firepower if you're attacked." He looked up at Joshua. "But we better get back to work."

"You right about that," Joshua said with a chuckle.

By 12:30 pm the packing was all completed. Everyone gathered in the house. Emilia had laid out all the food that wouldn't be taken.

"Let's eat up, quickly," she said. This won't travel and we should grab a bite before we set out."

They began to eat standing in the kitchen.

"Just like the Israelites in the old testament," Rodney said.

"What do you mean?" Emilia asked.

"Nowadays they eat the Passover meal standing in remembrance of when they had to eat and run to get out of Egypt. Kind of like we're doing now."

"Didn't know you were a Bible scholar," Emilia said.

"I'm not, but I was raised in church."

"Good for you. We don't see much going on with the churches nowadays. Bit disappointing to me. We could use more Christian charity in the world now."

"Seems like the bad ones rise up when law and order collapses," Jason said.

"Damn straight about that," Joshua said.

"Don't swear," Emilia said. "Things bad enough without swearing about them."

They all heard it at once. The sound of an engine, coming from the north. Jason, Rodney, Clayton and Billy reacted at once. They dropped their food, grabbed their weapons, and went to the windows.

"Is it the militia?" Joshua asked.

"Sound like just one vehicle," Jason said. "You three stay in the house. We'll go outside and see what's going on."

Jason and the others slipped out of the back door and went around to the corner of the house. They watched as an older car drove into the dirt yard. A man got out. He slipped a rifle over his shoulder and yelled to the house.

"Joshua, Emilia. You in there?"

There was no answer from the house.

"He knows them," Clayton whispered to Jason.

The door to the farm house opened and Joshua stepped out.

"What do you want, Sam?" He called out.

"We're looking for the three men that I sent here. They were to ask you about some strangers that might have come through here. Heard they kidnapped the Chairman."

"Don't know nothing about that. Haven't seen them. Your men ain't exactly welcome around here."

"What happened to your arm? How'd you hurt it?"

"None of your business, but hurt it yesterday working around the trucks."

"And you say you didn't see them?"

Just then Emilia stepped out beside her husband.

"Sam, if Joshua says he didn't see them, then he didn't see them. You calling him a liar?"

"No Emilia. I ain't. It just seems odd, them never showing up."

"Well you can ask them about that when you see 'em. How'd you hear about something in Knoxville anyway?"

"The radio. I get information about what's going on, what to watch for."

"You get instructions about how you're supposed to bother people who just want to be left alone? Acting like a busybody, you know that."

Sam started to answer, but Emilia cut him off. "And I know you have it in for Joshua. You'd like to take over our business. You can't be trusted. Why don't you leave us alone?"

"Emilia, I don't have time to discuss all that with you."

"You don't want to answer my question. That's what."

"Well I'm going to have to ask *you* some questions, since you say my men never came here." Sam started forward and the other two men got out of the car. "Go around back and check things out," Sam said to them.

"Sam you stop," Joshua shouted. "You got no right to come snooping on our property like this."

"Yes I do. I'm authorized as the Area Administrator. Now just settle down. We'll look around and I'll get a statement from you. After that we'll be going. If you got nothing to hide, you got nothing to fear."

Emilia went back into the house. She ran back through the kitchen to the back door. She opened it just as Sam's two men came around the house to find themselves confronted by four armed men. They quickly put up their hands and Billy disarmed them.

"Tarnation," Emilia exclaimed. "What are we gonna do now?"

"Let's all go inside and get Sam settled down," Jason said. "We can figure things out from there."

The group marched back in the house. Sam was standing in the kitchen with the rest of the family.

"What's going on?" He said, seeing the four men.

"Just unshoulder your rifle...carefully," Jason told him, "and you won't get hurt."

Clayton took Sam's rifle and stepped away.

"Now sit down," Jason commanded.

Rodney had the other two men sit on the floor while Clayton covered them.

"Joshua, you're gonna be in a heap of trouble. These here look like the men General McKenzie is looking for. What you want to be hiding them for?"

"We ain't hiding them. We're being hospitable. They're passing through and asked for something to eat, so we gave it to them."

"You can't be aiding criminals," Sam replied.

"How do we know they're criminals? We don't have anything telling us that?"

"So, what happened to my men? Did they come here?"

"I don't give a hill of beans about them. I expect they're like you, crooked as a dog's hind leg," Emilia said. "We don't have anything to do with them."

"Well you're gonna. The Chairman put me in charge and he's got the militia behind him."

"Bunch of busybodies," she replied. "Useless as tits on a boar hog."

"Enough of this," Jason said. "Are you in communication with this general?"

Sam shook his head. "Radio's back at my office, up at Hartford."

Jason looked over at Rodney. As soon as they left, Sam would head back to the radio and contact the general.

Jason nodded to Joshua to follow him. He stepped towards the rear door. Emilia followed them outside.

"What do you want to do?" Joshua asked.

"Don't kill them," Emilia said. "That don't seem right."

"Can't let them go. They'll have the general after you and us both." Jason thought for a moment. "We'll tie them up, here in the house and give both of us a head start. Do they know where you're going?"

"No, no one but kin know about the place. I expect half of them are already there," Joshua said.

"We figured this day would come. Not the way it did, but something would happen and we'd realize it was over here...time to go," Emilia said.

"Let's do it," Joshua said. "Time to get going."

They trooped back into the house. Jason directed the men to be tied up while Joshua and the family completed their preparations. When they were done, they gathered out in the yard.

"You sure know how to stir things up, don't you?" Emilia said.

"I'm sorry," Jason replied. "Didn't mean for this to involve you."

"As I said, we knew this time was coming."

"You sad to say goodbye?" Joshua asked her.

"Some. It's a good house. Gave us good shelter and we had good times here. But nothing lasts in this world, only the next. This time's past. Time to look to what's next for us and Enoch. Different world now, with different values."

"Ain't wrong about that," Clayton said. "We got room in Hillsboro for strong folk like you."

"I told you. Don't much care for city life. We'll do fine with our own back in the hills. Surprised you came out to the flat lands."

"Like you, things change, so we trying something new. You all take care of yourselves."

Hands were shaken all around and the Nutters got into their vehicles and drove off.

Chapter 27

Y ou boys are in some deep trouble," Sam said when
Jason and the others came back into the house.
"The General and Chairman ain't going to go easy
on you. Running around, breaking the laws. Did you do
something to my men? You kill them?"

"You got a big imagination," Jason said.

"I crawled over to the window, I seen the Jeep leave
with the Nutters. That looked like the one my men used.
Only way they'd have it is they've been killed or taken
prisoner."

"You gonna kill us?" One of the men asked in a fearful
voice.

"Not unless you make us," Jason replied.

"We can't let them loose," Clayton said. The man
turned to Clayton with a frightened look on his face.

"We won't turn them loose. Just leave them tied up
here. Someone'll find them sooner or later.

"You can't do that," Sam said. "We'll starve."

"You won't starve. You'll die of thirst before you'd
starve to death. We'll leave you some water. I expect the
General will find you before a day goes by."

"He won't know where to look for us," Sam said.

"We'll leave your car where it can be seen. I'm betting
he knows about the Nutter's place and will come and check
it out. In any case, you'll probably figure out how to get
free before then." Jason turned to the others. "Let's pack
up,"

They put the three men in different rooms, each with a pail or basin of water near them. Jason figured keeping them apart would slow down their getting free. It was a half hour after Emilia and Joshua had departed before they headed out of the door.

To the north they heard the sound of multiple engines on the interstate. They could see the troop truck weaving through the abandoned cars on the freeway.

"Damn," Jason exclaimed. "We have to get back across the creek and up the ridge."

"We should be going down the east side," Rodney said.

"Yeah, but we'd have to cross the highway. They'll catch us out in the open. We can do it later, let's get out of here."

The men took off and splashed through the shallows of the Pigeon River, pushing into the thickets on the far side. They stopped to look back at the compound. The vehicles were just turning into the yard.

"Hell," Rodney said. They'll see us if we try to climb the ridge. We'll be exposed."

"Let's make our way downstream," Clayton said. "Maybe we can find some cover to get up on the ridge. Once we're up there, they can't get to us. We'll just pick them off and melt back into the woods."

Jason nodded and the men started pushing through the thicket along the bank of the river. They were on a flat area along the river's edge. It showed signs of regular flooding. Thickets of willows and short grasses, bent to the water's flow, grew in the rocky soil. They kept low, stepping around the larger stones, worn smooth from the regular erosion of the water. There were many puddles that couldn't be avoided. The men stepped through them as quietly as they could.

Shortly they heard shouting. The General's men had found Sam and the other two men. Now they ran out into the yard yelling and pointing to the river. Some of the men started across the yard.

"They coming," Clayton said.

Jason nodded and unshouldered his rifle.

"They know we're over here, somewhere. Can't let them get across. Spread out, but stay in sight of one another. I'll take the first ones out. While they're re-grouping we'll try to keep moving downstream." The men nodded.

Jason lay down, fitting himself against the rocky ground. He ignored the puddles that soaked through his clothes. After getting a sight line, he waited until the men got to the bank. They stopped at edge of the water and stared across it. Finally, the three of them stepped into the water. They were close together which wasn't a good idea.

Jason fired. Three quick shots rang out. He only needed to move his aim an inch for each figure. The three men went down into the water. Two hung up on the rapids and the third washed downstream in the current.

The men in the yard ducked back around to the front of the house when they heard the shots. Jason and the others began to move south. They went as carefully as they could, making sure they stayed well screened from the yard.

Suddenly Clayton whispered, "They coming again."

The militia hadn't pinpointed the shooter's location, which had now changed as well. Jason crept forward in the damp ground. He carefully slid his rifle through the brush and sighted the men in the yard. He could get off a few shots without being located, but then he'd have to back away and move.

"We near any cover going up the ridge?" He asked over his shoulder.

"About fifty yards downstream there's a split in the face of the slope. Some of the bank slid down. It gives us some cover if we crawl, Clayton said."

"They won't see us?"

"They may see us, but if we stay low, they can't hit us. Ain't the best, but we can crawl to the top."

"I'll buy us some time. You guys get down there and start up."

"We aren't leaving you," Rodney said.

"Don't worry about me. Just get started so we're not all bunched up. I'll follow. When you make the ridge, you can cover me."

Let's go," Clayton said.

Jason heard the men shuffle off downstream. He watched the yard. Two shooters were lying prone on the grass, barely visible from Jason's vantage point. He guessed there was some discussion going on about who was going to try the river next. Probably no one wanted to expose themselves to his fire. *The fear of a sniper. You never see the death coming.* A grim smile spread on his face.

He swept his scope around the yard. No one moved in the open. There were some rifles pointing out of the windows. Then farther up river he saw movement. Four figures dashed for cover near the bank. The river was deeper there, with no rapids to wade through, but the men must have thought it was safer, being farther away from where they guessed Jason was hiding.

Jason switched his sights to the spot where the men had disappeared. It was fifty yards further away. He made a mental adjustment to where he'd place the reticle when he took his shot.

A moment later he saw a body slip down the bank and into the water which was chest high. The man held his rifle up over his head and started forward. Jason waited. When he was half way across the river the second man slipped into the water. Still Jason waited. The third followed. The first man was nearing the west bank. It was time to act.

He fired. The first man lurched to the side, his rifle flew out of his hands. In a moment his body slid under the water, pulled by the current. Before he disappeared, Jason fired again and the second man collapsed mid-stream. The third man now turned back. Jason's shot hit him as he climbed up the bank where he had entered. He was slammed forward and then slid down the bank. His body spun in the current and began to float downstream.

The two men lying in the grass at the house started shooting. They were aiming across the river, but Jason could tell that they still hadn't located him. They hadn't seen where the shots had come from. He pulled back and began to follow the others.

When he arrived at the cleft, he could see the rest of the men nearing the top. Jason cradled his rifle ahead of him, being careful to keep the muzzle out of the dirt and not hit the scope. He started crawling up the cleft. The dirt broke loose from the face in places and he slid back some feet. The loosened rocks and dirt clattered down the slope. *If they look carefully, they'll see the dirt sliding, even if they don't see me.* He could only hope that the others would reach the top and give him covering fire. They had climbed while everyone was focused on Jason's shooting.

As Jason was crawling, some shots rang out. He could hear the deadly whistle of the bullets overhead, a short, sharp zing that meant death. *Keep going.* The shots came closer. Some of the bullets hit the edge of the crease he climbed, showering him in a spray of dirt and stones. Then he heard return fire from the ridge, short and steady. The deadly whistling stopped and Jason redoubled his efforts to crawl up the slope.

In a few moments he had made the top and scrambled into the brush and rolled behind a boulder to catch his breath. Clayton and Billy stopped firing. Rodney reached out a hand and patted Jason on the shoulder.

"You had them completely focused away from us. We scrambled up the cliff with no one seeing us."

"What do we do now?" Clayton asked as he crawled over to where Jason was lying. Billy kept watch, taking an occasional shot when someone showed in a window.

"We have a commanding position. We can hold them off for a long time up here. They'll be reluctant to try the river, especially with us above them."

"They probably calling the others, so their numbers going to get bigger," Clayton said.

"They'll fan out and cross where we can't get to them, upstream and downstream. Try to pinch us in," Rodney said.

"I agree. Now's the time to melt away, put some distance between us and them," Jason said.

"But we on the wrong side of the river," Clayton said.

"Yeah. We'll have to deal with that later," Jason replied.

Clayton waved Billy over to them and the four men faded back into the forest and turned south.

Chapter 28

General McKenzie was not happy. The area administrator was found tied up in the farmhouse. From what he said, it seemed as though the men who had taken the Chairman prisoner and escaped Knoxville, had killed some of his men and fled across the river.

Sending men across Pigeon River had proven disastrous. The shooter had killed six of his men with sniper-like precision. This situation was more than he had anticipated. He knew the men were bold, but now he realized they were skilled and disciplined shooters. Even though there were only four of them, he had to be careful.

The first thing he did was to radio his other team and order them back to the I40 corridor. He knew the men fleeing had to cross I40 somewhere in order to get back to Hillsboro. He'd plant a team to the south to watch for them and send another team across the river to track them.

After assembling his men in the yard, sheltered from any shooting from across the river, he picked out four men who knew the woods. They were in the militia but they were country boys. They could hunt and track animals. He sent them a mile upstream to ford the river, out of sight of any shooters. They were to head south and try to locate the fugitives' trail.

The other team had two dogs with them. When they arrived later that night, he would send them across the river to pick up the men's scent. They would then track them down the old-fashioned way, with dogs and men, hounding them until they were worn out or gone to ground. *We'll get you. The dogs'll find you.*

Jason and the others moved at a steady pace through the woods with Clayton and Billy leading. Their experience in the woods showed as they navigated around thickets of wild rose that always tried to reach out to ensnare them. The two had the ability to find the subtle game paths that offered an easier way through the brush. It reminded Jason of how he had learned to come to grips with the forest; to not fight it, but work his way through it, with his eyes shifting from the detail close in front of him, to scanning ahead for the best route. Once a person got into the rhythm the walking became easier. Still their pursuers would have men adept in the forest as well. And he was sure there would be pursuit.

"We got to think that they might have dogs," Clayton said looking back at Jason.

"Not many dogs left that didn't go wild," Jason said.

"Still, there's a good possibility they got one or two. They get our scent, it's like marked highway for them. They won't have to tramp around looking for where we went. They just follow the dogs."

"They work them day and night?" Rodney asked.

"If the dogs are strong enough."

"Don't like dogs tracking me," Billy said. "They catch you, they tear you up."

"We'll have to go through the night," Jason said as they hiked along.

"Be slow going, even with the night vision goggles," Clayton said.

"If they have flashlights, they can keep up a faster pace," Rodney said.

"If the dogs are strong, they move fast," Clayton said. "Seen men have to run to keep up with a dog on a scent."

The four walked in silence. They followed ridges and flat areas as much as possible over the rugged terrain. The problem was the grain of the mountains ran generally northeast to southwest so their direction of south involved them going over ridges and down sometimes steep slopes. Adding to their difficulties was the fact that the flow of the mountains was confused in this part of the chain, breaking up into a confused jumble of ridges and closed valleys, sometimes cut by creeks with steep banks.

Some sections had generations-old trees that left the understory clear and almost park-like. These, however, were few. Most of the terrain, especially on the south and west facing slopes, had thick undergrowth from the increased amount of sunlight penetrating the canopy.

They hiked on in silence, following Clayton and Billy. Large boulders, fallen thousands of years ago from the upper ridges often blocked their path, forcing them to scramble around them. Some were house-sized and overgrown with mosses and other plants growing in the soil that collected in their crevasses. When they got to a ridge, Billy, would climb a tree to look for any pursuit and to try to see the interstate. There was little to see.

As the sun began to set, the men stopped to eat from their meager rations. Their hurried departure from the farmhouse caused them to leave behind some of the food Emilia had left for them.

They ate sparingly and took some sips of water. The day had been hot. They were tired and sweaty. The night sounds had not yet started up. Only a few crickets had begun their mating calls.

"Listen," Billy said.

Everyone looked at him. The quiet conversation Jason had been having with Rodney stopped.

Then they heard it. Dogs barking and baying, faintly in the distance.

"They got dogs," Billy said.

"And sounds like they got our scent," Clayton said.

When the dogs arrived, McKenzie had most of his men across the river. They had confirmed the shooters' place on the ridge and that the men had left. The dogs' handlers were old hands in the woods. They guided their canines to the area at the top of the ridge and the dogs quickly picked up the scent. Much barking and baying ensued as the dogs strained to be on the chase. For them it was a fun game in the woods. For the men, on both sides, it was a matter of life and death.

The General split his men into two teams. Ten men went with the dogs and their handlers. They would try to link up with the four men who left earlier and run down the fugitives. The rest, about thirty men, would head down I40 and set up posts near where he guessed the escapees would try to cross. If the trackers didn't catch them, he hoped this group would intercept them.

With the men assembled, the group set off through the woods at a fast trot with the dogs, straining at their leashes, leading the way. They knew the men they were chasing had a good head start, but they were moving fast and, with lights, could keep going through the night.

Jason looked at Clayton. "Are we going to be able to stay ahead of them?"

"Not sure. What I'm sure about is we got to keep going through the night. They won't be stopping. Those dogs can probably run through the night."

"We better get at it. You and Billy use the night vision goggles. We'll follow behind you."

The group set out. As darkness came, Billy and Clayton put on the goggles. Even with the goggles the pace was slower. Billy complained it was hard to see details. They got snagged more often in the thickets. The ridges, now going in all directions like a crazy quilt pattern, confused them and slowed progress.

"Walking in the water help throw the dogs off?" Rodney asked.

"I seen dogs follow a scent in the water," Clayton said. "I think it's an old wives' tale. Besides it would just slow us down to wade around in a creek and then get out on the other side. Maybe if we was at a large river, we could just swim downstream far enough to throw 'em off, but not these small creeks we crossing."

The group stumbled along, egged on by the distant barking which came and went.

"If we don't hear them, it just means they on our trail," Clayton said.

When the dogs were solidly on the trail, they quieted down and just pursued. When they lost it for a moment, they cast around rapidly and let out furious barks to announce they had picked it up again.

The group pushed on through the night, stumbling, getting caught in thickets, freeing one another and then stumbling along again. The climbs were sometimes steep with them clawing their way on all fours to the top.

At one ridge they stopped to drink some water. The moon had come up which now made it easier for Jason and Rodney.

"Can't wait for the sun to come up," Billy said. "These goggles are a pain."

"Try it without them now that the moon's up," Jason said, "but I bet you'll see better with them on. I know Rodney and me are still stumbling along, even with the moonlight."

The night slowly gave way to the gray of dawn. Clayton and Billy took off their goggles.

"We can speed up," Clayton said, "but the others will too."

The men set off jogging. They were bone weary, bruised, wet and tired. But they forced themselves into a broken trot through the forest, dodging trees, rocks, and thickets; going around the large boulders that had fallen from the ridges long ago. They scrambled up the slopes and slid down the other sides. One wouldn't need a dog to track them. They had disturbed the ground so much in their passing they left a trail easy to see. The men following the dogs could move faster, though.

There was no talking now, just heavy breathing and constant motion. When someone tripped and fell, the closest person stopped to give him a hand up. Without a word they would then set out to catch up with the others who had kept moving.

At the top of one especially steep ridge, they stopped. The other side looked too dangerous to try to slide down. It went from very steep to vertical with house-sized boulders strewn at the bottom of the slope.

Billy was leaning over with his hands on his knees, trying to catch his breath. Clayton had slumped to the ground with his back against a large rock. Rodney and Jason leaned against two trees.

"We may need to start thinking about a place to make a stand," Rodney said.

"Don't want them to just catch us running. If they gonna catch us, better it's a spot we can defend," Clayton said.

"Problem is we don't know how many are behind us," Jason replied.

"Even with two to one odds, we can probably take them," Rodney said. He turned to Clayton, "Those dogs attack us when they catch up?"

"Depends on how they was trained. Bloodhounds are pretty gentle. They just the best at tracking. If they're using German Shepherds, they could be trained to attack when they catch you."

"Hate to shoot a dog," Jason said. "If we have to make a stand, we'll pick a ridge, like this. They'll be struggling up it and we'll be spread out on the top and pick them off. If the dogs don't attack, we can leave them alone." He lurched away from the tree. "But I'm not ready to take a stand. Let's figure a way off this ridge."

They hiked along the ridge while examining the slope. Finally, Jason pointed down.

"It isn't getting any better. I say we go down here. It's steep but not a cliff. We can slide down from tree to tree so it's not a free-fall. Remember, they have to navigate this as well."

The men nodded and, one by one, started down the slope.

Chapter 29

It was near summer and the sun was strong. There was little breeze in the forest to alleviate the growing heat. Sweat poured down Jason's face, stinging his eyes. His shirt was soaking wet and his pack was chaffing his shoulders. They could hear the dogs occasionally when they lost and then rediscovered their scent.

"Dog's gettin' closer," Clayton said with labored breath.

They had just descended down a steep slope into a flat area that was partially cleared. There was a dirt road running along the floor of the valley, following a slow-moving stream about fifty feet wide. It was unlike the other creeks they had crossed which were narrow, rocky, and fast moving with sharply cut banks.

"Looks like someone grew hay in this field," Clayton said.

"Might be a cabin on this road, in one direction or the other," Billy said.

"We don't want to go there," Jason said. "It'll only bring them trouble."

Across the creek the ridge was steep. The men waded through the stream. Their feet struggled in the soft bottom mud. The ridge was steep enough to force them to crawl up on hands and knees. They stopped for breath along the way, leaning against the smaller trees that clung to the slope, and then pushed forward through the rocks and dirt.

At the top they all stood there panting. Looking down, Jason could see the cleared floor of the valley and the stream winding through it.

"This looks like a good spot to defend," he said.

Rodney nodded in agreement. "They'll be exposed in the field and wading across the stream will be slow with that muddy bottom. We can pick them off easily."

"Any that make it across will have to come up this slope right in our line of fire," Clayton said.

"So, no warning? We just take them out?" Billy asked.

Jason turned to him. "You want to negotiate with them?"

"No, but I'm thinking, we're just going to shoot them without giving them a chance to turn back? Seems wrong somehow."

"Don't seem wrong to me," Clayton said. "They coming after us. We ain't coming after them. Seems like they made a choice, now they pay for it."

"Billy, what do you think they'll do if they capture us?"

Billy's face screwed up with consternation. Jason could see his concern and confusion.

"I guess it wouldn't be good for us. They'd surely put us in prison, maybe even kill us, since we shot some men back at the Nutter's."

"I don't want you to have any reservations. You've shot men before, defending your home, defending Lori Sue..."

At the sound of her name, Billy's face fell into sadness.

"I'm sorry to bring her up, but I doubt these men are much different from the ones we defeated in Hillsboro. They may not be the leaders or organizers, but they are part of the muscle that keeps those men in power. We have to protect ourselves. By taking them out we do that. Plus, we send a message to not mess with Hillsboro."

"I guess you're right. I just had hoped that I was on a different path, when I left with Rodney. Looks like we're still stuck in the same mess as before."

Jason didn't respond. Billy had a point, but there was nothing he could do about it. The situation was dictated by outside forces. He had to respond in the best way he knew to defend what they were all struggling to achieve, some sense of normalcy and peace so they could rebuild their lives.

"We don't shoot the dogs, agreed?" Jason asked the group.

Everyone nodded.

"If they got German Shepherds, how do we know they won't attack?" Billy asked.

"If their handlers turn them loose, watch them when they come up the slope," Clayton responded. "They come with ears pinned back, teeth bared, they're gonna attack." He paused. "Got to take them out then."

Jason let that be the last word.

"Let's spread out. Everyone get behind some cover. Make sure you got a clear line of fire to the field. Stay in sight of each other in case we have to move or retreat. We'll wait until they're all in the field before we fire. We want them all out in the open. Don't shoot the dogs' handlers."

The men spread apart, each picking a spot to lie down. Then they waited. How long it would take, no one knew, but the pursuers would come, and they would be ready for them.

There was a burst of barking and baying, much closer this time. The four men waiting all glanced at each other.

"One of the dogs is a blood hound from the sound of him," Clayton said.

The men focused intently on the clearing. There was the sound of branches snapping along with shouts from the men. The pursuers were coming down from the opposite ridge.

"Remember, wait until they're in the field. Hold your fire until I shoot, then let loose," Jason whispered.

Everyone sighted their rifles. Except for Jason, they were all shooting M16s with iron sights.

"Set your fire selector for three-round bursts," Rodney said. "You'll be more effective that way until you zero in on the distance."

The distance, not more than one hundred yards, made the shots easy for Jason with his M110. He expected to carry the load in this firefight.

The sun beat down. The crashing in the woods beyond the field grew louder and the dogs burst into the field, dragging their handlers with them. They rushed to the water's edge and would have jumped in, if not held back. As Clayton had guessed, one was a bloodhound; the other was a Shepherd. The handlers stopped and waited. A moment later the rest of the men emerged. Jason counted ten of them.

They were all armed with what looked like M16s. They had on uniform shirts with various work pants, jeans, and boots. To Jason's eye, the men looked beat; they were all out of breath and covered with sweat and forest debris from their slide down the slope.

The pursuers walked up to the men holding the dogs. The man in charge started talking with the handlers, pointing across the stream. The dogs barked and bayed, straining at their leashes, still eager to be on the hunt. Jason placed his sights on the guy who looked to be the leader of the group.

His shot hit him in the head. The man collapsed where he was standing with the back of his head blown open. The others on the ridge opened fire. A flurry of bullets rained down on the field, with many missing their mark.

After Jason's first shot, two of the militia dove to their right seeking the cover of some larger rocks by the stream's edge. The handlers pulled their dogs to them and dropped into the tall brush to their left, covering their dogs as they lay on the ground. The rest of the militia turned and bolted for the woods.

Rodney's shots hit one of the men before he took two steps. Jason moved to the fleeing figures and hit one of them in the center of his back. The other shooters from the ridge hit two more of the men. The remaining three men made it to the cover of the trees.

The men in the woods began to return fire, their shots were beginning to close in on the ridge where Jason and the others lay. He could hear their deadly whistle as they flew overhead and could see the dirt and rocks fly where they hit the ground.

"Keep the two behind the rocks pinned down," Jason yelled. I'll try to pick off the ones in the woods. Don't just shoot blindly into the trees."

The three men began sending a devastating amount of fire down to the rocks, pinning the shooters down. Their rounds hit the boulders and the ground, splitting off shards of stone and throwing up chunks of soil.

Jason concentrated on the woods through his scope, looking for muzzle flashes. With each flash he noted the shooter's location. He had a cleaner shot at one of the men. There were no large branches to deflect his round. He watched, ignoring the other shots coming out from the trees. Then he saw the barrel of a rifle swing out from behind the tree trunk. Jason squeezed off a round, aiming just above the barrel. The shooter's rifle flew up and fell to the ground.

At that moment someone from the rocks shouted out the word "surrender". Jason and the others saw a pair of hands waving in the air from behind the boulders.

Rodney looked over at Jason who nodded.

Rodney shouted down to the men, "Throw out your rifles and stand up with your hands in the air and you won't be shot."

"Promise you won't shoot?" the man yelled back.

"Do what we say and you won't get shot," Rodney replied.

"Don't shoot us or the dogs," one of the handlers shouted. "We ain't armed."

"Do the same thing. Stand up and put your hands in the air," Rodney shouted.

As the men began to stand, Rodney shouted to the two left in the woods, "Come out with your hands up and you won't get shot. Don't and we'll kill you before you can get back up that slope."

The field was still. The two militia men stood nervously with their hands in the air. The handlers were standing with their dogs held close. Neither dog was barking or baying. They sensed it was best to keep still.

"You hear me in the woods?" Rodney shouted again. "Come out now. If you don't then your friends might die and we'll shoot you down and leave you to the coyotes and bears."

The men in the field now called out to the two to come out.

"They don't show themselves," Jason said, "Clayton, you and Billy split up and go around the field. Finish them off in the woods."

Before Clayton and Billy could head down, the two men appeared at the forest's edge with their hands in the air.

"Come forward about half way," Rodney shouted. He turned to Billy. "You stay up here while we go down to secure the prisoners. Anyone makes a wrong move, shoot him."

Billy nodded. He had a grave look on his face.

Jason, Rodney and Clayton scrambled down the hillside and waded through the water. The dogs, smelling them and knowing they had found what they were chasing, started jumping and straining at their leashes.

"Hold them dogs, less you want 'em shot," Clayton said.

"We'll hold 'em," one of the men said. "They ain't dangerous. It's just a big game to them."

"Game or not, I don't want them in my way," Clayton responded.

Jason, Rodney, and Clayton patted down the two at the creek. They made them lie down in the field with their hands behind their necks. Clayton guarded them.

Rodney and Jason went over to the two who came from the woods and repeated their search for weapons. When they were lying down, Jason went to the men who were shot. Of the six men shot, four were dead. One of the men still alive had been shot in the chest. Jason could hear the sucking sound as air flooded the lungs. He found a wallet on the man and used it to cover the wound. He could only tie it down, which made for an imperfect seal but it was the best he could do. The man was already losing consciousness. Without a hospital, the man would probably die within an hour.

The second man had a shattered left shoulder and arm. Two bullets had hit him. Jason cut up the man's shirt and tied it over his wound to stop the bleeding. His lungs were not punctured, but his shoulder was badly damaged. He was in a lot of pain, but in no immediate danger of dying.

After bandaging the man as best he could and checking him for weapons, Jason came back to the four uninjured men. Using belts he had removed from the dead men, he secured the captives. When that was done, he waved Billy down from the ridge.

Jason assembled the four prisoners. He had them sit in the field, far enough apart so they couldn't touch one another with their wrists secured behind their backs.

"Clayton, why don't you take the men with the dogs aside and see what you can find out. I'm wondering if we need to worry about them or not."

Clayton nodded and motioned to the men to walk off with him.

"There's two injured," Jason said to Rodney. "One's not going to make it—sucking chest wound—the other one will live, but his shoulder's going to be messed up."

He squatted down in front of the men. "Who's in charge here?"

No one spoke. Jason looked them over. Three of the men looked pretty young. One of the men was older, maybe thirty. He had a harder look about him.

He moved over in front of the older man. "What were your orders?" He asked.

The man didn't speak.

"Better start answering my questions. I got a few of them. It's a pain in the ass to deal with captives. If you don't tell me what I want to know, I might just kill you here and we'll be on our way."

"You wouldn't do that," one of the younger men said. He had a fearful look in his face.

"You willing to bet your life on that?"

The young man stared at him with wide eyes and then lowered them, looking at the ground.

"He's afraid to tell you the truth," the older man said. He stared straight at Jason. "We was told to bring you four back...dead or alive."

"Now we're getting somewhere," Jason said. "You're a tough SOB, but an honest one."

"Now that we know the truth we don't have to play around. I've got two choices. I can let you live and we go on our way, or kill you and go on our way."

"You should let us go. We didn't have a choice about going after you," the younger man said. "We won't follow you."

"He don't know that, idiot," the older man said.

"You want him to kill us?"

"He's gonna do what he wants. Makes no difference what we say."

"That's where you're wrong, hard ass," Jason said.

"You give me what I need, I'll be happier. Might let you live."

"Whaddaya want to know?" the younger man said.

"Start with you name," Jason said.

"Gill," came the reply.

"How many men did the general send after us? There were more than you ten at that farmhouse."

"He just sent us with the dogs."

"The other team join him?"

"How'd you know about them?" the older man asked.

"What's your name?" Jason asked looking back at the man.

"Ed."

"I figured he'd want to follow both possible routes we might have taken. Now, did they join up?"

"Yeah," Gill said.

"How many of them are there?"

"Don't tell him nothin' else," Ed said.

"What's it to you? I don't want to get shot." He looked at the ground and mumbled, "Didn't want to come on this chase anyway."

"You just wanted to wear your uniform, carry a gun and tell people in town what to do. That it?" The older man's voice dripped with sarcasm. "When real enforcement work comes, you don't want no part of it." He spat on the ground.

Jason looked over at Rodney. "I'm going to take Gill over where I can talk to him privately. You keep talking to Ed. Maybe you can help him see the light."

"Be my pleasure," Rodney said. "Since I spent some time in the company of the militia, I found out what they think of a black man. Now I'll be happy to let them know what might be in store for them if I don't like what I hear."

Jason walked Gill away from the others and sat him down in the grass.

"Now Gill. I don't know what Ed's going to say, but I guarantee he'll talk to Rodney. See Rodney's a Master Sergeant, did tours in Afghanistan and Iraq. He knows all about hard asses. Killed a lot of them as well. Me, I shot Ali Babbas from the roof tops in Iraq. But I've killed more men back here since the power went out than I can count on both hands."

He leaned up close to the young man. "What you need to understand is that I don't mind killing, when I need to do it. You've chased me and my men through the woods for two days and nights. Now you're going to tell me everything you know because it won't take much to make me shoot you and leave you here in the woods."

Gill was shaking now.

"I don't know much, but I'll tell you what I know."

"Did the other group join up with the general?"

Gill nodded.

"How many men does he have?"

"We started with about fifty men."

Jason did some quick calculations. Fifty men less the six killed at the Nutters, less the ten men in the chase, left thirty-four men to worry about.

"What's his plan? Where's he going with the remaining men?"

"I think he was going to go down I40 and set up somewhere to intercept you. If we didn't catch up with you."

After more questions, Jason went back over to where Rodney was standing with the other prisoners. They walked off to talk privately.

"From what the kid says, the general's got about thirty-four men left. They're going to try to catch us somewhere further down I40. They know we need to go across the highway."

"That's pretty much what Ed told me."

"You got him to open up?"

"I told him about my duty tours and some of the interrogation techniques I learned from some CIA guys I had the chance to work with. It seemed to impress him."

"You never told me about that."

"There's some truth to it, but it's mostly embellished. Makes for good stories, though." Rodney grinned. "He said a lot more. He said the Vice Chairman, that Cordell guy, and the General, decided that they'd probably divert from their pending action against Johnson City to Hillsboro. They figured, even before getting the Chairman back, that he'd want to send troops to 'teach us a lesson' he said."

"Does he know how many men they'd send?"

"He didn't have any idea. Not that high up and not that bright." Rodney paused to think. "But they must have over five hundred men in the militia, the way Ed describes it. They're pretty well organized."

"Damn. Five hundred. That's going to be ugly."

"For everyone," Rodney said.

Chapter 30

Jason and Rodney went over to the men holding the dogs. The animals were acting friendly, wanting to jump up and be noticed. They eagerly sniffed around the two. These were the scents they had chased through the woods on their big adventure.

"You boys work for the General? Are you in the militia?" Jason asked.

"No sir. We was just brought in to track you. Didn't know what was up except that ten men came with us."

The other man added, "We figured you were escaped prisoners. We did that before the power went out...track escapees along with lost people."

"What do you think?" Jason asked Clayton. "Think we can set these two free and they won't cause us any trouble?"

"You don't have to worry none about us. We'd be happy to just go back the way we came."

"We don't mind tramping through the woods with the dogs," the other man said.

Jason ignored them, looking at Clayton. These were country men, used to the woods. They had something in common with Clayton.

"I think these boys are okay. They just trying to get along. Keeping their dogs alive was hard enough. I guess there ain't many choices whether to work for the Chairman or not around Knoxville."

"Where do you boys live anyway?" Jason asked.

"We're south of Knoxville about fifteen miles near Pinter Gap. Up against Chillowee Mountain."

"You making it there?"

"Yes sir. We got some farming and hunting. This work, with the dogs, gives us some extra to buy things we need in town. Ain't too bad long as we left alone."

"And you're left alone? The Chairman hasn't recruited you into his militia?"

"No. Some others in the area went and joined. Mostly single men who had no family. He gets the rest from town. Most of the militia seem like city boys to me."

"I think we can let you go back the way you came. You're not armed. You'll leave that way. We see you again, we'll shoot to kill, both you and the dogs," Jason said.

"You won't see us. We be happy to just go back home."

"I expect you'll have to report to someone. I don't care about that. You tell them what happened here will happen to others if they keep after us."

Jason motioned for the two men to go and they headed off back the way they came, pulling their dogs with them.

"They'll have to keep them on a leash so they don't start back after our scent," Clayton said.

"That's their problem."

"Billy," Jason called out. "Keep a watch on those for me. Rodney, Clayton and me need to talk together."

Billy nodded and Rodney walked over to Jason and Clayton.

"What do you propose we do with these four?" Jason asked.

"And the wounded men," Rodney added.

"One of them is probably already dead, but the other one, yeah. He needs to be considered as well."

"I don't fancy killing them," Clayton said. "Happy to if they's shooting at us, but now it don't seem right."

"I agree, but it's awkward, Rodney said. "They could just follow us, if any of them have any idea how to track. Then they make a bunch of noise when we get near the interstate. Try to attract the other men."

"They could. *If* they can track us and *if* they're near enough to the others. There are miles of road where we can cross. We can pick the spot," Jason said.

"They could head to the interstate and find the militia. They could help them narrow down where we are. Make it easier to find us."

"I think we can chance it," Jason said. "The older guy, Ed, might want to do that. I suspect the younger ones have had enough. They barely survived getting killed."

"What about the wounded man?" Rodney asked.

"We'll make a trace for him. The others will have to drag him along with them. They'll be responsible for him." Jason looked around. "This road goes somewhere. We can send them east on it, towards the highway. That's where they'll want to go after we leave. It will take them the rest of the day to reach it, and we'll be long gone to the south."

"And if they connect with the militia?" Rodney asked.

"They tell them what the militia already knows. We're heading south and trying to get back to Hillsboro. They'll also tell them we're very dangerous. The General still won't know where we'll try to cross."

"Makes sense to me," Clayton said. "Let's get this done and get going. We got lots of woods to walk before we get back."

A half hour later, with the trace made and the injured man strapped on it, Jason sent the four men down the road.

"Remember, if we see you again, you're dead men."

"You won't have to worry about us," Gill said as they started down the old road.

Jason and the others watched until they were out of sight and then waded across the stream to continue their trek south.

It was early evening. Jason and the others were hot and tired. They had been hiking at a fast pace for six hours since the shootout and had been up for more than thirty-six hours. Coming down off a ridge, they came to another small stream rushing its way out of the valley to join the Pigeon River. There was as flat area next to the creek under a tall canopy of beech trees.

"This looks like a comfortable spot," Clayton said. "We all dog tired. Let's stop, make a fire, eat some food and boil some water for our canteens. I could use some sleep."

Billy sat down with his back to a large beech and closed his eyes. Rodney and Jason looked around.

"Looks okay to me," Rodney said. "We need a rest."

"Ain't no one gonna see a campfire down here. We're lost to the militia with no dogs tracking us. They won't have a clue."

"You're right," Jason said. He shrugged off his backpack and sat down heavily. "I am tired."

"And we have two more days of hiking to go," Clayton said.

Jason lay back on the soft ground. "Don't remind me."

After a few moments, Billy and Clayton got up and gathered some dead wood for a campfire. First small twigs and dried pine needles to start, then larger sticks until the fire would be hot enough to support a branch too large to break. Billy carried over a four inch in diameter limb to feed into the fire as it burned. They kept the fire hot but small. It burned clean and not only boiled their water, but gave warmth and cheer as the evening's damp set in.

Clayton and Rodney rolled up two larger logs for them to sit on. They heated their few remaining MREs in the water and ate in silence. Clayton refilled the small pot with water for boiling. After it had cooled, they would pour it into their canteens and repeat the process. Water was more important than food with the hot days.

The cicadas kept up their mating chorus. Hundreds of them trying to outdo one another created a surprising din. Through the din they could hear the peeping of frogs from the creek calling out for mates. There was little conversation.

Jason watched Billy. The young man sat with a scowl on his face. He had not spoken a word during the evening's activities.

"Billy, something bothering you?" Jason asked.

Billy shook his head.

"You're looking a bit glum and you've been quiet all evening. What's on your mind?"

'It ain't nothin'," he replied.

"Must be somethin'," Clayton said. "Got you all shut up."

Billy had been toying in the ground with a stick. He threw it into the dark, beyond the fire.

"If you gotta know, I ain't happy about going back. I left with Rodney to start over. Leave all that sadness behind me. Now I'm going back."

He looked at Jason. Through the firelight Jason could see the anger in his face.

"You shoulda just paid the ransom. Then me and Rodney would be on our way to Missouri. Now we're back killing people. There's always a lot of killing going on around you."

Jason sat on the log, looking at Billy. He wasn't sure what to say.

"You sure they'd let you go after they got paid?" Clayton asked.

"That's what they said," Billy said. He turned back to Jason. "You said they'd probably be coming to Hillsboro since they can't let you get away with what you did. How's that help things? They'll just be more killing."

Jason looked back at the young man. He knew how much sorrow Billy had experienced. His dream to go off with Rodney and put it all behind him was now smashed.

"I'm sorry this causes more pain. I know it's hard. I made a decision that sending the money wouldn't help. It might not have freed you and Rodney and it certainly wouldn't have stopped Knoxville from coming after Hillsboro. It seems we are a rich target. They'd come sooner or later."

"Well, they certainly coming sooner now you did what you did."

Jason raised his hands. He wanted to give Billy the respect his opinion deserved even if he thought it wrong.

"Not sure I'd get easy treatment from Knoxville," Rodney said. He looked over at Billy. "Not sure they'd just let me go when they got the money. I'm a black man. You didn't know what happened when they separated us. It wasn't pretty. There's still some racists in Knoxville." He paused. "Hell, there's still racists everywhere, not just in Knoxville. I've seen it all my life. I just let it roll off my back, ignore it for the most part. Those fools are ignorant and don't represent most of the people I've dealt with." He leaned over towards the young man. "But from some of the things said, the taunts, I'm not sure I'd have been free to go."

He leaned back against the log. "So, I'm glad Jason did what he did."

Billy was silent for a moment. "But there'll be more killing."

"We livin' in dangerous times," Clayton said. "Got to accept that and deal with it."

"I just want to put that behind me!"

Billy's voice rose in anger or frustration, Jason couldn't tell which.

"I killed another man just today. When is it going to stop?" Billy asked.

"We've all been involved in killing since the power went out. Only Rodney and I have done it before—in the Army. But now there's gangs and outlaws, dictators like the Chairman, and no laws or enforcement to deal with them. So, we have to deal with them on our own."

Jason looked Billy in the eye. "Let me ask you. You willing to live under someone like the Chairman? You willing to get in line, obey his orders, live by whatever he decides are the rules, just to live peacefully?"

Billy dropped his head and looked at the ground. "I don't know. Just know I'm tired of the killing."

"Just think about it for moment. Any killing we've done has been to defend ourselves. We don't attack others, we aren't trying to dominate them, conquer them. That's what the Chairman and Stansky, guys like that, try to do. But we aren't going to allow it to happen to us or the ones we care about."

Jason stood up. "If that means killing, then so be it."

He walked off into the darkness.

There was a silence at the campfire. After a minute Clayton spoke up.

"He be right. Rodney too...about that racism. I never been around many blacks until I fought with Rodney. You also, I bet. But we be brothers now. We helped save each other, made lives better for our people."

"Billy," Clayton pointed a finger at him. "you did that too. You defended your valley, you dealt with Stansky, gave him what he deserved. Lori Sue may have died, but she died helping someone that needed her. She fought against that bad man, stood up to him. It's what we have to do now. Defend ourselves."

"We'll go to Missouri yet," Rodney said. "I still plan to go and I still want you to come with me. But for now, it looks like we have to fight another battle, take down another bad guy."

"You think we can go?" Billy asked. There was a hopeful tone in his voice.

"I do."

"But they'll be more killing in the meantime."

"Probably."

"It's hard," Billy said finally with some sadness.

"It is. It doesn't do one much good, but it's necessary in these times," Rodney said. "Don't give Jason too hard a time. He's a warrior, a defender. I've seen such men. They run to danger when others need help. Maybe this was a mistake. I don't think so, but maybe it was. Right now, it doesn't matter. We're set on a path and that means having to defend ourselves against the Chairman."

"And we better be good at it," Clayton added.

Chapter 31

Clayton awoke before dawn. He stirred the other men. "We best get moving. Sky's getting lighter, enough to see by. Better walking when it's cooler and we got a lot of ground to cover."

The men slowly got up and stretched their sore, cramped muscles.

"Sleep okay?" Jason asked Rodney

"Like a baby."

"Liar," Jason replied with a grin on his face. He turned to Billy. "You okay about last night?"

"Yeah. I'm okay. This ain't your fault. You just doing what you can to help. And I *am* thankful for getting out of that jail, even if it means more fighting."

"Good. Hopefully we can get back to Hillsboro without any more confrontations. We've got a good chance of avoiding the rest of the General's men."

They checked their campfire and then set out across the stream, hiking south.

"We could avoid I40 altogether," Jason said when they had stopped mid-morning. "We just hike to the south of the highway and come up on Hillsboro from the south. Use the state route when we can. They'll be watching the interstate."

"Good idea as any," Rodney said.

"Any towns we got to be careful of?" Clayton asked.

"There's a few," Jason said, "Chandler, Mill Creek, Bentonville. They probably have people in them and they'll be suspicious of strangers. It shouldn't be hard to go around them if things don't look right."

The men hiked on, now buoyed by the thought of avoiding more shooting.

By the end of the day they were past the point where the interstate highway turned east and headed towards Hillsboro, passing north of the town. They camped while still in the woods. The next day they would be out in farming country.

"We'll reach the state road tomorrow and follow it. If there's no problems, we can be in Hillsboro in two more days," Jason said.

He could sense everyone's eagerness to be done with the trek. He and Clayton had been camping for nearly two weeks and, for the most part, living on the rations they had brought with them. They were nearly out of food now and would finish the trip on empty stomachs. It didn't worry Jason. They had their weapons, ammunition and water. They could go for days without food if necessary. Tomorrow they would start eating up the miles.

The General moved his troops down the interstate. He figured the place he had the best chance to intercept the fugitives was where the highway turned east, although he held out little hope they would actually encounter the men. There were just too many places they could go around his position. He guessed they would be too smart to just walk blindly along the interstate. They had already shown themselves to be more clever than that. Maybe the trackers had been successful and his men had caught them.

With that thought in mind, General McKenzie and seven militia troops departed the larger group in two Humvees to drive back north. Hopefully he would find the trackers. If not, he'd go on to Knoxville. He needed to be a part of the planning for whatever the Chairman had in mind for Hillsboro.

McKenzie did not intersect with the trackers on his way back to Knoxville. When he arrived, he went straight to Chairman Horner's office. It was nearly evening. The Chairman was talking with his assistant, Phillip Cordell, when the General came in.

"Did you catch them?" Horner asked.

The General plopped down on a chair and opened his jacket.

"No. We caught up with them at a farm along I40. They killed six of my men and then fled into the woods, heading south. I got two dogs and trackers and sent them in pursuit along with ten of my men. I haven't heard back from them."

"Do you think they'll be successful?" Cordell asked.

"The dogs were on the scent, so it's just a matter of catching up with them. Those guys are good fighters, good shots." McKenzie paused thinking about how easily they had shot six of his men. The militia never saw them and never got off a good shot at them. "They're woodsmen and know how to move fast in the mountains. It could be days before my team catches up to them." He shrugged. "So, we won't know for a while."

"What about the rest of your men?" Horner asked.

"I sent them further down I40. The fugitives have to go east at some point, so they're going to set up where the interstate turns towards Hillsboro. Still it's like trying to find a needle in a haystack. These guys are savvy enough to just hike around any ambush we set up." He shook his head. "I don't hold out much hope for catching them."

Horner slammed his fist down on the table. "Damn it! We can't just let them get away. We'll look incompetent. Others will think they don't have to obey. Then where will we be?"

McKenzie hunched forward in his chair. "I've been thinking about that. We were planning on a campaign against Johnson City. Maybe we should shift our focus to

Hillsboro. It's a richer target and we send a message that they can't get away with what they did."

"We were hoping to get them to just go along with us. I wanted to get them under our influence without having an all-out fight."

"I agree. Their giving in to our ransom demands would have been a good signal. But they didn't to do that. And not only that, they came here, into this office, and took you prisoner. That action has to be answered."

Cordell spoke up. "So, we should go to war with them? That could be costly. You didn't hear what that guy said, the leader, to Tom. They have the whole population armed and defenses set up. He said it was the Swiss model."

"Maybe if we do this right, we won't have to engage them in battle," Tom said.

Cordell and McKenzie looked at him.

"What do you have in mind?" Cordell asked.

"How many men do we have signed up in the militia?"

"Five hundred and fifty, give or take a few."

"How would it look to show up at Hillsboro's door, figuratively speaking, with, maybe three or four hundred armed men, *and* some artillery. Then we give them a chance to talk to us. Negotiate the recapture of that guy, Jason. The one who taped the shotgun to my neck—"

"And make them pay reparations for what they did, kidnaping you and killing our men," Phillip added. "That just might work. We could show others we won't stand for such treatment, intimidate Hillsboro, and never have to fire a shot."

"What do you think, Mike?" Tom asked the General.

McKenzie sat quietly, turning the idea over in his head. "We'd have to be ready to fight...to back up the threat. It can't be a bluff."

"Okay," Tom said.

"We have to go ready to do battle, the whole nine yards," McKenzie said.

"That wouldn't be a good thing, if it happened," Phillip said.

"If we're not ready to go that far, then I say we don't go. We find some other way to respond," McKenzie said with a firm voice.

"That son of a bitch manhandled me. Taped me to a shotgun, then he lectured me as we drove away, and left me tied and blindfolded on the side of the road." Tom was standing now, pacing back and forth behind his desk. "He can't get away with it. He has to pay." His eyes were shining with anger.

"Maybe we do this in stages," Phillip said. He always looked for a middle ground, sometimes between what the Chairman wanted to do and what the General recommended. "We send another emissary and demand the return of this Jason to stand trial for what he did."

"We haven't got our last emissary back," McKenzie said.

"I know, but this time a crime has been committed. We can frame it as the kidnapping of the Chairman and breaking two men out of jail who were arrested for breaking our laws."

"What law did they break, exactly?" the General asked Phillip.

"Make one up. Trespassing, violating our security by not getting a pass to travel through town, not registering when they tried to walk around our security perimeter. You can find something. Let's recast the ransom into a fine to be paid to release them. Then this guy comes and attacks our Chairman and breaks more of our laws."

"We'd be seen as being civil about this, treating this as a civil matter," Tom said. "It just might work."

"I can get some arrest warrants drawn up. We have a judge who'll do it. I can go there and present the warrants," Cordell said.

"We can try, but it won't work," Mike said. He heaved a sigh. It had been a tiring excursion, chasing the fugitives, with nothing to show for it. This scheme would not be successful, but he could see the Chairman's buy in.

"If it doesn't, we go to the next level. The one you propose," Tom said. "The fact that we come peacefully first to settle the issue legally, as a civil, matter might sow discord in the city and cause them to negotiate rather than fight."

Phillip added, "We might not get them to turn over Jason, but they could pay reparations. We make a point, we get some loot, and we put Hillsboro on notice not to mess with us. All good things."

The conversation continued well into the night.

Chapter 32

The next day the men broke camp early. There was renewed energy in the group fueled by their eagerness to get back to Hillsboro. An hour's hike brought them out of the forest and into farm country.

The forest was timeless. While you were in it, you would never know the power had gone out and civilization in the U.S. had collapsed. Maybe, if you were very observant, you would look up and wonder why there were no contrails in the sky, tracers left by high-flying jets on their way to New Orleans, Houston, or some other major city. The sky remained empty of such signs of civilization and commerce.

Now hiking in inhabited country, one could see the devastation: abandoned fields, abandoned farmhouses, cars left on the roadsides. The signs of loss would only increase as they drew closer to more urban areas. The signs of loss dampened everyone's spirits which had been buoyed by nearing the end of their trek.

They came to a local road heading southeast.

"There's a good chance this will intersect a state route going east," Jason said.

"We're going by dead reckoning now?" Rodney asked.

"I have the map, but I'm not sure where we are on it. So, yeah, pretty much," Jason said.

At a rise in the road they could see a cluster of houses gathered around a crossroads. It looked like there was a gas station with what had been a convenience store and a dozen or more houses along both roads. Jason studied the scene through his binoculars and then handed them off to Rodney.

"You see any activity?" Clayton asked.

Jason shook his head. "It all looks abandoned."

There seemed to be no enthusiasm to take the time to hike a couple of extra miles in order to detour around the village. The urge to get home was growing.

"I agree," Rodney said. "Looks empty."

"Let's go," Billy said. "I'm tired of all this walking."

Jason looked around. Rodney and Clayton weren't disagreeing.

"All right, but keep a careful eye out. Be ready to respond if you see any danger."

They walked towards the houses, about a mile and a half away. Twenty minutes later they were approaching the crossroads. They walked in two-by-two fashion, Jason and Rodney ahead with Clayton and Billy behind. At Rodney's insistence, they kept a space of about ten yards between the two pairs.

There was no talking now. The empty houses stared out on the streets. Some with their doors open and windows broken, evidence of their violation. A few looked like they hadn't been raided and might still be habitable, if only someone were around to live in them.

Suddenly Billy stopped and swung his head to the right.

"You see something?" Clayton asked in a low voice.

The two men in front stopped and turned to look back at Billy.

"I thought I saw something moving, to my right. Something or someone disappeared around the corner over there," he pointed to a house they had just passed.

"Think we should investigate?" Clayton asked.

"Let's just keep going," Jason said. "But keep alert."

The men began to walk again. This time they all heard it. A crunching sound, off to the right.

"Steps?" Clayton asked.

They could see nothing. When they started walking again, Billy turned and walked backwards. His back tingled when he turned away from the sound they all had heard. He could imagine a bullet slamming into him, right between the shoulder blades.

"Feels kind of creepy," he said.

"You gonna trip and fall on your ass, walking like that," Clayton said.

They walked a short distance further with Billy shuffling backwards.

"What's that?" Billy said with a sharp voice.

The others stopped and turned.

"What'd you see?" Jason asked.

"Something. A shadow? Something came out from the corner and ducked out of sight. It went behind that car, the one at the curb."

"You're sure you saw something hide behind the car?"

"No, but I think I did."

Rodney called out. "If you're hiding behind the car, come out with your hands in the air. We mean you no harm. We're just passing through, but we don't want to get shot in the back."

Nothing.

The men spread out across the road

"Come out now and you won't get hurt," Jason said.

The four started walking forward with their rifles at ready. A high, thin voice called out from behind the car, "Don't hurt me."

The men stopped.

"We won't, but come out so we can see you," Jason called out.

"No shooting? No hurting?"

"That's right. Just come out."

A gaunt figure slowly arose from behind the car. A man dressed in rags. His hair was long and matted. His shirt and pants in tatters and his shoes were broken down boots now tied up with rags to keep them together.

"Did you see them? Did you talk to them?" The figure asked.

The men lowered their rifles seeing this apparition was obviously unarmed and looked to pose no threat.

"Are you alone?" Rodney asked.

The figure hesitated. A thoughtful look on his face. "Just me and some friends. Everyone else run off or were taken. I'm taking care of things until they get back. Somebody has to do it."

"Where are your friends?" Rodney asked.

The man's face brightened. He broke out in a twisted smile, showing missing and broken teeth.

"Follow me," he said and turned towards the gas station and store.

The four men followed, now back on high alert.

The apparition entered the store and turned to smile at the men.

"Where are they?" Jason asked.

The man just kept smiling and then swung his hand around. Behind him were life-sized cardboard figures hawking different products; a NASCAR driver holding up a soda bottle, a tennis star holding a sports drink, someone in a Carolina Panthers uniform holding another power sports drink. In addition to the figures, a wall near the checkout counter was full of NFL backdrop posters touting the football league and some light beer.

"We're keeping things together while everyone's gone," the man said. He looked down at the floor. "'Course I don't know when they're coming back." He looked back up at the four men, his eyes flickering with anticipation. "You see them?"

"See who? The people from this village?"

The man shook his head.

"Then who," Jason asked.

The figure looked around, past the men, through the windows. Then he spoke in a whisper. "The visitors. The aliens." He looked around again and leaned towards the men. "They took everyone away. Those that wouldn't go, they put to sleep, somehow, and they never woke up. I hid in a cave. Didn't come out for weeks, till I was sure they was gone. You see them?"

Jason shook his head.

"Well you better hide when they come. They take you for sure."

"The aliens?" Rodney asked.

The man nodded with his lips pressed firm.

"We talk about why they came here, why they shut off the power and put people to sleep. Why they took people away. They're from a dying race, near as we can guess. They need something from us. They experiment on us, take our body fluids to help them figure out how to make new aliens."

The four men stared in wonder at this skinny figure in his tattered clothes. His feet wouldn't be still, shuffling and tapping on the floor. His arms waved around haphazardly as he talked.

"We hear them sometimes. They come at night. They still looking for people, but we stay hidden." He looked over his shoulder at the figures. "Me and my friends. We're keeping this place open until the others come back."

"You hear them?" Jason asked.

The man nodded his head up and down furiously. "We can see their lights, but we stay hidden. Can't let them catch us."

"How do you live?" Clayton asked. "What do you eat?"

"We got plenty to eat," the man replied. "Lots of rats, squirrels."

"That all?"

"Sometimes we eat the wood sorrel growing in the yards and fields. Got water from a well."

"And you sleep here?" Jason asked.

"My friends stay here. I go over to the house down the street, especially when it's cold. Got a good stove to keep warm. My friends don't like to go out, so I meet with them over here most days."

"And that's all you do?"

"We talk about things. How to avoid the aliens, when the others might be coming back. We ain't seen many other people in a long time, so we don't get much news. You say you never saw them, though."

He now looked almost confused. "You think they gone?"

Rodney started to speak but Jason caught his arm.

"We don't know if they're gone or not. We've been in the woods for some time," Jason said. "Do you mind if I talk to my partners outside for a minute? We'll be right back."

The man watched as Jason led the group out of the store.

"Why'd you stop me?" Rodney asked.

"The man's crazy. We can see that. You saying the aliens are gone or there are no aliens might shatter this world he's created."

"You want to let him go on with this fantasy?"

Jason looked back into the store. The man was talking to the cardboard figures, gesturing wildly with his arms. "It's how he survives. He's lost his sense of reality. Look at his friends."

Clayton shook his head. "Be a lot of other crazy people around if they was as good at surviving as this one. What he heard was probably refugees or gangs passing through."

"Should we bring him with us?" Billy asked.

"What good would that do?" Clayton asked.

"It just seems wrong to leave him here."

"He seems to be doing all right," Clayton said.

"I don't think he'd want to go," Jason said. "He'd probably think we want to take him to the aliens. We should just leave him alone."

Rodney nodded in assent as did Clayton.

"Guess you're right. He's made it this far," Billy said.

The men went back inside.

"We have to go now. Got a long way to travel. We'll keep an eye out for the others from here. We'll let them know you're asking about them.

"Tell them they can come back. I've kept everything like they left it."

"What is your name?" Jason asked. "We should tell them your name."

"It's Noah Frank Lynn."

"Noah Franklin," Jason repeated.

"No. Noah *Frank Lynn*. My middle name is Frank."

The men said goodbye and turned to go. Noah stood in the doorway watching them as they walked down the street, heading east.

"Watch out for them. You hide when you see 'em. Don't let them catch you," he called out.

After an hour of walking, Rodney suddenly spoke up. "Noah Frank...Lynn. NFL"

The others looked at him.

"NFL, National Football League," he repeated.

Jason smiled as they continued their journey.

Chapter 33

By the end of the second day since leaving Noah behind, the men reached Hillsboro and passed through the south-western gate, near where the water channel had been cut to power the mill.

Clayton cut through the town to depart from the other side and join his family on their farm. Rodney and Billy went with Jason to his home. When Anne saw Jason coming through the door, she jumped up and nearly tackled him, throwing her arms around him in a huge hug. After nearly smothering her husband, she gave each of the other men joyful hugs while Sarah hugged her step-father. Jason then went in a bedroom to peek at his son who was sound asleep.

"Let him sleep. He can see you in the morning," Anne said softly. She held on to Jason, as if afraid he would disappear if she let him go.

"Come sit down. I'll pour each of you a drink and get you some food."

"We should clean up," Rodney said.

"You do smell a bit ripe, but for now just sit. As the song goes, 'rest your weary feet a while'."

Anne brought out some whiskey she and Jason had brought from the valley farm. She poured everyone a half glass, neat.

"Here's to a successful rescue," she said raising her own glass of water. Rodney looked at her.

"Still nursing," she said, then turned to start a fire in the stove. She and Jason had brought the wood-burning kitchen stove from their farm house to their house in Hillsboro.

"How does ham and eggs with some tomatoes and onions sound?"

"That sounds great," Jason said. He started to take off his boots but Rodney stopped him.

"Don't. You'll stink up the kitchen and spoil those great cooking aromas Anne is going to produce."

Billy just smiled as he sipped his drink. He was still not a great fan of whiskey, but now understood its role in social settings. And the fact that it relaxed him didn't hurt.

After a large meal, during which Anne and Sarah coaxed some tidbits of the adventure from Jason and Rodney, Anne sent the men off to wash. She heated a large tub of water from the tank outside which they carried to the bathroom. There was still no running water, but everyone had a tank that collected water from their roofs. In addition, there were numerous wells that had been dug around the city and people could go to those locations and pump water to carry back to their homes.

Grey water from sinks and bathtubs was allowed to flow into the waste system. The town had no way to process it and just passed it along, back into the river downstream. Work was in progress to create a large complex of drain fields to pipe the water into. There were severe penalties for dumping black water into the system. It happened and could be handled, but with great difficulty. If the perpetrators were found, their drains were either sealed up with concrete or disconnected from the sewer lines.

The hot tub of water was blended into the cold and each man was able to get at least a luke-warm standing bath. The soap felt like a luxury after weeks of camping.

Now washed and fed, Anne showed Billy and Rodney where to sleep—pads on the living room floor—and she and Jason retired to their bedroom.

"Tomorrow you need to report to Kevin. The town council is going to want to meet to debrief you and ask you lots of questions," Anne said when they retired to the privacy of their room.

"Yeah. There's a lot to talk about."

"You're probably not going to like all you hear from the council."

"I'll deal with that tomorrow. Right now, I'm home and have you in my arms. I can't think of anything beyond that glorious fact."

"And you shouldn't either," Anne said as she wrapped herself around her man.

The next day Jason, Rodney, and Billy went to the police headquarters to see Kevin. After much joy and hugging one another, the men sat down.

Kevin shook his head. "I can hardly believe you were successful. I know what Anne said at the council meeting. It was a brave statement, but I still thought it wasn't going to end well. No one but Anne, and maybe Catherine, thought you'd make it back."

He got up and poured some tea for the men. "Tell me about it."

Jason, along with Rodney recalled the events as Kevin listened with rapt attention.

"Damn, I never would have thought of that, a mutually assured destruction setup. If they killed you, they would be killing the Chairman. He must not have liked that."

"We had some time to talk as we drove out of town with him. He's a dictator with a dictator's mentality. For him control is the key to the future and control needs to be in his hands, not the citizens," Jason said.

"In dangerous times, that can be a good thing. Decisions made faster. One is able to react more quickly to threats. That's why, during war, our president becomes the Commander in Chief. After war is declared, he can operate with his generals without everything having to go through congress."

"I get that, but is that how we should live while we're trying to rebuild civil society? Seems to me we have to find a way to normalize life while we remain flexible and quick to act on threats."

"If you can figure out that balance, someone should elect you to run the country," Kevin said.

"I don't think there's much of a country right now. That's something we'll be dealing with at some point, but for now, we're in that city-state stage of society."

"Can you find a place for Rodney and Billy to stay? Sleeping on our couch and floor is going to get old quickly."

Kevin turned to his sergeant. "I never thought I'd see you again so soon."

"Me either."

"You still going to go west?"

"Yes. But I think now we should wait a few weeks to see what the fallout is going to be from our rescue."

"You think there'll be repercussions?" Kevin turned back to Jason.

"I do. It may involve an all-out attack on Hillsboro. They were planning on taking over Johnson City, but they may turn their attention to us."

"We're a much more formidable opponent than Johnson City."

"That's why I'm not sure. But I think the Chairman can't let this go unanswered. Too many people know what happened. The word will get out and he can't afford to look bad, especially to his own citizens."

Rodney nodded in agreement. "That's why I want to stay around for a while. Billy too, I think." He turned to Billy who nodded in agreement.

"I'm still going with Rodney, when he's ready to leave. This is still a sad place for me."

Kevin got up. "I guess I better go see Steve. Get him to call a council meeting."

"The sooner the better," Jason replied.

"I'll arrange some place for you and Billy to stay," Kevin said to Rodney.

"I think I'll go out to see Clayton. He should be at the meeting," Jason said. "By the way, where is Catherine?"

"She's in Taylorsville, being a diplomat," Kevin replied.

"How's that going?"

"Only okay at best. All the surrounding towns are suspicious. Not much has changed since you left, but they're slowly coming around. If what you say is true, we'll need them on board to help us out."

"Could be a tough sell," Jason said.

"We'll cross that bridge when we come to it. Tell Clayton we'll have the meeting the day after tomorrow. It takes more time to get things arranged nowadays."

The men got up to go.

"I'll go out to Clayton's farm with you," Billy said. "Maybe he can put me up somewhere. Be less sad than staying here in town."

"I'm going to go see my troops," Rodney said. "Kind of miss them, even Tommy."

Chapter 34

T wo days later the town council gathered in their usual chambers in the city hall building, the modest but appropriate venue where the town's business had been run for generations. Steve Warner, the acting mayor, an electrician who had led the internal resistance to free the town, was presiding. A number of citizens who had been alerted were at the meeting. Along with Rodney and Billy, Kevin and Charlie Cook, the previous police chief, there was Anne and Sarah.

"I want to thank you all for coming on short notice. As you can see, Jason and Clayton have returned after successfully rescuing Sergeant Gibbs and Billy Turner. I've called this meeting so we can hear their report of what went on."

There were other opening comments by members of the council. Jason could never understand the need for such. It seemed like when someone got elected to a public office, they felt obligated to always have something to say. Finally, Steve motioned for Jason to stand and speak.

He began by re-introducing Clayton, who had been key to getting Rodney and Billy freed. Jason also wanted to be sure the council understood the contribution Clayton's people were making. He didn't want them to feel estranged from the town's people. The two groups needed each other too much to become distant and disconnected.

After the compelling story of the tense time in the Chairman's office, the flight south and the gun battles,

Jason sat down. There was a hushed silence. Then Steve spoke up.

"I guess we all should congratulate Jason and Clayton for what they did. We took care of our own and showed Knoxville that we are not to be messed with."

The room burst into applause. Clayton looked embarrassed.

"Mr. Mayor," Raymond Culver spoke up from the dais as the applause died down. "May I make a comment?"

Steve looked over at Raymond. He had come to learn in his short two weeks on the job that Raymond Culver could be a pain in the ass. He often took a contrary position, but he was not easily dismissed as his formidable intelligence had to be dealt with and his arguments answered.

"Go ahead Mr. Culver," Steve said.

"We do appreciate Mr. Richard's success. Many of us didn't hold out much hope for his mission. We worried that it might end in loss of life, to him and his partner and to the prisoners. We're happy he and the others returned safely." He paused before continuing.

"But I do wonder the effect this will have on Knoxville. It seems as though Jason put their leader in a very dangerous and embarrassing position. They might react badly to that. That may not be helpful to us. Our future may be best served by establishing peaceful relations with Knoxville and this act might have set that back if not made it impossible."

"I hear your point Ray," Steve said.

"I just think that we should discuss some sort of peace gesture. We should be ready to show Knoxville the olive branch of peace, not the hard stick of war and conflict."

"From what we can tell, the men made it back and the pursuing militia gave up and probably returned to Knoxville. We can discuss how we might make overtures to Knoxville, but for now I don't think we need to do anything but celebrate everyone's safe return."

There was much more discussion with all the council members wanting to tease out the details of the rescue. The encounter with Noah Frank Lynn caused a mixture of mirth and sadness in the chamber. Everyone was touched as well as amused by the story of the survivor, but it also reminded them of their loss.

After the meeting, Anne insisted that Clayton, Kevin, Rodney, and Billy come over to their house. She was making a pork loin that someone had given her to celebrate Jason's return. With the hotter days, the gift needed to be eaten, so Anne had invited friends, including Charlie Cook and his wife, over. Clayton's wife, Lizbeth, had come to town with him, so she would join them as well.

The meal was sumptuous for the times. Cooked in the oven of a wood stove, the aroma of the wood fire could not help but permeate the meat. With the loin, Anne had cooked some of the root vegetables she had kept over the winter, carrots, beets and potatoes.

The meal was eaten with great enthusiasm and little conversation. Everyone appreciated a full meal in these days. With little power and no refrigeration, one had to learn old ways to enjoy good meals. The positive was that most food was generally fresh to the benefit of everyone's health.

"I know you have much to talk about and I want to talk with Lizbeth and Mary," Anne announced when the meal had ended. "So, you men go into the living room. Me and the ladies will clean up."

"Let us help," Jason said. "He got up and grabbed a couple of plates. The others followed his example and the dishes were soon stacked in the kitchen.

"Thank you," Anne said. "Now go. It's too crowded in here."

The men retired to the living room.

"What do you think the fallout will be from your actions?" Charlie asked after they sat down. "Do you think they'll attack us?"

"I don't really know the answer to that," Jason said. "We learned that they have around five hundred men in their militia. And, as I told Kevin, I don't think they can let this go unanswered. They have to respond in some fashion."

Charlie shook his head. There was a worried look on his face. "I'm not being critical, but there'll be people who will criticize you, if they think your rescue will bring danger to the town. No one needs that so soon after we fought Stansky."

"That's not fair," Kevin said in a strong voice.

"I'm just voicing what some people may think. You, we, need to be prepared for that reaction."

Jason sighed and relaxed in his chair. A full meal, lovely wife, good friends; life was, at this moment, pretty nice, he thought. Except for the subject of discussion. That brought home the level of instability and stress that still haunted their lives.

"Look," he said. "I don't need to answer for what I did. When I stepped down from being mayor, I became a private citizen. As such, I could do what I want. I haven't broken any laws. If I wanted to go off and rescue some friends, that's my business...and Clayton's as well. There's no law to stop us."

"You're taking the position that you acted as a private citizen? The problem is, as you already said, Knoxville may not see it like that," Charlie replied.

Jason lifted his hands in a gesture of surrender. "It's done. I wasn't going to leave Rodney and Billy held captive."

"Please understand," Charlie said. "I've been a police officer for thirty years. I can see the reaction that is coming. I can also see the relevant laws, such as they exist, that might apply. You refused to pay the ransom, abused the courier. Those were official actions, before you stepped down and acted as a private citizen—"

"Taken with council approval," Jason said.

"Okay, Charlie," Kevin said. "I think we get your point. Some may bring it up, but Knoxville might not respond in such a way as to start a war. No one wins if there's a war between the cities."

"We get to warring," Clayton said. "We maybe have to go back to the mountains."

"You don't want it to come to that. No one does," Rodney said.

The conversation went on until the women came into the room. Their presence expanded the scope of conversation to daily living and the efforts to restore the pieces of modern society: schools, medical care, power, sanitation. The children growing up in the post EMP world would not know of a different one; children like Jason and Anne's son, Adam. Most adults wanted to be sure they learned what the United States had been and, therefore, what it could be again.

"Speaking of children," Jason said. "When are you and Catherine going to start a family?"

"We're working on it," Kevin replied with a shy grin.

"Enough said. To think we'll be grandparents." He beamed at Anne. "We're not that old."

"It will be different. Their baby will have an uncle barely older than themselves," Anne said.

"Odd times for sure," Mary said.

The rest of the week brought no news regarding Knoxville and the worry began to settle down in everyone's mind. Jason and Anne started talking about whether to move back to their farm in Hidden Valley. Only Tom and Betty Walsh, along with Claire Nolan still lived there. Tom and Betty helped Claire who had lost her husband, Andy, in the battle with Big Jacks and was getting a bit frail. The Sands had moved with their daughter to Hillsboro before the revolt. John was now helping with rebuilding projects in town.

Both Jason and Anne loved the valley, but it was now much more isolated. Sarah was seventeen and would not want to move back. She liked the increased interaction with people in the city and had found friends her age. Plus, she got to see her boyfriend, Tommy Wilkes, someone who Jason and Anne figured would be a son-in-law someday. The better education opportunities for Adam in town also played a big part in their considerations.

Ten days after they had returned, the guards at the northwest gate stopped a Humvee flying two flags. One representing the City of Knoxville and the other plain white.

A man got out of the back and introduced himself as Phillip Cordell, Administrative Assistant to Tom Horner, the Chairman of Knoxville. He said he had come to talk to Hillsboro's mayor, whoever that might be, about a transgression on the part of one of the town's citizens.

The vehicle was escorted to City Hall.

Phillip Cordell was brought into the mayor's office and introduced to Steve Warner.

"You're the mayor?" Cordell asked as he shook Steve's hand.

"Acting mayor. I'm filling in since the position became vacated."

"Who was the previous mayor?"

"Not important," Steve said, trying to avoid any interrogation. He had been told Phillip was from Knoxville and he didn't anticipate this was a goodwill visit.

"You have the authority of a fully elected mayor? I ask because one doesn't know exactly how cities are organized these days."

"Indeed." Steve gestured to a chair. "Please sit down. Can I get you something to drink? We have a small amount of whiskey left and water."

Cordell shook his head. "I'm fine, thank you."

Steve sat back in his chair and tried to look relaxed. "What brings you this long way?"

"We had an incident recently. I think you may already know about it. We were holding two men from Hillsboro, who had broken our laws. Two men from your town infiltrated our city, kidnapped our Chairman, terrorized his secretary and the office guard, and broke the two prisoners free. I set up an expensive and time-consuming chase to rescue our mayor and recover the fugitives. That resulted in the deaths of twelve men from our militia. All killed by those four men."

Steve just sat there stony-faced. His hands clenched in tight fists below his desk. Cordell sat across from him, waiting, staring at him. He had one eyebrow raised in a dramatic questioning gesture. Finally, he spoke again.

"I'm sure you are aware of what I am talking about. I came a long way to discuss this outrage with you and what we can agree to do about it."

"Mr. Cordell," Steve began. His mind was racing. He had hoped this day wouldn't come and he hadn't prepared any rebuttal in advance. "Your premise seems to be off base, so I'm at a bit of a loss as to how to respond. We received a ransom demand. A person from Knoxville delivered it. It was for one hundred pounds of gold. You realize that kidnapping and holding someone for ransom is against the law. Against city, state and federal law. It looks to me like you, or someone in your city was the perpetrator of a crime. We sent a team to rescue our hostages from a kidnapping."

Steve leaned forward. "Now what do you want to talk about?"

Cordell smiled. He was not shaken by Steve's response. "I think you may have misunderstood the message. Couriers are not the most efficient method of communication. We were asking for the payment in order to pay the fines for the two men we were holding."

"The fines were for exactly what crimes?"

Cordell took some papers out of his pocket and placed them on the desk.

"Here are arrest warrants for a Jason and Clayton, last names unknown, and the two prisoners." He shoved the papers across the desk. "As you can see, they're signed by a judge. You are obliged to honor these orders. I'm here to return the men to stand trial."

He sat back with a slight smile on his face. "The warrants list their crimes. The men we arrested trespassed into the city without registering at an entrance gate. They attempted to elude discovery to avoid proper registration, and they refused to pay the transit fees we charge for people to pass through our jurisdiction on the interstate."

"The federal interstate highway?"

"The very same...that runs through the city, inside the city limits, over which we have jurisdiction since there seems to be no federal government." Cordell continued, "Jason and Clayton committed kidnapping, assault, threats of bodily harm to multiple people, committing a felony with an unregistered weapon, and," he paused for effect, "murder."

"I see the document and I hear what you're saying but I go back to the origin of these actions. Contrary to what you state, there was no confusion in the courier's message. Your man was quite clear in his demands. I doubt he made that up or distorted a message about paying a fine for some minor infractions into a demand for a ransom."

"So, you don't believe me?"

Steve smiled. "Mr. Cordell, I'm finding it hard to accept your story."

"And you don't want to honor these legal arrest warrants?"

"Considering the circumstances, I don't think I can."

"Perhaps I should speak to our courier, to help clear things up."

"I don't think that can be arranged at this point. It could be interpreted as you trying to manipulate your courier's statement to align with yours."

Phillip Cordell sat there for a moment. Steve could see he remained calm. The man seemed to be an experienced negotiator, a good choice for an assistant to a tyrant.

"There is a requirement for you to honor legal arrest warrants. Are you putting Hillsboro above the law?"

"I'm not a lawyer, just an electrician. But from what I know, there is no state government and maybe no federal one as well. You're aware of that reality. So what we have are two cities, city states if you will, each sovereign, with no current treaties between them." Now Steve paused for effect. "From what I see, this arrest warrant is based on a flawed premise and I doubt our citizens could get a fair trial in such a case."

"Let me get to the crux of things," Phillip said. "If you pay a reduced fine and turn over the man or men responsible for shooting our militia, we'll drop the issue."

"I can't do that. I only have your word for the shooting and if it is so, there's a good possibility they were acting in self-defense."

"Is that what they told you?"

"It's what I heard."

"You didn't get a report when they got back? You didn't get debriefed on this supposed rescue? I'm surprised."

"What happens here is the town's business and not yours. I find your request not valid and in conflict with the facts as I know them. I'm sorry, but I can't help you."

He started to rise. Phillip held out his hand to stop him. Steve stopped and sat back down. As soon as he did, he was angry with himself. The gesture and his response gave Cordell more authority over the meeting than the man should have had.

"Do me the courtesy of letting me bring my proposal to your council. I assume you have a town council?"

"We do. But I'm not going to let you have the floor at a council meeting." He paused for a moment to think. "I can call a meeting to present your demands, but that's the best I can do."

Cordell sighed. "At least do me the courtesy of being able to attend the meeting, even if you won't let me speak on my behalf."

Steve stood again. This time all the way. "I'll give it some thought."

He led Cordell out of the office and grabbed one of his staffers.

"Escort Mr. Cordell to the hotel and set up two rooms for him and his escorts."

"Yes sir."

"They are not to leave the hotel. Arrange to have a dinner and breakfast tomorrow brought to the hotel."

"Yes sir."

Steve turned to Cordell, "I'll try to get the council together on short notice. I assume you don't want to spend much time in our city."

Steve shook his hand and watched as the man departed. He had an ominous feeling about where events would go from here.

Chapter 35

I t took some effort, but Steve managed to round up the nine members of the council to meet the next day at noon. There was much talking going on among the members when he walked up to take his seat on the dais. He looked around and was glad to see that Kevin had been able to recall Catherine so she could attend.

Kevin, as Police Chief, had seen the arrest warrants. He had gone over them with Charlie Cook who pronounced them reasonably correct. Charlie was not on the council but was in attendance in the audience. There was a smattering of citizens at the meeting. Steve guessed some of the council members had contacted them to attend. He could see some of Raymond Culver's support sitting there.

Steve opened the meeting with a recap of Phillip Cordell's visit the prior day and the existence of the arrest warrants. He explained his doubt about the story given him by Cordell, noting the courier had presented a far different story with a clear demand for ransom. It was hard to think the courier had been confused regarding his instructions and his message. Because of this discrepancy Steve thought the arrest warrants should not be honored. It looked like another attempt to extort money from Hillsboro with the addition of turning over their citizens to what would not be a proper trial.

When he finished, a cacophony of voices broke out with everyone, both on the dais and in the audience talking at once. Anne gripped Jason's arm tightly. Jason sat there, grim-faced. Steve pounded his gavel until he got the room under control.

"The audience will not speak. This is a council meeting. You may only speak if I agree to it and call on you. Council members," he said, looking both right and left, "you will all have time to make any points you want. But you must wait until recognized. We will have order in this chamber."

Hands shot up. Steve recognized Kevin first. He hoped he would put this issue into its proper context.

"The courier's demands were independently corroborated by various council members other than myself. We all came to the same conclusion. Rodney Gibbs and Billy Turner had been captured and were being held for ransom. One hundred pounds of gold. Let no one here doubt that was the reality we faced—"

"And Jason abused that courier. Cut off his finger," one of the council members shouted.

"And he stepped down as mayor for that," Kevin responded as Steve pounded his gavel again to get order.

"If I may continue," Kevin said. Steve nodded to him. "I viewed the arrest warrant. It is unprecedented and not easily dealt with since we have no state government and no federal presence. In addition, Knoxville is in a different state."

"What's your bottom line," someone from the audience called out.

"Silence!" said Steve in a loud voice. "I see you. Another outburst and I'll have you thrown out of the meeting."

The man scowled but didn't respond.

"My bottom line is this. First, Cordell's story conflicts with what we *know* are the facts presented to us. It represents a reinterpretation of events to put Knoxville in a good light. Second, there is no precedent for this action even if it were legitimate. We'd have to sign a treaty with Knoxville that established such things. Because of these two points, we cannot give in to the man's demands."

There were murmurs of both support and dissent as Steve gaveled for quiet.

Other council members got their turn to speak. Bob Jackson, the man who had led the effort to restore the water mill to provide electric power, spoke in support of Kevin's position. Others were on the fence. Dr. Morgan asked about consequences.

"I'm not in favor of bloodshed, battles between cities," she said. "We just got through that horror when removing Stansky. I get to see the ugly backside of all that fighting. It's not pretty and made worse by our limited medical supplies. We need to consider the consequences of saying no to this man.

"What would you have us do?" Steve asked.

Dr. Morgan paused. She liked Jason. She knew he was the catalyst that freed the city, that he was the one who, along with Kevin, had directed the fighting to defeat Joe Stansky. Her face reflected her conflict.

"I don't know. I'm not in favor of turning Jason and the others over to Knoxville, but there must be another way beyond refusing all their demands. Maybe we could have a trial here where we could insure its fairness?"

There were some snickers from the audience.

"A middle ground for sure," Steve said. "We should keep it in mind, but I doubt Mr. Cordell will go for that."

After more comments, Raymond Culver finally raised his hand and was recognized.

"We all owe a debt of gratitude to Jason and all the others who fought to free Hillsboro from Stansky's tyranny. We are the better for it."

Steve waited for the "but" that usually accompanied Raymond's friendly comments.

"This situation, however, cannot be dealt with by simply saying we must defend Jason and the others at the peril of our city." He began to warm to his topic.

"It seems to me that Jason is a fighter and prone to impetuous behavior. Some would say dangerous behavior.

We know he abused the courier against all norms of decency and civilized behavior. He acted like the gangster we recently displaced.

"Then he convinced the council to not pay the ransom demand and set off with his cohort in arms to wage a personal war on Knoxville because they detained two of his friends." He paused for a moment. "And he did this with the support of some people we put a lot of trust in." Raymond now was looking directly at Kevin.

"If we had not followed his direction, the two men would have resumed their journey and Knoxville would not be knocking on our door with arrest warrants and possible threats. We would be at peace with no crisis and left alone to continue our rebuilding.

He now stood as the room silently stared at him. "We have to put this aside. We cannot follow this out-of-control fighter who steps on civil rights and resorts to violence to solve problems." He pounded his fist on the dais. "We have to turn him over to the Knoxville authorities for his unlawful actions in their city. Actions which only bring discredit to Hillsboro. I don't want us to be led down a violent path by this man who has lost any moral authority to lead this city. He cannot dictate Hillsboro's policy by...his words...or his actions."

He sat down. There was a smattering of applause but the room remained mostly silent.

"Jason," Steve said, "since you are the focus of this discussion, would you like to say something on your behalf?"

Jason didn't answer for a moment. He looked forward, his eyes focused on the wall behind the dais. The town's shield and motto were there, "*Honor omnia*", honor in all things. Slowly he stood.

"I seem to be more than the focus of this discussion," he began quietly, "I seem to be on trial without a court or judge."

"You're not on trial," Steve assured him. Jason didn't acknowledge his remark.

"The town's motto, on the wall behind you council members, translates into 'honor in all things', or 'honor above all'. That is how I have tried to live my life. I don't apologize for what I did to the courier. I felt I needed to do it for the sake of Rodney and Billy. However, I realized after that action, I could no longer officially lead the city. I shouldn't lead it anyway even though I helped free everyone. All of you."

He stopped to look at all the citizens who were now on the council and then turned to look over those in the audience.

"You, collectively, let a gangster take over this city. I saw it in the months after the EMP attack. I had a business in this city. I contributed to its taxes and its civic affairs. I left that after the attack and set out on my own. Should I have stayed and fought it? Who knows? What I do know is that no one else did. Everyone was content to let the gangster take over and run the town as long as he kept you safe. Trading off your freedom for security.

"It looks like you're about to do it again. If you bow to Knoxville, like Raymond suggests, they won't stop. There will be increasing demands to give over authority to them, to abide by their rules until you will have accepted another tyranny into your midst. Raymond Culver was comfortable with that. He made sure he had a comfortable position in the old tyranny and he will do so in the new one. He's clever that way."

"I object," Raymond shouted.

"Silence!" said Steve. "You had your say, made your point. Jason has the floor by my recognition. I'm giving him his say."

"Beyond that point," Jason continued, "if the council wants to turn me over to Knoxville, I will not accept that. I will leave town. You can banish me, like was done in medieval times, but I will not allow myself to be taken prisoner by a tyrant or his lackey. I'll take my family and leave. I'll rely on myself, like I've done before."

"You're going to refuse a lawful arrest warrant?" One of the council members asked.

"Let me be very clear on this. No one will take me into custody. It will be dangerous for anyone to try. Do not doubt me on that point."

He sat down. Anne took his arm and pulled it tight to her.

Steve worried that Jason's last comment only served to convince others of what Raymond had said, that he was prone to violence.

"Let's call the vote," Raymond said.

Steve was not sure where this would end up. Kevin, the Chief of Police, was also Jason's son-in-law. Would he resign also? Would he refuse to serve the warrant if the council voted to accept it? Would Catherine resign to follow her family? It began to look like a disaster was forming. There was much hushed conversation on the dais and in the audience.

"Steve," Dr. Morgan called out, "I'd like to have someone in the audience speak. I invited her here because she has something important to say."

"Call the vote," another council member said.

"I'll hear from the person Dr. Morgan is talking about. Go ahead."

Janet Morgan nodded to a woman in the audience. She was in her thirties, attractive with a shy face, now looking very nervous, even scared. She stood up.

"My name is Helen Chambers. I came here only a few weeks ago. I'm a nurse, so I went to the hospital and Dr. Morgan gave me a job. I was on my way here with my husband when we were attacked by a gang, four men. They killed Martin and took me prisoner."

She went on to describe in a choked voice how she had been repeatedly raped while tied down.

"They probably would have just killed me when they got tired of me, or made me their slave, if I gave in to them. I had no options. Then Jason and his friend, Clayton came along. They killed the men and freed me. I was terrified, of the men *and* of my rescuers. I was nearly out of my mind. But those two men..." she broke down for a moment. "They were so kind and patient. They understood how traumatized I was. They gave me time to get myself together and helped me to arrive here safely."

She looked around the room, her face now firm and set, and began to speak again in a more confident tone.

"These men represent the best in this town. They are honorable. They acted with compassion and used deadly force against the evil people that had captured me. It seems we need such people in these times. I hope to become one as I heal and get stronger."

Helen now pointed her finger at the dais, letting it sweep across the council.

"Shame on you if you banish this man from town. Shame on you if you don't defend him. He represents your best and if you cast him aside, you are not worthy to live free. You condemn yourselves to slavery, the slavery of expedient choices, the slavery of the easy way over the right way even if it is hard. I could not live in a town such as that. A town that didn't have the pride to defend their best."

With that she sat down. Applause now began, quietly, in one corner of the room. It was taken up by others and soon spread through the whole audience. Steve quickly put a motion on the floor which gave the council three choices: one to reject the warrants, two to accept the warrants, or three to advise Cordell that a treaty would have to be negotiated and signed before any warrants could be served on Hillsboro citizens.

With a voice vote, the council went down the line approving the third option. When the vote came to Raymond Culver, he knew he was outnumbered and voted with the majority. Cheers went up. Anne hugged Jason, Catherine came up to give him a hug. Kevin came down from the dais and congratulated Jason.

The next day Steve Warner notified Phillip Cordell of the council's decision.

"In the absence of state of federal authority, we need a treaty between the two cities. We're glad to work on that with you so we can begin to cooperate and help one another."

"This is not a good way to begin cooperation."

"I trust you will take back the message that your warrants are not enforceable here in a different city and state."

He arranged for Cordell to be escorted to the city gate. There he could collect his courier and take him back. Steve did not accompany them to the gates. He didn't want to have to engage in a discussion about the courier's missing digit.

Chapter 36

W hen they got home, the whole family gathered in
the living room.
"I can't believe some of them wanted to hand
you over to Knoxville," Sarah said in disgust.

"Never mind that now," Jason said. "This isn't a
victory. A lot depends on what Knoxville decides to do
about this rebuff."

"It's a clever play, changing their story just enough to
put them in a good light and cast you and Clayton as the
bad guys," Kevin said.

"Yep. And it almost succeeded."

"That woman, Helen, saved the day," Anne said. "Her
story was compelling. I shudder to think of what might
have happened to us, me and the girls, if we had lost some
of the battles we fought."

"It's still a wild place out there," Catherine said.

"That's why I don't let you travel to the surrounding
towns without an armed escort," Kevin said. "We still have
anarchy. No state or federal government."

"I do wonder about that," Jason said. "I keep expecting
to see federal agents, or the army showing up any day." He
shook his head. "But back to the point, we need to be ready
and figure out a way to anticipate Knoxville's response."

"Send out spies?" Anne asked.

"We could," Jason said, "but it would be dangerous for
them. Maybe we set up sentinels along the probable
routes. If they're going to attack Hillsboro, they'll bring a
large force. Lord knows their militia is big enough. A

couple of hundred soldiers on the move should be easy to spot."

"They'd come down the interstate. It would be the easiest route," Kevin said.

"I agree," Jason said. "They'd have to bring support vehicles, along with troop trucks. It would be slow going, but easier than trying to navigate back roads which might not be passable by large vehicles." He thought for a moment. "We need to talk with Clayton."

"What do you have in mind?" Kevin asked.

"I have some ideas I want to run by him. We'll need his clan's help. I'm not sure how much support you'll get from the council to put together a militia to stand against a large force. They supported me now, but that may fade away in the face of a strong response from Knoxville. In any case we'll need to be warned if they come here."

That night Jason and Anne sat on their porch.

"You're going to see Clayton tomorrow?"

"Yes. I'll start early. I may be gone one or two nights."

"You're not planning to go to war with Knoxville, are you? You've done enough already."

"I'm planning on making sure my family is safe. Frankly, after today, I'm not sure how much loyalty I want to give to this town."

"Don't let Ray Culver get to you. There are people like him in every group. You have the support of many on the council, including Steve." She pulled him close to her. "And remember, your daughter and son-in-law are pretty well integrated into the city."

Jason sighed. "Yeah, Chief of Police and Ambassador at Large. Who would have thought we'd end up like this?"

"It's not such a bad life, is it?"

"No. It's just that the bad guys are still out there and it seems we have to deal with them ourselves."

"Vigilance is the price of freedom. That was a World War Two slogan. After, it didn't have a lot of meaning in people's lives...but it does now."

Anne reached over and kissed her husband. *And worry is the price of vigilance*, she thought.

The next day Jason and Kevin left to visit Clayton at his farm outside of town. They arrived that afternoon and sat down to talk.

Jason recounted what had gone on at the town council meeting. Clayton scowled as he listened.

"Seems like the town's already forgot about what we did for them. They ready to throw us over for their safety," he said with some bitterness in his voice.

"Not all of them. And they all voted in the end to send Cordell back empty handed."

"Still, it don't matter," Clayton continued as if he hadn't heard Jason. "I'd a done it anyway. Billy's kin. Got to defend our kin."

"That's what we need to talk about," Jason said. "If you remember, I proposed forming a group of rangers to maintain a watch out beyond our borders. In today's world, we can't just wait until danger comes calling at our gates. We need to know in advance what's coming so we can be ready for any threat."

"What you want from me?" Clayton asked.

"I want to create that ranger group using some of your young men and some of the town's militia. Kevin can gather the town's recruits."

"And do what?"

"We create a group. We send them out, fifty to one hundred miles. They watch the major roads. Those are still the main travel routes. And they let us know when danger approaches."

"How they gonna do that? We don't have radios. And how we gonna watch in all directions? You going to need a large group. We can't have all our young men out. They got to help on the farms."

"You're right," Jason said. "But for now, we concentrate on Knoxville. If they're going to respond we only have to watch one route, the I40 corridor."

"How they gonna let us know if they a hundred miles away?"

"We talked about that," Kevin said, "on the way over here. The group would drop off watchers in pairs along the route. They'd position themselves on high ridges with long sight lines. Each pair builds a signal fire that can be seen from the rear. When the first one sees any militia coming, they light their fire. Then as each watch post sees a signal fire, they light their own. Within minutes, we can get the signal relayed back to us that a group is on its way."

"We won't have any details, but we'll know there's a force coming. That's enough," Jason said.

Clayton looked thoughtful. "Might work. How much time we get out of it?"

"It's about a hundred and fifty miles to Knoxville. I figure it will take them four or five days. If we place watchers pretty far out, we can get four days' notice," Jason said "Each pair of watchers or rangers, will head back to Hillsboro after they light their signal fires. We'll need them here," Jason said.

"Okay, but how do we deal with them if they come? My people are outside of the city. We could get overrun."

"Yeah," Kevin said. "We don't want to fight them at the city barriers. If they bring any heavy weapons they could just stand off and pound us into submission."

"You think they got heavy weapons?" Clayton asked.

Kevin nodded. "They might. They could get them from the area National Guard armories."

"Hillsboro got them?"

"Yes, but we don't want to get into an artillery duel. We lose. The city will be damaged along with all the progress we achieved. We can't let them destroy the city.

"So, we go attack them before they come."

Jason shook his head. "There's no appetite for that. We don't know for sure what Knoxville will do. We offered an olive branch by suggesting we engage in treaty talks for mutual cooperation. We have to see if they take us up on the offer."

Clayton made a sound of disgust. "Not much chance. I heard what that Chairman was saying. He wants everybody under his control."

The men talked through the afternoon. They agreed that two ranger teams would be formed, made up of volunteers from the Jessup and Early clans and the city militia. It would be strictly a volunteer effort not needing any town council mandate or approval. Kevin would oversee the organization. The groups would be mixed together further tightening the connection between the city and the two clans. Clayton, Rodney and Jason would see to their training.

"We have to keep this simple," Jason said. "There's not much time. All we want them to do is to place themselves along the route and light a fire large enough to be seen by the scouts behind them."

"How many we gonna need?" Clayton asked.

"I think a dozen. If they spread out twenty to thirty miles apart, the fires should be able to be seen. The farthest post will be near Knoxville so we should get an early enough warning.

"And if they come, what you got in mind?" Clayton asked.

"Guerilla warfare Jason replied.

"And the heavy weapons?"

"Can't let them get near us," Kevin said.

"They could have 105 or 155 millimeter howitzers. The 105 can fire nearly nine miles and the 155 can reach out nearly fifteen miles."

"Damn," Clayton said. "We'd never see them."

"Right," Kevin replied. "And they could just lob shells into town, everywhere. All they need is to have someone with experience in artillery."

"You tell the mayor and council about all of this?"

Jason shook his head. "Wasn't my part to do. I was sort of on trial. Besides it wouldn't have helped to panic the council."

"I guess you right. Seems like they don't have much backbone."

The groups were quickly formed. From the clans, Clayton had to pare down the number of volunteers. For the teenagers it seemed like a exciting camping adventure in the woods for a week. Kevin had little difficulty as well recruiting from the militia. His recruits were generally older but included some teenage citizens who also thought the assignment sounded like a good outdoors adventure.

The teams were assembled and equipped to stay out in the field for a week. They practiced how to set up large bonfires without starting a forest fire. Rodney severely admonished them to make sure their fire pit was completely cleared and to make sure they had a clear line of sight to the next watch position behind them. The plan was to set up on ridgetops or rocky outcroppings. As soon as they lit their fires, they were to head back to town. In no way were they to engage the enemy.

Chapter 37

Sarah offered to join the ranger group, but neither Jason nor Anne would allow it. She was only a little disappointed, never being quite the warrior her sister had become. Her boyfriend, Tommy Wilkes, however, had joined, which worried her greatly.

Tommy insisted he would be the best choice to be one of the two sent out the farthest. He would be better able to assess the composition and strength of any advancing force, thereby providing Hillsboro with valuable information when he returned. The rangers lighting the subsequent fires would not have even seen the advancing troops, only the ones lighting the first signal fire.

The next step was to discuss with Steve Warner how to prepare for any aggression on the part of Knoxville. As Chief of Police and also in charge of the militia since that group had been purged and integrated to the police force, Kevin could make contingency plans. If something other than direct police work was required however, he would need to bring it to the town council. Something like defending Hillsboro against an attack from Knoxville would come under that directive.

"The council won't like this," Steve said.

"Won't like me being prepared?" Kevin asked.

"You know what I mean. Ray Culver is going to get some mileage out of this. He'll go back to his original theme that Jason led us astray by not paying the ransom."

"We aren't being attacked, we're just preparing for the possibility."

"You and I know that, but some may see it otherwise."

"Well I have to do my job. It would be a dereliction of duty not to prepare."

"I agree," Steve said with a sigh. "I'll defend your actions and we'll get approval. But be prepared to weather a shit storm from Culver. And remember, we can't put the town on a war footing for an extended period. We're still in rebuilding mode."

The town's ranger group was sent out after only a day's training. They moved fast, driving up the interstate in a convoy of three civilian cars. Cars that could be left abandoned on the highway, if necessary, as the rangers dispersed into the surrounding hills.

One by one the cars dropped off as the occupants headed into the forest. Tommy was the last. He was paired with Morgan Jessup, Clayton's oldest son. They drove on towards Knoxville. The two grew increasingly tense as they got closer. If they ran into the convoy while on the road, they might be detained. Both had purposely dressed as civilians. Tommy carried a civilian variant of the M16; Morgan carried a 30.06 bolt-action rifle. They hoped they would look like any other wandering souls trying to survive and find a community in this new world.

When he got near Newport, Tommy stopped the car. Morgan pointed to a sharp ridge on the east side of the interstate that stood out. It looked like just the place to use for watching and signaling. It would be a hard climb and they wanted to get there before nightfall. After taking a bearing on the ridge, the two young men shouldered their backpacks, climbed over the deer fencing, and headed up the slope into the forest.

Morgan led the way. He moved effortlessly through the woods, just like his father. Tommy struggled to keep up but was not going to let the younger teenager best him.

They jogged through the later afternoon, pushing up the slopes which got ever steeper. Finally, they had to crawl their way up on their hands and knees. They paused only for a moment to catch their breath at any flat area before going on.

It was all uphill now as they closed in on the ridge. The sun was dropping in the west when they came out on the exposed rocks. The two young men stood there gazing west into the light of the sun's afterglow. The high cirrus clouds to the west looked like they were on fire, bathed in a mixture yellows merging into orange and red. They stood quietly, absorbed by the beauty of the Tennessee hills now glowing in the evening light. Finally, Tommy broke the silence.

"We should set up a place for the signal fire."

Morgan nodded. He began to look around. "We need a clear sight line to the rear, from where we came."

They explored the ridge in the gathering dark until they found a place where the pressure had distorted the ridge line, causing part of it to jut out to the west. It was enough for one to look back to the south. You could see miles of the interstate and the mountains on either side. The two smiled.

Morgan began to scrounge the nearby brush for kindling and windfalls while Tommy cleared the area that would form the base of the fire. They would set up a fire with dried wood to make a large, hot blaze. Fresh wood, chopped by them, would then be added to create additional smoke in case the blaze was hard to see in the sunlight.

Tommy, being older at twenty-three and in the militia, took the lead. Morgan was seventeen, but every bit Tommy's match in size, strength and speed, having grown up in the mountains, hunting, trapping, and building shelters.

"Make sure that area's clear," Morgan said. "If it catches some of the grass and moss, the fire can go into the cracks and spread. Start a big forest fire that way."

When the area was clear, they began to build up a tower of dry wood with the tinder and smaller sticks at its base. Then the two set about cutting live branches to add smoke to the pyre. The trees on the ridge were small and stunted. They would be dense, owing to their slow growth and burn slowly, creating more smoke.

"I'll take the first shift," Tommy said. They would watch twenty-four hours a day. At night a convoy would be easier to spot from vehicle headlights. During the day, they would need to watch more carefully through the binoculars they had brought.

Daybreak came without incident. Tommy and Morgan had each gotten only about four hours of sleep during the night. They assessed their signal fire construction and, with a few additions to the structure, decided it was ready.

They ate in silence, dried venison and water. Morgan scrounged through the brush for some edible plants. Ten minutes later he came back, his hat filled with berries and leaves.

"What's all that?" Tommy askes.

"Huckleberries and wintergreen," Morgan replied.

"Looks like blueberries."

"It does. I think they're related. The berries aren't as dense as what you get on blueberry bushes." Morgan popped a small handful in his mouth and offered his hat to Tommy. "Tastes about the same. 'Course these are not too sweet, it being early in the season."

Tommy sampled the berries. "Not bad. You're right about the sweetness."

"Still good for energy." He picked up some of the leaves and started chewing on them. "Try the leaves. Like brushing your teeth.

Tommy took a few. He chewed for a few seconds as Morgan watched him. Suddenly Tommy's face lit up.

"It's like the chewing gum." He exclaimed. "That's amazing."

"Makes your mouth feel good," Morgan said.

"Probably helps for bad breath. We got more of that since the power went out. Living with the guys in the militia, it gets pretty rank sometimes."

"Show 'em where to find the mint."

"You sure know a lot about the woods," Tommy said.

"Grew up in them. Comes naturally."

Tommy looked reflective. "We need to know about these things since the EMP attack."

"Old ways are always worth knowing about. They're reliable. It's how we lived before we came down to Hillsboro and started farming." He looked away to the far hills. "Farming's better, I guess. We get more food. Can put up extra reserves."

"Like money in the bank," Tommy said.

Morgan smiled at him. "Yeah, that's it."

After finishing what Morgan had gathered, they got comfortable to watch. Neither was sleepy, so they took turns scanning the highway through the binoculars and making small talk.

"You think they'll come today?" Morgan asked.

"No way of knowing. Lieutenant Cameron...I mean Chief Cameron, I guess he's not a lieutenant anymore. He said they might not come at all, Sergeant Gibbs, Rodney, thinks they probably will."

"Kind of hope they don't. It'll be boring sitting here for a week or longer, but better for everyone if they don't come."

"You're right about that."

They sat in silence for a while as Tommy looked through the glasses.

Finally, Morgan spoke up again. "You going with that girl, Sarah? Jason's daughter?"

"Yeah. I'm gonna marry her."

"When you gonna do that?"

"She's only seventeen, so I guess I'll have to wait a year."

"Ain't she too young for you?"

"Her sister's married to Chief Cameron and he's about nine years older than her, so no. We're only six years apart." He turned to Morgan. "You got a girl?"

Morgan poked a stick into the rocky ground. "Nah. A couple girls hang around. They ain't bad, but I don't want to settle down. I like being in the woods, like this ranger thing. Maybe do something like this for a while."

"I'm not sure how long this group's going to stay together. I kind of like it as well. Beats being in a barracks with ten or more smelly guys."

"And you ain't one of them?" Tommy looked at him with a questioning look. "One of the smelly guys," Morgan said.

"Hell no. I chew wintergreen, keeps me fresh. I rub it on my pits as well."

Morgan grinned. "That's just stupid."

Later Morgan was watching through the binoculars. He saw some movement on the highway. They had focused their vigil on the turn where the highway first came into view.

"Got something," he said.

"Let me take a look." Tommy reached for the glasses. He studied the scene for a few moments.

"Military vehicles. I see some troop trucks and some Humvees. Light the fire."

He put down the binoculars as Morgan began to strike a flint with his knife, throwing sparks at the tinder. After a few strikes some of the pieces began to glow. He bent down and cupped them in his hands and gently blew on them. A tiny flame erupted. Morgan placed it in the rest of the tinder and began to blow it into burning. Soon the tinder was fully lit and the twigs started crackling.

"It's going. Soon as the larger branches catch, we can leave," Morgan said.

They watched as the pyre grew larger and hotter. Soon it was blazing.

"Let's go," Morgan said.

"Not yet," Tommy replied. "I need to get more information about this convoy. He moved away from the fire and looked through the binoculars again.

Tommy studied the vehicles. He wanted to get a count of the transport trucks and note whatever was included in the convoy. The information would help Kevin and the others to figure out how many men were coming.

"Come on," Morgan said. "We can't stay. They can see this fire. They'll know we're up here spotting them."

"Wait. Got to see the full convoy to know what's coming."

"We don't want to get caught. Then no one'll know what's coming."

"We won't get caught. You get us back to the car and we haul ass back to town. The convoy won't catch us once we get to the car."

He kept watching.

"Holy crap," Tommy said.

"What's up?"

Tommy got up from where he had been sitting, cradling the binoculars on his knees to steady them.

"They got two howitzers...and a tank. Shit. We can't let those weapons get near the town. Let's get out of here."

Before he was finished Morgan had turned and put some of the fresh wood on the now roaring fire. Thick, white smoke rose furiously in the heat column. It was carried high into the sky.

Then they turned and ran. The two young men flew through the woods, risking a turned or broken ankle in their haste. They slid and tumbled down the hills they had crawled up the day before, sometimes losing their backpacks or grip on their rifles in their falls. They only stopped to gather them and then set off on a run again.

What took four hours was completed in an hour. They slid down the last embankment to the highway fence and clamored over it. Reaching the car, they threw their backpacks into the back seat. Morgan held the weapons as Tommy started the car, turned it around, and headed off as fast as he dared, weaving in and out of the abandoned vehicles.

Chapter 38

As soon as Tommy and Morgan got back to town, Tommy went straight to Kevin's office and told him to get Jason. A half hour later, Tommy was giving his report.

"Could you tell what size howitzers they were?" Kevin asked.

Tommy shook his head. I'm not that familiar with the artillery. What about the tank?"

Again, Tommy shook his head. "I'm sorry to seem so dense, they were far away. It's not an Abrams, I can tell you that."

"M60 Patton, I'll bet," Jason said. Also very bad news. We might be able to stop the howitzers before they get to town, but I don't know how we stop the tank."

"If it's an M60, it can shoot over four thousand yards. It can blow open our wall and drive right through," Kevin said.

"With the infantry right behind it," Jason said.

Tommy looked worried as did the other two men. Kevin dismissed Tommy and told him to remain close to the militia barracks.

"From where Tommy said he saw the convoy, we have three days, maybe four, to get ready," Kevin said. "We'll need the mayor and the council, but we have to start our mobilization now. We can't do this sequentially."

"Aren't you taking a risk?"

Kevin looked at Jason. He felt more in control now, having been battle tested during the fight for Hillsboro and now confident in his abilities. "We don't have a choice. The council's approval is just a formality. If they don't approve mounting a defense, are we just going to lie down? You're not going to stand around and let the town deliver you to Knoxville. You're going to fight or retreat to the valley." Kevin pointed to his chest. "I'm going to fight, defend this town. I'll assemble my militia and work with Clayton. We'll repel these guys and settle up with the council later."

Jason smiled. "I'm on board with that. Looks like we're going to piss off some of the council again. You may lose your job, you know."

"Can't worry about that now. Let's talk to Steve and then we have to get busy."

The two men rushed over to city hall to see the mayor. They pushed past the receptionist who was trying to be officious, asking them about an appointment.

"No one makes appointments these days," muttered Kevin as they entered Steve's office followed by the very irritated woman.

Steve looked up from some paperwork with a surprised expression on his face.

"Tell her she can go," Kevin said, pointing to the receptionist.

"Thank you for trying to do your job, Alice, but it's okay. I can meet with these men."

When she had closed the door, Kevin spoke. "We just got a report from the rangers we sent out. There's a force on its way from Knoxville. They're three days out."

"Uh oh," Steve said.

"They've got two artillery pieces and a tank," Kevin said.

"Oh my God. That doesn't sound good."

"It's not," Kevin replied. "I know you have to bring this to the council, but I have to get my forces together to defend us. I can't wait for the council to meet and talk about this. I've got to start...this afternoon."

"But that's getting ahead of ourselves," Steve said.

Jason remained silent. This was Kevin's scene to play out. Jason understood he had already been discredited and couldn't take the lead.

"Steve," Kevin said. "I'm going to muster a defense force with or without the council's approval. I'll have Clayton's clans helping as well. There's nothing we can offer Knoxville at this point. Jason is not going to hang around only to have the council turn him over to Knoxville's people. That's just not going to happen."

"Now you're acting like Jason," Steve said.

Kevin leaned over the desk. "Steve, this is an existential threat. Life or death of this city. I have to engage the enemy *before* they get to our gates. You don't want to know what will happen if those guns get in range, or if that tank can make it to the wall. They can tear apart this city."

He stared hard into Steve's eyes. "You get me cover with the council, or you don't. I'm going to do what I can to keep this force from killing our city. If you need to find another Chief of Police when this is over, that's fine with me. Remember if it comes to that, be thankful for that problem. It means you still have a functioning city."

Steve sighed. "I should have known things wouldn't be smooth going. What are you going to do?"

"I'm going to mobilize our militia. We'll fight a guerilla battle, hopefully far enough away that the town never realizes it. You get an approval from the council if you can. Some people may notice the mobilization going on, but make sure no one tries to stop it." He leaned his fists on the desk. "I won't allow that to happen."

Kevin straightened up. "We have to go now."

"I'm on your side, you know," Steve said.

Kevin looked at him. "I know. I think you also know I'm doing what I have to do." He turned and left the office with Jason.

Outside Jason stopped Kevin. "I should go talk with Clayton while you pull the militia together."

Kevin nodded. "We have to leave as soon as possible."

"Tomorrow at first light," Jason said.

"Tomorrow."

They both headed back to the police station. Jason grabbed one of the old cars used by the department and headed out of town. Kevin gathered the six cops at the station and sent one to the building housing the militia and the other five to run down the militia members that were off duty and, hopefully, at their homes.

An hour later, Jason pulled into Clayton's farm yard. He found his friend in the barn repairing a broken plow.

"Figured I'd see you soon," Clayton said when Jason walked in. "When Morgan got back, he told me what was coming. He wasn't sure what exactly they are, but I know they ain't good for Hillsboro."

"You're right about that. We have to stop them well before they get to town. The artillery could have a range of fourteen miles and I can't fully describe what that tank can do."

"Can we use mortars?"

Jason shook his head. Tank's too armored. Mortar fragments would just bounce off it."

"We got any artillery to shoot back?"

"We've got a howitzer and there's an artillery piece over in Taylorsville." He paused. "The biggest problem is that we shoot and miss, we kill trees or some roadbed. They shoot and miss, they hit buildings and kill people. We'd have to be precise, they can be sloppy and still destroy the town."

"Not a good trade-off."

"I agree. The only way to deal with this is to put a guerilla force together...today. We have to engage them while they're on the way here. Ambush them, stop their advance. If they attack back, we retreat into the forest. Then we come back and do it again."

"You think that'll stop them?"

"It's our only hope. Kevin's mobilizing the militia right now. We need you to round up as many of your clan as you can. We mix the groups. The militia will benefit from your clan's skills in the woods and you'll benefit from the militia's firepower. We should be heading out tomorrow."

Clayton stared hard at Jason, then put down his tools and headed to the door. "Not much time. I'll get my boys on it."

Chapter 39

The clansmen filtered into the city from the late afternoon into the evening. They had been instructed to go to the militia headquarters. It was the same building used by Joe Stansky. The facilities were considered the most practical, having been set up for the purpose of housing a large group. This militia, however, had been purged of men tainted by misplaced loyalties or criminal records.

As soon as the men arrived their weapons were checked and extra ammunition provided from the militia's reserves. Most of the clansmen had 30.06 or 30-30 rifles with a smattering of AR15 variants. One man had a Henry chambered in .44 magnum. There was no ammunition for him. He was offered an M16, but refused, preferring his more familiar weapon.

The men with the AR15's chambered for .223 ammunition were told to exchange their rifles for M16s unless they had a large amount of ammunition. The militia had a plentiful supply of M16s along with the 5.56 mm ammunition. The AR15s were at risk for jamming or worse if they shot the slightly larger NATO round.

The militia officers moved quickly, knowing their impending deadline for departure. When the clansmen had been checked out and given additional ammunition, Kevin assembled the group. There were seventy-five men gathered in the courtyard. Kevin stood on roof of a Humvee and addressed the men.

"The civilians you see among you are all volunteers. This operation we're going on has not yet been authorized by the city council. There is no time to wait for their approval. Therefore, this has to be a volunteer mission."

He scanned the group. Between himself and Clayton, they had been able to round up just fifty-five militia and twenty clansmen.

"There is a military convoy on its way from Knoxville. They are headed here and we have to assume their intention is to attack us. They're equipped with two artillery pieces and a tank. This along with mortars, machine guns and rifles. We don't know how many there are, but I estimate from the number of vehicles in the convoy, they have over two hundred men."

Kevin noted that all the clansmen came with their backpacks and some form of bedroll and tarp for sleeping and protection from rain.

"This force assembled here will go out tomorrow morning," he continued. "Those in the militia will be provided backpacks. You'll carry rations for five days. You'll have water and purification tablets which will let us drink from available ground water sources. You'll carry extra ammunition in your packs.

"This is going to be a guerilla campaign. We don't have the forces to directly engage the enemy in any frontal assault. We'll attempt to stop the convoy from reaching our city by ambushing them. If they attack, we retreat. Then we come back to do it again. They will have the superior numbers and weapons but we will use the forest to our advantage.

"We're defending our city, our families, the progress that we have made. If anyone feels they can't go, you can leave now. There will be no repercussions, but everyone going must be committed to not letting this force reach our city. Their guns and their tank can destroy us. We can't let that happen."

There was shuffling amongst the crowd. Four men left, quickly and without incident. The rest were told to get their packs, load up with food and ammunition, and wait in the courtyard.

Kevin moved to a separate room with his officers to organize the group, with Jason and Clayton joining him.

"I'm going to divide the men into two groups," Kevin said. "Each group will position themselves on either side of the interstate. We want to be able to fire on the convoy from both sides. I'll coordinate overall between both forces. Rodney Gibbs will lead one group and I'll lead the other. We'll communicate by radio between the two groups. We'll be most effective if we coordinate our attacks."

Jason took Kevin aside for a moment. "I'm going to grab the M107 .50 cal rifle in the warehouse. I'll place myself way ahead of your forces and start sniping them. I'll leave tonight so I can be in position ahead of you. I may be able to give you more time to find a good spot to set up. Good job with the plan. Just be sure to get out on time."

Kevin nodded and Jason left the meeting.

He hurried to the warehouse to retrieve the M107 and ammunition.

When Jason arrived at the house, Anne met him at the door.

"What's going on? I saw some of the police going down the street, knocking on doors."

"They're rounding up all the militia members who were not at the barracks."

"Why would they do that?"

"Knoxville is on the march. They're coming to attack us."

"Oh no!"

"Our scouts saw them, a sizeable military convoy from the description."

"What does that mean for us...for you?

"I don't know. The council will blame me, but I don't know what they'll do about it."

He brushed past Anne and headed to the bedroom. Anne followed.

"What are you going to do?"

"We have to stop the convoy before it gets here. They have some heavy weapons that can destroy the town." He rummaged through the closet and pulled out a gun case. "I'm going to go up the highway and try to slow the convoy down by sniping them. Shooting from the surrounding hills."

"Haven't you done enough?"

Jason stopped and turned to his wife. He took her hands in his. "This is about saving you and our family...as well as saving the town. They're really one and the same now. I can help with that by doing what I know how to do. What I was trained to do."

The concern on Anne's face did not disappear. She sighed.

"I don't want to lose you, that's all. I need you, Adam needs you, and the girls still need you."

He pulled her into his arms. "The best way to do that, to protect all of us, is for me to help out how I can. Kevin's leading a group that will go out to fight the convoy. They'll use ambushing tactics and avoid a direct confrontation. My shooting will only help."

"Does Catherine know what's going on?"

"I assume so. I haven't talked to her."

"It sounds dangerous...what Kevin is doing."

"More dangerous than what I'm going to do, really. I'll be fighting from a distance. He'll be much closer."

Just then the front door opened.

"Jason," a voice called out. It was Catherine.

"I'm in the bedroom. Come on up."

Catherine walked into the room. She had her backpack and rifle with her and looked ready to head into battle.

"Where are you going?" Jason asked.

"I heard about the convoy. I'm going with you."

"Did you talk to Kevin about this?"

Catherine nodded. I saw him just after you left. He told me what you were going to do and I want to go with you."

"Now both of you are going?" Anne said with alarm.

"I can't stay out of this fight," Catherine replied. "Kevin agrees. I was in more danger during our fight with Stansky."

"She's right," Jason said.

He kissed Anne. "We have to get going. We have to get out in front of our ambush force. We'll try to slow the convoy down. That's the role we can play. You take Adam and Sarah and go to the south side of the town. You'll be farther away from any shelling if the convoy gets through. Find a basement to stay in."

"How much time do we have?" Anne asked.

"If we don't slow or stop them, three or four days. Check with Steve. He'll probably be initiating plans to get as many people to safe areas as possible. If the town is overrun, get out and head to the valley. The others there will help you. We'll meet there if things go bad. Your job is to protect Sarah and Adam."

Anne nodded. The fear on her face was now replaced with determination. Jason could see her courage rise to the challenge they faced. It was the same when she fought with him to defeat the gangs that had attacked their farm in the valley.

"We have to go," Jason turned to Catherine. "You take my M110. You used it well before. I'll carry the M107." He turned back to his wife. "Take your rifle and pistol with you when you go to find shelter."

With Anne's help they packed some food and water bottles along with purification tablets. Both brought waterproof ground cloths, a thermal blanket, and change of socks; dry feet were important in the field.

"Kevin gave me one of the cars the police use. It'll help us get down the highway quickly."

"Is there danger of any outlaws ambushing us?" Catherine asked.

"Always. Chance we have to take. We need to move fast."

They both kissed Anne goodbye and headed out the door.

Jason would risk using the headlights during the night. He knew it would alert anyone watching the interstate but he needed to move fast. When the moon rose later, he would try to turn them off and navigate by moonlight.

Catherine kept her M110 ready in the front seat. The big .50 cal M107 was laying alongside of her where Jason could reach it if they were attacked.

"Watch the overpasses and interchanges as we approach. They're favorite spots for ambushing. We may get lucky and no one will be out at night, but we can't be too careful," he said.

Three hours out, Jason saw a barricade of cars set up just before an exit ramp for the small town of Chamberlain.

"That's not just abandoned cars. That was set up." He slowed the car down and brought it to a halt in between two abandoned cars. They were sixty yards from the barricade. "We can jump out and get cover behind these cars if there's someone at the barricade."

They sat and watched. Jason cut the engine. Catherine quietly unlatched her door. Jason cradled the .50 caliber rifle in his lap and did the same. They rolled their windows down. The night was still. Nothing moved.

"Should we go ahead?" Catherine asked.

"Just watch for a few more minutes. Someone may be trying to figure out what we're up to. If there's someone there, I want them to show their hand while were in a good defensive position."

Then they both heard it. It sounded like footsteps on pavement, up ahead, behind the car barricade. Then they saw a shadow move past a gap in the cars. After that, nothing. No sound or sight.

"Someone's there," whispered Catherine. "Do we just wait?"

"Patience. They'll show their hand soon enough. We can't go forward. We'll have no cover once we're past these cars."

Catherine remembered Jason's mantra, "Let the enemy show itself."

Finally, a shadow emerged over the trunk of a car. "Come out with your hands in the air and you won't be hurt," it called out. The shadow included what looked like a rifle aimed at them.

Catherine looked over at Jason.

"Let me go first," he said. "If they shoot, I'll draw the first fire. You go a second behind me. Get behind the hood of the car next to you. You'll be protected by the engine."

Catherine nodded. Jason sprang from the car, Catherine a moment later.

Shots rang out and the bullets whistled past as Jason and Catherine ducked behind the cars.

"Stay down," Jason called over to her.

He crawled around the backside of the car which was stopped partially sideways on the highway. He peeked around the front tire. There, silhouetted against the night sky, was the figure doing the shooting. Jason aimed his rifle, the figure dropped behind the trunk. Jason lowered the rifle and fired three rounds through the trunk at the level he guessed the figure was crouching. He heard the clatter of the rifle on the pavement.

Not hearing or seeing any other evidence of another shooter, Jason called out to Catherine to cover him and ran forward bent low to the pavement.

As he expected, the man behind the trunk lay in a bloody heap. Two of the .50 caliber rounds had hit him. They were powerful enough to penetrate an engine block. They had easily gone through both metal sides of the car and torn apart the body.

"Don't come back here," Jason called out. "It's not pretty."

Catherine stopped short.

"The .50 cal makes a nasty mess when it hits soft tissue." He looked around. "Someone'll be coming soon, they'll have heard the shots. Let's get this car moved," he pointed to the compact on the end of the line. "We can drive around on the shoulder if we can push this farther off the road."

They got the car in neutral and both of them put their shoulders to the car to get it rolling. They ran back to their vehicle and started it up. Jason threaded it through the blockade and accelerated down the road. Shots rang out behind them. Catherine ducked down to the floor. Jason's weaving through stalled cars had the effect of blocking a clear shot at their fleeing vehicle and soon they were out of effective range.

"Desperate times still," he said as they motored on.

"There can't be much to steal from anyone now," Catherine replied. "There's fewer people on the roads and fewer supplies. You'd think they'd just start farming somewhere."

"I guess some of them don't know how or can't imagine doing anything involving hard labor. Frankly I'm not that interested in their motivation, just in avoiding them."

They pressed on through the night. Jason killed the headlights when the moon came up. He had to go more slowly, but it felt better not to advertise their passing so clearly.

By daylight Jason was getting worried.

"We're closing in on the convoy. Both of us are moving towards each other. We can't get caught on the road, so I have to guess when it's time to bail on the car and take to the woods."

"How far have we come?"

Jason looked at the speedometer. "About sixty miles. It's slow going with all the abandoned cars and trucks."

"What do we do when we stop? Do we set up there?"

"We'll go into the forest and keep moving forward as fast as we can until we encounter the convoy. Then we go to work."

Chapter 40

General McKenzie felt good. He was moving at a steady pace even though he was taking the time to clear vehicles from the interstate. It was a time investment for the future. When they had Hillsboro under control rapid transport between the two cities would be helpful. He stopped the convoy each night to keep his troops rested and to make sure they did a good job of clearing the abandoned vehicles. It was work better done in daylight.

He thought about Jason's comment that Tom Horner had related to himself and Phillip about Hillsboro having a Swiss-style armed civilian militia. *Fat lot of good that'll do them. Wait until they experience the 105 Howitzer.* His two artillery pieces, even without the tank, would bring Hillsboro to its knees. They would be begging to discuss terms with him.

McKenzie let himself have a moment of thinking about the accolades he would receive for subduing Hillsboro without a major conflict, loss of life, or property. *Proper intimidation, that's the key.* It would all be played out in four days.

In the evening he let his mind wander to how the capitulation would play out. He imagined bringing Jason and the other man back in chains to parade in front of the town's people as example of their power...his power. Maybe he would bring back the current mayor and some other leading figures as insurance of the town's compliance with whatever he ordered. A smile crossed his face when he thought about that scene; like a Roman general returning from his conquests.

Hillsboro for its resources, then Johnson City. With the eastern front secure, they'd go after Nashville and then on to Memphis. They could establish an empire from the Piedmont to the Mississippi. Tom's vision seemed possible. *And if the feds come around, they'll have to deal with us. We'll be too large and powerful to ignore.*

"Get some sleep," Jason said. "I'm going to drive through the day and cover as many miles as I can."

"Will we stop after today?"

"Let's see how far we get. I'd like to get a hundred miles out. I don't think we can risk getting any closer while on the interstate."

Jason drove on while Catherine tried to sleep in the back seat. By mid-afternoon, he stopped, exhausted. He'd been driving all day and the night before.

"Can you drive for a while? Even slowly. I have to rest and we need to keep pushing out."

"You trust me behind the wheel?" Catherine asked with a mischievous grin.

"You can drive. I showed you and I know Kevin let you drive the Humvees. If you can drive one of those, you can drive a car. This is much easier to maneuver. Just don't push it. Pick your way along."

"Yes sir," she replied giving him a mock salute.

"Smart aleck," Jason said. He climbed into the back seat and with a long sigh stretched out his body across the seat. "Nothing like these old cars with their long bench seats."

Catherine carefully threaded her way through the abandoned cars. In the few clear places she accelerated, briefly touching fifty miles per hour at times.

"Don't scare me," Jason called out from the back seat.

"Don't be a back-seat driver. Just relax and rest. I'm slowing down when it gets crowded."

Three hours later, Jason awoke with a start. Catherine was slowly trying to make her way around a multi-car pile-up involving a tractor-trailer that had happened over two years ago.

"Where are we?" He said as he sat up.

"How would I know?"

"I mean how far out are we?"

She looked at the odometer. "About one hundred and twenty-five miles." She pointed through the windshield. "This is going to be tough going. I may have to go back and cross over into the other set of lanes to get around this mess."

Jason looked at the sky and then his watch. "Let's stop here. We must be getting close. We'll go on foot."

He got out of the car and stretched. After shouldering their backpacks, they grabbed their rifles, headed across the highway to the west, and into the woods. They climbed into the hills before turning north to follow the interstate.

"We have to move fast," Jason said. "Cover as much ground as we can."

They set out at a trot, snaking around the dense brush and wild rose brambles. Catherine soon took the lead. She was light-footed and readily found a way through the trees and rocks. The two carried on with their rifles held low in one hand, swinging back and forth.

Jason felt a surge of adrenalin coursing through his body. He had to hold himself in check to not sprint forward. Their jogging pace was one he could keep up for long hours. He could see by Catherine's graceful, economic movements that she could as well.

His whole body tingled with energy and anticipation. The fatigue that had enveloped him in the car was now washed away. The nap helped some, but Jason knew it was more than that. He was energized by being in the woods again; by being on a mission again, helping to save people. He was using his skills as a sniper and a woodsman and he had to admit that the effect was invigorating. His senses were sharpened. The complex smells of the woods: pine, leaf mold, an occasional whiff of a forest herb, and the dank and darker odors of a creek making its way through a hollow, all registered as they jogged along.

His mind and body absorbed all his senses could distinguish. With a pang of guilt Jason realized that this experience, this type of mission, made him feel alive. He loved Anne, their son, Adam, and the joys of life with his family, but this, being in the woods, racing to do battle with the enemy, brought a sharpness to his being that city life could not give.

They leapt the smaller creeks, splashed through the larger ones, never stopping. The climbs were slower, sometimes requiring them to scramble hand and foot up a slope. They would pause for a moment to catch their breath and, without a word, set out again. Throughout the afternoon they would occasionally head back towards the interstate which followed the river valley to scan the road for signs of the convoy. Then they would move back from the ridge and continued north. They jogged, slid, and clawed their way forward. Along the way, Catherine found some faint game trails which improved their pace.

The afternoon had turned into evening. Jason indicated they should head towards the interstate again and then stop to eat something. They sat quietly, eating the dried venison and pork they carried, washing it down with water.

"We have to be getting close now, don't you think?" Catherine asked.

"Yeah. We'll keep going after a short rest, but we should check for the convoy more frequently."

"Do you think they're moving at night?"

"No way to know for sure." Jason looked out over to the highway. "My guess is that they're not. Stopping will keep his men fresh and avoid any accidents or problems with clearing the road. It would be more difficult at night." He turned back to Catherine. "We'd have seen them by now if they had been going day and night."

"You're doing well," Jason said, changing the subject. "You still move more easily than I do in the woods."

"I learned it from you."

"But you've taken that skill beyond me."

"Maybe it's just that I'm not as large as you, so it's easier."

Jason smiled at his step-daughter. He had taught her to shoot along with the rest of the family, but she had taken to it and excelled. She was a natural sharpshooter and had played an important sniper role in the battles they had fought together. His smile broadened as he thought that such an attractive girl was also so adept in the woods...and so deadly.

"Did you feel it? He asked.

"Feel what?"

"The energy. Being in the woods, being on the hunt, running to engage the enemy."

Catherine smiled and looked down at the leaves where she sat. She seemed almost shy now.

"I felt it. Not sure what to think about it."

"It's what a warrior feels, the rush of engaging the enemy. The rush of fighting to protect others, the ones you love. You have that in you. I could tell early on." He paused for a moment. "And you have the skills to go with that instinct."

"I'm not sure how I like the killing though. When Bird got wounded and died, that shook me."

"I know. But it didn't stop you from doing your job in the later fight. And it didn't stop you from going with Billy to help Lori Sue. That's what a warrior does, run to the battle in order to save others."

"I couldn't stay away. Billy needed help, Lori Sue and Donna needed help."

Jason smiled and nodded.

"Does that make me a freak? I want to have a family someday, be normal."

"Not sure how we'll define normal in these coming years." Jason said. "But, no," he continued, "feeling like you do doesn't make you a freak. It makes you strong. You and Kevin will raise strong boys and girls. They may not have the warrior spirit, but they'll be strong people, like your sister, Sarah. She's strong, but she isn't a warrior."

Catherine sat and pondered what Jason had said for a few quiet moments.

"What do we do when we find the convoy?" she asked.

"We start shooting, sniping."

"We start killing them, just walking along?"

Jason shook his head. "That may happen, but first we'll try to stop the vehicles, the troop trucks, the Humvees, the artillery pieces which are set up on wheeled carriages."

"What about the tank?"

Jason shook his head. "Can't do anything about the tank. But it probably won't go on without the rest of the convoy."

He got up and stretched his arms. "Let's go. We can move in the dark, just more slowly."

They grabbed their gear and started through the woods

Chapter 41

Kevin departed the morning after Jason and Catherine left. He sent twenty of his men out ahead in pickup trucks. They were to try to get one hundred miles up the road and stop to wait for the rest. The main body of men set out on foot in a quick march. Kevin's plan was to drive them day and night, allowing only an hour rest every six hours. He assumed the Knoxville force would only move during daylight. While he risked exhaustion, he knew that he needed to get as much distance between him and Hillsboro as possible.

He couldn't expect his small force to stop the convoy with their first skirmish. It might take repeated ambushes followed by retreating and regrouping, during which the convoy would move forward. His men would have to backtrack quickly towards town, moving faster than the convoy, to set up another ambush. Kevin knew he needed as much territory as he could establish to give him the space for repeated attacks to wear down the approaching force.

The town council met in emergency session the day after Kevin departed with his volunteers. Steve Warner presided. He was feeling overwhelmed since taking over from Jason. Few council meetings had been routine, filled with progress reports on electrification and other projects aimed at bringing back some of the services lost from the EMP attack. Most had been crisis meetings with his loyalty being questioned at times. Today would be no different.

When he announced that an attack force was headed to Hillsboro pandemonium erupted. Steve's further announcement that a volunteer defense force had departed the day before without any council authorization only increased the discord. After a long minute of gaveling the session back into order, he tried to explain in more detail what had taken place.

Immediately Raymond Culver stood up and interrupted him.

"We don't need to hear all the details. Especially if you're going to shade them to make this action seem less treasonous," he said in a loud voice. "These men went out to engage in an armed battle with another city without our approval. In effect they have unilaterally started a war with Knoxville."

"I wouldn't put it quite that way—"

"I'm sure you wouldn't," Raymond said, interrupting him. "You have always excused this behavior starting with Jason's actions. And speaking of him, he's the one who led us to this point. He decided to not pay the fine demanded by Knoxville and to kidnap their leader instead. He started this mess and should be put in jail or banished from the city."

Others now joined in with Culver's opposition demanding a motion to sanction Jason and Kevin for their actions. Steve knew he had little support. With Kevin and Catherine gone from the chamber, there was only Bob Jackson, who headed up the water power project, and Dr. Morgan, head of the hospital. However, Dr. Morgan's support was not all that assured. He was in danger of being seriously outvoted on any motion he allowed to come to the floor.

First of all," Steve began. "I'm not an apologist for Jason or anyone else."

A supporter of Culver tried to interrupt but Steve gaveled him into silence.

"I will not allow anyone to interfere with orderly discussions. I have the floor. If you don't want to abide by the council rules, I will have you ejected. I am the interim mayor, approved by this council. I run these meetings and I will have order."

He could only hope some of the council members would give him cause to be ejected. It could reduce his probable vote deficit.

"Secondly," Steve said, "Mr. Culver disingenuously refers to Knoxville's ransom demand as a fine. We've been through that bit of revisionism started by their spokesman, Cordell. I, along with most of you didn't buy it then and I don't buy it now. In spite of Raymond's repetition, it remains a falsehood."

He paused for a moment. Someone started to speak, but Steve gave them a sharp look and they stopped.

"My last point is that the group that left town was an all-volunteer group. There is no precedent for what is happening, but there is no edict that people can't come and go without council's approval. We are not a police state. If a group feels they need to defend themselves, individually, then they have the right to do it."

"Were you aware of this group and what they intended?" Someone shouted out.

Steve looked at the man. "One more outburst from you and I'll have you ejected."

There were two armed men from the Police Department in the chamber to keep order. They were under Steve's orders as acting mayor.

"To answer your question, yes. As I just said, there is no law or edict that would cause me to tell the men they were acting illegally."

A hand went up and Steve nodded to the member.

"Where is Jason? And for that matter, where is Catherine? She's a member of the council and not present."

"I assume they both left. Probably with the volunteer force. Jason was present when I met with Kevin but I didn't speak directly with him. The volunteer force was organized and directed by Kevin. As far as I know Jason had nothing to do with it."

Raymond Culver now requested the floor.

"We have to intercede. This has gone far enough. First Jason, now Cameron, our Chief of Police. We are betrayed by these men. I move that we send an emissary out to meet the convoy and consider their demands. We can avoid an attack if we can get to them before this foolishness erupts into an open gun battle. It's still not too late to consider what it will take to allow us to live in peace with Knoxville."

"Hear, hear." Another council member called.

Steve looked over at Bob Jackson who was conversing with the town's only legal guide, Andrew Smithfield, a lawyer who settled personal injury claims before the EMP attack. Andy got up from consulting his rule book and whispered to Steve.

"That is not a legitimate motion," Steve said after listening to Smithfield, "All motions must come from me as Chairman of the council. A floor motion needs a super majority to get accepted for discussion and vote."

"How many is that?" One of Culver's supporters asked.

"Seventy-five percent of the council. That's nine members, so the motion needs seven people."

"It should be seventy-five percent of those present," Raymond shouted.

"Not according to the rules.

A long discussion ensued, barely under control, but not disorderly enough to give Steve an excuse to eject anyone from the meeting. After motion, counter motion, and appeals to arcane parts of Robert's Rules of Order, all of which nearly had Andy Smithfield to throwing up his hands in disgust and confusion, Steve had to accede to a vote using the present quorum of members. The vote now needed only five members to pass.

After closing arguments on both sides of the issue, Steve called the vote. Raymond Culver had three other council member's support. Bob Jackson voted against the motion as did Steve. Dr. Morgan, thankfully, joined him in a nay vote.

"The motion offered by Ray Culver will not be considered," Steve intoned.

"What are we here for, then? If it's not to try to mitigate this irresponsible action on the part of Cameron?" Raymond asked with some bitterness.

"We need to be discussing what we do to prepare for an attack," Steve said.

The council soldered on. Steve could see a hardening of the division in the group. Ray Culver had coalesced a group around him that wanted to radically reduce the role of the militia in the life of Hillsboro. This position seemed to Steve and others to be suicidal. He realized that the issue would be one that all of Hillsboro's citizens would have to participate in. And to do that they would need a clear picture of the world outside of their city. The world with its lack of structure and laws.

By morning Jason and Catherine were running on empty. They slogged on through the night with an ever-slowing pace. The moon rising after midnight had made the latter part of the night's running somewhat easier; but that was offset by their growing fatigue.

They reached a hilltop as the sun was coming over the hills to the east. Jason called a halt. They headed back towards the highway to check out where they could best set up.

A half mile ahead the hills on each side of the road squeezed close. The road twisted and turned and there were a larger number of wrecked and abandoned cars creating a bottleneck on the southbound lanes. The two of them walked forward along the mountain ridge until they came to a spot where it dropped away to the river below in a steep, rocky cliff. The position presented a clear line of fire to the choke point in the road.

"This looks like a good spot," Jason said. "We have a clear line of sight to the road ahead. The convoy will have to stop to clear the wrecks. They'll be vulnerable to our shooting. We may be able to hold them up here for a full day."

"How far is it?"

Jason took out his spotting scope.

"It's about a half-mile. Seven hundred and forty yards."

"That's getting near the end of my range with the M110."

"Yeah. It will be difficult shooting. Your scope is set for one hundred yards, correct?"

Catherine nodded.

"Just dial in the correction out to seven hundred yards. You'll be close and can adjust on the fly from there."

"Can I do any damage from this distance?" Catherine asked.

"Oh yeah. You can take out tires. You can take down personnel if we need to do that, keep them pinned down. I'll try to disable some of the vehicles, with the .50 cal. The 107 can carry out to almost two thousand yards, so I'm well in my range. Remember, the farther we shoot from, the safer it is for us."

They set up their shooting positions and then settled down to wait.

"You go to sleep," Jason said. "I'll take watch for three hours."

Catherine didn't object and settled herself on the ground as comfortably as she could. Within minutes she was asleep.

The twenty men sent ahead by Kevin stopped on the second day. They had reached eighty-five miles and were at a place where the highway got pinched by a bluff on the east and the river on the west. The median was eliminated to fit the highway through with minimal blasting of the steep slope to the east.

Tommy Wilkes led the advance team. He called a halt and set the men to climbing the ridge. Once on top, he radioed Kevin.

"Mile eighty-five. We've stopped. Waiting for you to catch up."

"Roger that," came the reply. "We should be there in six hours."

Few words were used in case Knoxville was on the same frequency.

Tommy had the men set up shooting positions. They were three hundred feet above the roadway. It would be easy shooting. It would also be hard for the opposing force to assault their position.

That same morning General McKenzie got his convoy going after a quick morning meal. He had a half dozen armored personnel carriers, four transport trucks, some loaded with supplies, some with troops. In addition, there were a six Humvees, four of them with .50 caliber machine guns and two of them towing the howitzers. A tanker truck loaded with diesel fuel brought up the rear. The M60 tank had a range of three hundred miles so if there was little maneuvering, it could get to Hillsboro and back on one tank. Two of the personnel carriers were loaded with ammunition for the tank, the howitzers and the men's rifles. General McKenzie felt satisfied he had what he needed to bring Hillsboro under his control.

The convoy lumbered out. They would be half way to Hillsboro by the end of the day if they didn't run into too many blockages. He had decided overnight to move the convoy to the other roadway if it was clearer when they came to a blockage. It would save time. Two days on the road with two or three to go would get him to his objective.

"You going to turn the tank loose on the town when we get there?" One of his lieutenants asked.

McKenzie shook his head. "I'll let the town see it from a distance. I'll send a messenger out under a white flag to also let them know there are two howitzers dialed in on the town. They won't see them. I'll leave those teams behind, about five miles back. It won't take them many shots to zero in on the town."

"They won't stand a chance," the man said in admiration.

McKenzie noted the tone in his voice. After his victory the whole town would share that admiration and he would be as popular as the Chairman. He'd have more influence over Tom when this was all over.

"They'll give in after they understand what they're up against," McKenzie replied.

"Kind of wish we'd have to use the tank and howitzers," the lieutenant said.

"You got to witness the few practice shots we took. If we do this without firing another shot that just saves our ammunition for Johnson City or Nashville. You can bet we'll need to use them there."

The man smiled.

Chapter 42

That evening, Kevin's main force joined with Tommy's team. Kevin sent half of the men, under Rodney Gibbs' command, across the Pigeon River to climb the hills on the west side of the highway. The others joined Tommy's advance team.

"You picked a good spot," Kevin said when they were in position. "It'll be hard to counter attack us up this slope."

"I figure we can hold them here for days," Tommy said with much enthusiasm.

"I wouldn't count on days, but one day would be good."

"How'll they get to us?" Tommy asked.

"The tank's gun, or the artillery pieces."

Jason and Catherine kept watch through the morning. Around noon, they both heard the rumble of diesel engines. Jason scanned the road with his binoculars and spotted the convoy coming around a corner over a couple of miles north of their position.

"Here they come," he said.

Catherine put her earplugs in and lay down at her shooting position.

"Stay loose. They could be a half hour getting to our target spot. I'll take the first shots, try to stop the lead vehicle. Once the shooting starts, you shoot out some tires, cabs, anything that will disrupt them and sow confusion."

As the convoy got closer, Jason saw that it was led by an armored personnel carrier or APC. The heavily armored

vehicle had an M2 .50 caliber machine gun along with an
Mk19 grenade launcher mounted in an armored turret. *No
way I'm going to stop that.*

When the convoy reached the target area, Jason
sighted the second vehicle, a Humvee, also with a .50
caliber machine gun mounted on it. The Humvee had
lighter armor than the APC and Jason had a chance to
knock out the engine. *If I can stop the other vehicles, the
APC will stop.*

He sighted the grill and fired his rifle. The M107 gave a
solid kick in the shoulder and a loud report. Catherine
jerked her head around in response. The bullet skimmed
across the hood missing the cab. His second shot hit the
grill and ripped it open.

The Humvee stopped and three men leapt out to
crouch behind the vehicle. Jason sent more rounds at the
stalled vehicle, smashing the windshield and tearing
through the cab. The machine gun swung around and
started firing at the ridge. The gunner had not pinpointed
their location so he just sprayed the ridge, hoping to
suppress the sniper rounds.

Now the APC turned it's .50 caliber machine gun
towards the ridge and began firing. The rounds were
coming closer. Then the grenade launcher fired. This
weapon had a range of sixteen hundred yards and could
fire at a rate of forty to sixty rounds per minute. The
grenades started hitting the ridge to their left, exploding
the rocky bank. The operator fanned it closer to where
Jason and Catherine were position, moving the elevation
up as the rounds swept towards them.

Oh shit. Got to stop that weapon. Jason settled his
sights on the turret gunner, looking for a chink in the
shielding to strike at him. He fired off multiple rounds as
the grenades exploded closer and closer to their position.
The firing stopped before the grenades hit their position.
Must have hit the gunner.

Catherine was now sending shots into the convoy behind the two lead vehicles. Jason couldn't tell if they were effective, but her shooting had to help. She was methodical, seeming to place her shots to good effect.

He turned his attention to one of the transport trucks. He put multiple rounds through the grill, hoping to damage the engine, then placed two rounds through the windshield. The men in the cab had exited when the shooting started. Jason's next rounds went through the sides of the box behind the cab.

Confusion seemed to reign behind the lead vehicles as it took some time for the others to understand they were under attack.

General McKenzie was in the second APC when the firing started. He didn't hear the first shot, but he heard the subsequent rounds and the return fire from his men. He got on the radio.

"What the hell is going on?" He shouted.

The lead APC responded. "We're taking fire from the ridge across the river. Multiple shooters. We're returning fire with the .50 cal."

"Get the Mk 19 in action. That should shut them down."

He could now hear the booming sound of the grenade launcher. It had a injure-to-kill radius of up to fifteen meters. Once his gunner could zero in on the shooters' location, they'd be toast.

Suddenly the Mk 19 stopped firing.

"Move the unarmored vehicles down into the median," McKenzie shouted over the radio. "They're sitting ducks on the pavement. And bring up the tank."

There was a shuffling of vehicles as the trucks and Humvees turned into the median strip which sloped down a good ten feet below the level of the road. He could hear the clanking of the tank's treads as the tank came forward.

"Someone pinpoint those shooters for the tank," he radioed.

Jason saw the tank coming forward. It moved only enough to get to a clear spot. The barrel swung around towards the ridge.

"Uh oh," he said.

"What's wrong?" Catherine asked as she stopped firing.

"They're bringing the tank into action."

Just as he spoke the tank fired. Dust shook from its chassis as it rocked on its tracks. The round exploded into the hillside with a deafening impact.

"Come on!" Jason called to Catherine.

He slid back and grabbed her. "We have to get back," he shouted.

"We're out of sight. He can't see us," Catherine started to protest, but Jason just grabbed her and started running

He counted off the seconds. Two to adjust the aim; two to load and clear for the shot. At four seconds he threw them both to the ground and covered Catherine with his body. The next round tore apart the ridge top just next to where both of them had been positioned. The explosion was deafening. The frag, dirt, rocks and bits of trees flew through the air over them.

Catherine looked up at Jason, her eyes wide with shock. Jason didn't say a word, but grabbed her. They ran back another ten yards and threw themselves to the ground again. This time the round went high and exploded in the trees. Again, the frag flew all around them and two oaks fell down, their branches crashing over and around the two.

Catherine started to untangle herself but Jason stopped her.

"Just lay still. We have some cover now from the limbs. Better to stay under here. We only have a few seconds between shots. Can't get that far away."

"My ears are ringing. God that was loud."

"And lethal."

Jason noticed Catherine was shaking.

"Breath slow and steady. I don't want you to go into a panic."

They waited, but no more shots were fired.

"Is this what war is like?" She said after a moment.

"Sometimes."

"It's horrible. How can anyone stay alive with such terrible weapons?"

"As bad as that is, it can get worse. The howitzers are even more lethal. And they shoot much farther. If they get within range of Hillsboro, no one is safe."

She shuddered and tried to settle her breathing down. "I'm not sure I'm the warrior you say I am."

"Don't think about that now. Just calm yourself. It seems like they've stopped for now. They don't want to just expend shells exploding the woods. Since we're not shooting, they figure we've been killed, injured, or retreated back into the woods. They'll wait."

"Only shoot when they can kill us, right?"

Jason looked at her. He knew she was unnerved by her introduction to heavy weapons through being on the receiving end. It would unnerve the hardest recruit, let alone someone without any training. Mortar and rocket fire, as bad as they were, were the most lethal weapons Catherine had faced. She had done all right then and Jason knew she would rise to this challenge.

"That's how it works," he said in response to her question. "Our job is to not let them do that and to do it to them. General Patton in World War Two told a young recruit that he didn't want him to die for his country. On the contrary he wanted the young man to help the enemy die for their country."

Catherine looked at Jason, now appearing calmer. "Is that supposed to be funny?"

"No, just to the point. Nothing funny about it. If it helps, remember why we're doing this. Why we're out here and not back in Hillsboro waiting."

Catherine looked thoughtful and nodded her head. "To save others, protect others."

"You got it."

Jason started to pull branches away. They both staggered out of the tangle of limbs and leaves.

"Let's move south. They'll probably be working on the truck I shot up. They can leave the Humvee, but I suspect they'll need the truck, even if they have to tow it. We need to set up and do this again. Every hour we can slow them, soften them, is to our advantage."

"If we shoot again, they'll just bring the tank up again. And next time we may not be so lucky."

"That's true. I think the tank will probably lead the convoy, so next time we let it go by and then shoot up the other vehicles, those we can stop. I want to try to shoot out the tires on the artillery pieces."

Catherine gave him a questioning look.

"We'll hit hard and fast. We know what the response will be so we'll retreat sooner. If we have enough distance between us and the ridge, we'll be safe. They can't curve their shot over the ridge to drop on us."

"Adjust our tactics."

"Now you're thinking like a warrior again." Jason held out his arm. "Wait here, I want to crawl to the ridge and see what's going on."

"Oh no, you'll get shot...or you'll make them fire that tank gun again." Catherine's voice was filled with alarm.

"I'll crawl up for a peek. They won't see me. No shooting, I promise."

With the firing from the ridge stopped, General McKenzie arranged for the armored APCs, and the tank to line up on the highway while the other vehicles dropped behind them into the swale in the median of the highway. The tanker truck was guided in as well. It had to be protected.

"We need to get the truck running," McKenzie said to his lieutenant. "The Humvee may be too shot up to continue but we need the supplies that are in the truck."

"The cab's shot up, windshield gone. We can punch the rest of it out and drive without it. I'll have the mechanics check the engine."

A few minutes later he reported back that the radiator was holed and intake system damaged. "The mechanics think they can fix it. We have some welding torches so they can braze the radiator. I don't know what they're doing about the intake, but they said they could jury rig something. It'll take an hour or more."

"Just get it done and we can move on." The general looked over at the ridge, now showing the raw wounds of the tank's shelling. "If this is all they can muster, we'll be inconvenienced but not stopped." He had two men dead and two vehicles down. He was feeling less generous towards Hillsboro now.

Jason returned a few minutes later. "They've set up a defensive position and seem to be repairing the damage we've done. We can consider what we did a partial success. Let's move south as fast as we can to find another position."

The two turned south and began to run through the forest. Jason relished the exercise to release his pent-up energy. From the looks of Catherine's pace, he guessed she also was enjoying the exertion.

Chapter 43

Again, the two set tled into that jogging pace that ate up the distance. Skimming the ground going downhill and huffing more slowly uphill, they traversed multiple hills and valleys often accompanied by creeks. They kept their eyes on the ground to avoid twisting an ankle on a rock. They seemed to be dancing through the brush, with their feet moving sideways as well as forward as they picked their way through the undergrowth. Catherine would flick a glance forward every few seconds to confirm her path.

After two hours, Jason called a halt and led them towards the highway. They were at a lower elevation now with a limited view of the road. Hills to the north shielded their sight lines.

"This isn't the best spot, but I think we're running out of time to set up." He looked south. "Not much better options in that direction."

"Shouldn't we get to the best position possible?"

"We should, but if the convoy comes past while we're on our way, we'll lose them. We can't catch them once they go past." He paused. "This will have to do."

They went to work setting up their shooting positions. Jason pulled a log over for Catherine to use as a shooting rest. He moved ten yards away and set up behind another log. Both of them cleared just enough brush to see through with their rifle scopes.

"It's five hundred yards to where the road comes into view. Closer than I would like."

Catherine adjusted the turret on her scope. Jason studied the target area.

"The wind is blowing from the east. I can feel it here on the slope. It's about ten miles per hour." He studied the target area with his binoculars. "Looks like less wind down at the road. Call it five miles per hour at forty-five degrees."

"How do I factor in the angle?"

"Ninety degrees would give you about a six and a half inch drift. With the angle, figure three quarters of that," Jason thought for a moment, "say five inches."

Catherine made some adjustments to her scope.

"Of course," Jason said. "That's a very rough estimate." It'll take a shot or two to get it right." He looked up to the sky. "We might get some rain tomorrow with this east wind,"

"Maybe that will help?" Catherine asked.

Jason shrugged. "Who knows? It'll make *us* uncomfortable, I know that."

"We won't melt," Catherine said.

Jason considered her comment. She seemed to have recovered pretty well from the trauma of being on the receiving end of the tank's 105 mm gun.

It took a little over two hours to complete the repairs on the truck. The Humvee was left behind. General McKenzie was anxious to get going. He still didn't want to run at night, but did want to recover some of the lost time from the ambush. He arranged the convoy with the tank now in the lead and the APCs interspersed throughout the line of vehicles. If ambushed again, the armored vehicles would form a protective wall that the unarmored trucks could hide behind to protect them from the shooting. He'd rely on the tank and APCs to suppress the snipers.

He actually felt confident that he had dealt with this first attack. There had been no more firing from the ridge after the tank's gun went into action.

With the new positions set, the convoy started again.

They could hear the tank. Even from their shooting position five hundred yards away the clanking of the tracks and the diesel engine announced its approach. Both Jason and Catherine settled their rifles at the target area and watched.

"We shoot the unarmored vehicles. You aim for the trucks, I'll aim for the Humvees," Jason said.

The tank came into view. They let it proceed. The rest of the vehicles followed.

"Wait for my shot," Jason said. Both of them were lying on the ground, their eyes looking through their scopes.

When five vehicles were in sight, Jason started shooting at the first Humvee in line. Catherine immediately started firing at one of the following trucks. She first aimed for the engine bay through the radiator, then the cab, if the truck didn't stop. Jason's shots were also aimed at the grill of the Humvee, then the cab. Each of them steadily rained bullets down on the convoy. Their first shots missed their mark, but subsequent shots hit right on target as both adjusted their aim.

The tank swung its gun towards the hills but didn't fire. The gunner was trying to locate the source of the shots. Jason had crippled the Humvee. Catherine had stopped one of the trucks. The cab was shattered and the driver down. The others had exited and run for cover. An APC, the fourth vehicle in line also swung its turret towards the hill.

"Let's move to the south," Jason yelled.

Two .50 caliber machine guns had started firing at the ridge close to where they were shooting.

Jason and Catherine retreated from their positions, turned, and ran down the slope. Part of the way down, they turned and crawled back to the edge to begin shooting again. Vehicles now had begun to back up moving them out of sight. Catherine and Jason concentrated on the two trucks and two Humvees that remained in their line of fire.

The tank's 105 mm gun fired. The round hit the hillside near where Jason and Catherine had been shooting.

Catherine screamed at the sound of the shell bursting when it hit the ridge.

"He doesn't know where we are," Jason shouted. "Keep shooting."

He now tried to hit the APC tires. They were run-flat designs but shooting them would wound the machine if not disable it. The machine guns now found their new position.

"We've been located again," Jason called out. "Let's get out of here. The tank's gun will open up on us in a moment."

He knew the information was being passed on to the tank. The gunner wouldn't take long to line up the shot at this range.

They both ran as fast as they could away from the highway. Jason counted to four and grabbed Catherine, forcing both of them to the ground. He covered her and she held her hands over her ears. The first shot whistled over the lip of the hill and exploded against the trees. The round tore down three trees, one large trunk barely missing them, glancing off the large oak they were lying behind. The limbs and branches whipped down around them, smacking Jason repeatedly as he covered Catherine. The next shot exploded the hillside where they had been shooting.

Jason rolled over, groaning.

"Are you okay?" Catherine asked.

Jason nodded. "Just bruised. I must have been hit by a dozen limbs. Felt like someone was beating me with a bat." He struggled to his feet. "Let's go."

Catherine got up and they moved off to the south. Jason lumbered along. His body was sore all over. Soon they were running again, although Jason was going more slowly this time.

Over their shoulders another round exploded on the hillside. The concussion rocked them. After probably a half mile, Catherine stopped.

"How far do we go?"

"Let's try to get another mile south if we can. They'll have some damage to repair.

"I shot one of them up pretty well." Catherine said. She paused and looked at the ground. "I think I killed the driver. I know I hit him. He fell out of the cab."

"Does it bother you?"

"Maybe a little. Others I've shot have been shooting at me. This one was just driving."

"If he hadn't been assigned to drive, he'd be shooting at you, don't think otherwise."

"I guess." She took a deep breath and seemed to put the thought behind her. "Let's get on with it. You good to keep running?"

Jason nodded.

When the first shots hit, McKenzie ordered the convoy to stop. As planned the armored vehicles moved forward to shield the trucks. Unfortunately, one was already getting shot up along with another Humvee. The first APC had started firing at the hillside.

"If we back up," his lieutenant shouted, "we'll get most of the convoy out of the line of fire."

"Radio that out," McKenzie said. "And get the tank gun into action."

He knew it had shut down the sniping before but it hadn't killed the snipers. Maybe this time.

After the third tank round, McKenzie called a ceasefire. A few last rounds of the machine gun rattled off and the air was still. The armored vehicles were now protecting the trucks and Humvees still left in the shooting area. The rest of the convoy had backed up. When the firing had started, the tanker truck, last in line, had stopped. It was not in the ambush area and the driver wisely shut it down and then ran into the ditch in the median.

"What do we do now?" The lieutenant asked.

"Get a dozen men and send them after those snipers. There's only two of them. They need to get to the shooting position and find out if they're dead. If not send the men after them. I want them killed. I don't want a repeat of this another few miles down the road."

He stomped off to look at the crippled truck.

The lieutenant grabbed some men, and sent them across the river. He gave them a radio and told them to report when they got to the sniper's location. If there weren't any bodies, they were to head south in pursuit.

Chapter 44

Jason estimated they were almost two miles south when he headed back to the highway. The hill was higher than the last one and had a long sight line to watch the convoy advancing. It sloped gradually down to the river and could easily be charged, if the Knoxville force decided to attack. He and Catherine would have limited opportunity to shoot attackers who would be shielded by trees as they advanced up the slope.

Jason was worried but his option was always to retreat, if not to the south, then back into the woods, to the west. They settled down to wait and watch. *Always the waiting and watching*, he thought.

"Do you think we can repeat this all day?" Catherine asked.

"Maybe. Each time we ambush them, it causes a couple of hours delay and they lose a vehicle of two. The vehicle loss will take its toll. Those trucks aren't empty, so they'll have to overload the remaining trucks. If they're carrying troops, more of them will have to walk which means they can't cycle in and out. They'll move slower as a result."

"Yeah, but we only get a few shots in and then we have to run...before the tank fires at us."

Jason looked at his step daughter. She was so inquisitive and so deadly with a rifle. He wondered if the experience was damaging to her. The world they now lived in was nothing like before. She had experienced "before", so she would be acutely aware of how different things were.

"We may only get a few shots in, but we seem to be able to make them count."

Catherine didn't respond. She seemed to be digesting this new experience with heavier weapons.

"Our world is quite different now than it was a few years ago," Jason said.

Catherine looked at him.

"I wonder how you feel about it," Jason continued. "You remember how it was before the EMP attack. Do you ever think about the changes?"

She looked off into the woods. "Of course. Not every day, but often."

"Do you miss it? The life before?"

"Parts of it. I miss going to school." She sighed. "But I don't think I could sit in school now. Not after what I've been through, what I've done. The attack caused me to grow up fast...faster than Sarah."

"She's younger. I think she's tried to hold on to her childhood more than you. You were ready to be an adult."

"Maybe. I got to see the killing up closer than Sarah. It takes away one's childhood."

"I'm sorry about that."

"Don't be. It's not your fault. It's part of how the world changed. Had to put aside childhood."

"Well you seemed to have adjusted well. You have a fine husband."

"Kevin's been a rock. He's older, but emotionally we're not so far apart." She paused to think. "I guess I've always been more serious, even when I was younger."

"Sarah was the vivacious beauty, you were the quieter, more thoughtful one. That's what I observed when I joined the family."

"I think that's right. And if you hadn't found us, we might not be alive today." She took a swig from her canteen. "Shooting is thirsty work."

"It's the adrenalin," Jason said.

"You coming along when you did," Catherine continued, "gave me the focus to process all the changes. Learning to shoot, learning how good I was at it, gave me the confidence to face this new reality. I get tired of it, but I know I have the skills to survive and thrive in it. I just hope we can get to some level of peace in our daily lives."

"We all hope for that." Jason changed the subject. "Have you and Kevin thought about kids?"

"We've talked about it. We're both kind of ready, but the crises seem to just keep coming."

"Yeah, that's unfortunate. When the time comes, you'll have to change from warrior to mother. That's a whole different dynamic."

"And what do you know about being a mother?" Catherine looked at him with a grin on her face.

"You got me there. I only have second-hand info from your mom. She managed it pretty well, refusing to hide out and avoid potential conflict, even late in her pregnancy. It hasn't seemed to hurt Adam."

"Mom's my model when the time comes, for sure."

Suddenly they both turned. There was the sound of undergrowth crunching, a muffled voice. It came from below them, from the direction they had just traveled.

"They've sent a team after us," Jason said in a whisper.

"Should we spread out?"

Jason nodded. "Stay on the high ground. We'll need to try to figure out how many are coming, but we can't let them get too close. These rifles aren't the best in the woods with these scopes. You've zeroed at a hundred yards, adjust it down to fifty. My M107 is heavy and not so good for anti-personnel shooting. We'll be relying on your rifle."

Catherine nodded, her face set grim and determined.

"How many rounds do you have left?"

I've gone through a mag and a half."

"Load a fresh mag. I've only got ten-round mags for the 107, so you can keep up the firing if I have to reload."

Catherine started to go but Jason grabbed her arm.

"Remember to shoot only when you can see your target. They'll probably shoot at sounds so they'll be sending lots of rounds through the woods. If ours count it will unnerve them to see their buddies drop with each shot. Now be careful."

She nodded and moved silently away from Jason.

Catherine moved through the brush, careful to stay on high ground She stopped about fifty yards away from Jason who remained at their shooting position. She was protected by an oak tree with some boulders next to its trunk. *Good place to shoot from.* She lay down, partially behind the oak and the rocks. After sliding her barrel through a gap in the stones, she began to scan the foliage down the slope.

Wait until I can see more than one of them. I can't let them spread out and circle behind me. Catherine figured if they tried to out-flank her, she would have to retreat, even if it meant heading downhill. She had confidence that she could move faster and quieter, but their rifles, probably with open sights, would be better suited to the woods than her M110 with its powerful scope. Looking through the scope was difficult with all the foliage distorting her view downrange.

After a few minutes, she saw a shadowy figure, then another one. They were not well-disciplined, moving close to one another. *Got a chance.* After seeing five men coming up the slope, she aimed at the first figure and fired. The shot flew high. The man dropped to the ground, but Catherine fired low where she saw the figure disappear. Her second shot struck home. She saw the brush move and an arm fling out on the ground.

Return fire erupted. Catherine slid her barrel back so it couldn't be seen. She watched through the cleft in the rocks, trying to pinpoint the muzzle flashes. After a flurry of rounds, she heard rustling again. One man raised up and started forward in a crouch. Catherine slid her rifle out and hit the man in the chest. She pulled the barrel back again to wait out the flurry of shots being sprayed in her general direction.

Then she heard the heavier boom of the .50 cal. Jason had found a target. The shooting in her direction stopped. Shots were now being directed towards Jason. The big rifle boomed out again and then all was silent. She could hear men calling back and forth. They were still trying to pin down the shooter's locations. No one seemed to want to move. However, many men had been sent, Catherine guessed they were four fewer in number now.

There was no movement. Catherine heard muffled talking back and forth but couldn't make out the words.

Suddenly multiple rounds were fired, rapidly. It sounded like the shooters were sending three-round automatic burst in her direction. She hunkered down. When she heard branches snapping, she risked a look. Men were charging up the slope, firing as they went. Catherine slid her rifle forward and got off one shot that dropped one of the attackers. Then she scrambled back and turned to run through the woods, angling to her left. As she ran, she heard Jason's rifle firing.

After about thirty yards, she dropped behind a large tree and swung her rifle around it. *Got to take out anyone following before they zero in on me.* Instinctively she realized that she was playing a game of shoot, retreat, shoot again and repeat the process. Never allowing the enemy to pin her down. As long as she could retreat and set up another position maybe she could wear them down. They had to expose themselves to come after her while she could wait.

They want to kill me. They want to kill Jason and all we hold dear. She watched the woods, looking over the rifle sights, waiting to see the enemy. Her determination solidified. If they wanted to kill her, she would have that fate in store for them. Now calm and methodical, she waited.

One of the attackers stood up with his back to Catherine. *Must be protecting himself from Jason's fire.* Without hesitation, she took the shot.

Jason had watched as the men came up the hill. He heard Catherine fire. One of the men went down and the others started shooing wildly in Catherine's direction Jason waited until he had a clear shot and took one of them out. Now shots began coming in his direction, but without effect. They couldn't see him.

Another shot came from Catherine. That redirected the return fire. Jason raised up slightly and sighted one of the shooters. His next shot ripped through the man, flinging his body across the ground. The others dropped down to conceal themselves. Jason could see the leg of one of the men. He moved his aim forward an approximate amount and took a shot. The leg flopped up and swung to the side indicating a hit to the torso.

There seemed to be confusion in the attack. Jason took the opportunity to maneuver around more to the rear quarter of where he thought the men were pinned down. He was careful to not get into Catherine's path of fire.

Then a flurry of rounds rang out from the attackers and they started rushing uphill towards Catherine's position. He heard her fire once. Then he stood up and began firing at the charging men. He could barely see them through the brush. Against his training he let loose a volley of shots at the bodies as they ran upwards and away from his position. *Got to interrupt their charge.* He hoped Catherine was retreating.

He guessed he'd hit two men but he wasn't sure. The charge collapsed as the remaining attackers dropped to protect themselves from Jason's crossfire. Every shot from the M107 tore up the trees, ripping open trunks of a foot in diameter. Jason knew it was sowing fear in the men, even when he missed his target.

The remaining men forgot about Catherine in their fear of the .50 caliber rifle fire now coming at them from their rear flank. When they adjusted their concealment to protect themselves from Jason's shooting, one of them exposed himself to Catherine. He stood up behind a three-foot diameter tree to try to get a bead on Jason. She took the shot. The man was slammed up against the trunk and slid to the ground. One of the men now turned and fled back through the woods and that triggered a route of the few remaining attackers. Both Jason and Catherine fired a few rounds at them but didn't pursue.

Chapter 45

O f the dozen men sent out to eliminate the snipers, three returned. They had lost their radio and McKenzie had no idea of what had happened until they shuffled back to the convoy.

"What happened? Did you get them?" McKenzie asked after the men waded across the river and approached the convoy.

The men didn't answer right away. Their heads were down and when they looked up, McKenzie saw the fear on their faces.

They stopped when they got to the general and his officers. McKenzie grabbed one of them by the arm and shook him. "I asked you a question. Did you kill the snipers?"

The man shook his head, afraid, or unable to speak.

"Where are the others?" the lieutenant asked.

"Dead," one of the men replied.

"All of them?" the lieutenant asked.

The man nodded. "We never saw them, but they saw us. Every time they shot, one of us died. We tried to charge them, but they attacked us...from two sides."

"There are only two of them, not a squad," McKenzie said. "What the hell are you talking about?"

The men just looked at the general, fear still showing on their faces.

General McKenzie took a deep breath, working to control his rising anger. "You tell me that a dozen men are defeated by two shooters? And they killed nine of you?" There was no answer. "Get out of my sight."

McKenzie looked at his officers. "Come with me," he said in an angry voice.

Taking the men aside he began to lash into them. "What the hell kind of training are you doing with these men? A dozen men can't take out two snipers? Hell, they could have just charged them as a group. We might have only three walk back, but the snipers would be dead. Now they're still out there."

His chief lieutenant spoke up. "They may have gone up against military trained men. They're obviously effective snipers. Most of our men haven't seen combat. This is new to them. If the snipers had split up, they could have flanked our men and just picked them off." He paused to gauge the general's reaction, then continued. "If they're good woodsmen, our men may not have been able to pin them down."

McKenzie snorted in disgust. "Pin them down, hell he said they never saw them. What kind of force have you given me?"

"I can assure you, General, this group can fight. Give them a conventional battle, with the artillery softening up the enemy, the tank leading, and they'll charge and shoot and do what is needed to take ground."

"I'll have to reserve judgement on that for now. I hope you're right," he looked around at the assembled officers, "for all your sakes. After this is over, I'm doing a top-down review of our combat readiness. I'd hate to go up against a well-trained militia with men like that."

He stomped off to check on the truck. It hadn't been able to be fixed and the supplies it carried were being loaded into one of the trucks that had carried troops. Those men would have to walk and fewer marchers would be given some rest throughout the day.

General McKenzie assembled his tank commander and the drivers and gunners of the APCs and Humvees. He had three Humvees left with machine guns. Two were .50 caliber, the other one was 7.62 caliber.

"These snipers are still out there. We know they'll repeat their attacks. We can't continue to go a couple of miles and then get stopped for another two hours. We have to keep going. We know they're operating from across the river, to our right. So, we'll position our armored vehicles on the right side of the convoy. Each making sure you cover a transport truck. I want an APC next to each truck. The men will march in the median which is mostly below the roadway, so they'll be protected."

He walked back and forth as the plan clarified in his mind. He was not going to let two snipers stop his heavily armed convoy.

"Gunners, you keep your weapons trained to the hills on the right. I want spotters to locate the sniper fire immediately and I want all my gunners to light up that spot. If we do this right, they'll only get one round of shots in before we shut them down."

"Our weapons didn't take them out before, how do we know we can do it now?" The tank's commander asked.

McKenzie glared at the man. "We may take them out, we may not. The point is that we shut them down and keep going. If we're not stopping for a couple of hours, they can't keep pace with us and we'll leave them behind."

"What about the abandoned cars? We're going to be two wide now, not single file."

"We clear only when we have to. We go around. If there's one lane, the armored vehicles will move off the road to let the trucks go through the gap. Just keep yourselves alongside as cover. If the trucks get stuck, the troops will push them. No stops from now on, understand?"

Everyone nodded.

"Catherine," Jason called out after the attackers had fled down the hill. "You all right?"

"I'm okay, you?"

"Yeah." Jason walked towards her voice.

"You did great," he said when they met.

"I remembered what you always said. Wait for them to make the move, to expose themselves...and to retreat, not get trapped. Do you think we've stopped them?"

"No," Jason shook his head. "They'll keep coming. We should get into a new position. This time they'll be expecting us and we'll have to be careful of another attack from the woods."

"I think there'll be little appetite for another attack."

"Maybe. It'll be up to General McKenzie."

"What's he like?" Catherine asked as they trotted off through the woods.

"He's a real general. A hard ass like many. He's capable but, judging from the men who attacked us, he's not working with a lot of well-trained soldiers."

"That will help Kevin and the others."

The two continued their jog through the woods. Jason finally called a halt when they had climbed a particularly steep hill. They turned to the highway and came out to a suitably steep slope down to the river and highway. There wasn't a long sight line in either direction but for a quarter of a mile, they had clear shooting.

"With the steep slopes, we'll be relatively protected from an assault in the woods." Jason said. "Now we wait." He took a drink of water, draining his canteen.

"You need some of mine?" Catherine asked.

"No, I'll fill up at the next stream we cross."

Sooner than they had expected, they heard the sound of the approaching convoy. Both of them got into position, lying behind protection and looking through their scopes where the convoy would appear.

When it came out from the screen of hills, Jason saw that McKenzie had made some adjustments. While they were on a steep hill, it was not especially high. The result was that the armored vehicles were providing reasonable cover for the unarmored trucks. The tank had its turret turned towards the hills across the river, ready for firing as soon as their position was exposed. The others had their weapons aimed in the same direction.

As soon as they were spotted, all hell was going to break loose.

"Catherine," Jason said while still looking through the scope. "They've got eyes on the hills. They'll see our muzzle flashes. It won't take a moment for them to pin point us. We get one round of shots as fast as you can and then we run away. The tank and the rest will open fire and our position will be wiped out."

Catherine looked over at him, her eyes wide, and nodded.

"Wait for my first shot and then get off as many rounds as you can. When I shout 'Go!', run like hell."

Jason watched the emerging convoy. He had limited shots at the truck cabs, none at the grills and engines which were better hidden. Shooting the boxes behind the cabs would be useless. The trucks probably didn't carry any more men and he would only hit supplies. He could see the men marching in the median swale. All they had to do when the firing started was drop to the ground and they would be protected.

"Try for the truck cabs," he called to Catherine.

Jason's first shot went through the top of a cab, his next, lower, smashed through the windshield. He didn't know if he had hit anyone, he just kept firing. Catherine also targeted a truck cab with similar results but less damage. Jason turned a few shots to the first APC, trying to take out the gunner. After about four seconds in which he got off six rounds, he gave the shout.

Both slid back from the hill's edge, turned and ran back into the woods. The tank's 105 gun fired and the hillside just below their position exploded.

"Keep running!" Jason shouted. Four second later he shouted again, "Down!"

They both hit the ground as the second round hit the hillside, right where they had been shooting. The blast ripped apart some trees and frag and branches flew over their heads. They could hear the thump of the grenade launchers. These could be more dangerous, exploding just over their heads or, worse, dropping down onto them.

"South," Jason shouted. They sprang up and raced through the brush, with limbs and brambles tearing at their faces and clothing. Behind them the grenades started landing and exploding.

Catherine yelled out and fell to the ground. Jason stopped and ran back to her. Her jacket was torn on her right shoulder.

"You're hit," Jason called. "Can you move? We have to get out of here."

Catherine started to her feet. Jason grabbed her under her left arm and yanked her upright.

"Ow, that hurts."

He took a quick look at her shoulder. "We have to get further away. Come on."

He started pulling her along.

"You'll make me fall. Let go," Catherine yelled at him. The exploding munitions behind them were deafeningly loud. "I can move."

A few minutes later Jason stopped behind a large boulder that had broken off from the higher slope ages ago.

"We're safe here. Let me look at your wound." He dropped his pack and helped Catherine off with hers. Her jacket had a large rip in it. Below, her shirt was torn as well and a deep gash exposed across her shoulder blade.

"Is it bad?" Catherine asked.

"Probably painful, but not bad." He took out some antiseptic powder and sprinkled it over the gash. Then he put a cauterizing patch on the wound and finished with some tape to hold it in place. Catherine grunted in pain as Jason worked on the injury.

"There," Jason said when he had finished. "Don't try to move your arm much, you'll pull the bandage loose. I want